The Rainbow Maker

Mark Turley

Published by UKA Press 2004

2 4 6 8 10 9 7 5 3 1

First published in Great Britain in 2004 by
UKA Press
An Imprint of KMS Ltd
PO Box 109,
Portishead, Bristol. BS20 7ZJ

www.UKAuthors.com

A CIP catalogue record for this book is available from the British Library

ISBN 1-904781-17-9

Cover images by Anastasia

This book was prepared for print by
Associated Writing, Editing and Design Services

www.awed-services.com

Dedication

There are many people who probably deserve a mention in this section. But I want to keep it short.

So, for whatever it's worth, this is for my Dad, a man who made a few rainbows himself in his youth. He used to tell me stories on Sunday mornings, over cups of tea. They were usually about brave boys and dinosaurs. Unwittingly, I think, he started all this.

It's also dedicated to the memory of Jill, my mum, who taught me that all things in life are either 'nice, clean' or 'filthy, dirty.' I never realised how true that was until I grew up.

Thanks to both of you,
Mark
July 2004

HER MAJESTY'S OFFICE FOR INTERNAL AFFAIRS

15th January 2002

Official Memo

For the attention of the Home Secretary.

Please find below London statistics, as requested.

Current population:	7,950,000
Legal immigration:	27,000 per year
Illegal immigration:	11,000 per year (approx.)

Estimated no. of nationalities represented within population:

Small communities (<1000 people): 105.
Large communities (> 1000 people): at least 80.

Population Density:	4,709 per sq. km[1]
Pollution Levels:	High[2]
Average Property Price:	£200,000
Average Salary:	£22,000 p.a.

Social Welfare projects needed for regeneration: £4.5 billion (est.)

[1] Average figure: In certain inner city areas, overcrowding is more serious.
[2] According to the UN classification scale of urban pollution levels.

It is clear that London now meets all stress requirements as laid out in the Washington model for preliminary development of the BCR. The figure quoted for costs is the very minimum required to avert the predicted situation.

HER MAJESTY'S OFFICE FOR INTERNAL AFFAIRS

10th February 2002

Official Memo

Highly Classified. To be saved in secure file only.

Report on development of <u>Operation Black Cloud.</u>

a) Stockwell Riots 1980

64 police injured, approx. 110 civilians. 4 fatalities. 61 private vehicles and 56 police vehicles damaged or destroyed. 28 premises burned, 117 damaged. 282 arrests.

Most serious public disorder in England in living memory.

Public Enquiry headed by Lord Jarman. Members of enquiry not privy to details of Operation Black Cloud. Report concentrated on policing rather than causes, but still described a sudden and calamitous outburst of violence against the police and other civilians.

Confusion resulted in the press, especially with regard to the end of the disturbance, which was sudden and absolute – rioters simply dispersed calmly. Social analysts blamed anti-police attitudes, institutional racism and relative deprivation.

Operational status: Closed (successful)

b) Homerton Estate Riot 1981

A police van answering a 999 call regarding mass disturbance was surrounded and attacked by a group of nearly 100 residents, armed with machetes, bars and knives. Before the arrival of riot police, huge-scale damage to both public and private property occurred. Massed ranks of police officers in full riot gear suffered a sustained, vicious attack consisting of bricks and masonry used as missiles as well as physical violence. During this time there were 13 fatalities (all civilian), 65 police officers were injured and some 200 civilians.

Injuries to civilians were mainly caused by the actions of other civilians.

At 10.30pm a fire was started in a newsagent's on the first floor of one residential block. Attempts by police officers to help the fire crew resulted in further confrontation, more casualties and the death of a police officer.

Shortly thereafter, the rioters dissipated calmly and public order was fully restored.

Unfortunately death of police officer was leaked to press, the only fatality from both disturbances to become public knowledge. Coverage hysterical, source of leak unknown. Suspected internal source, possibly within police force. Story of murder of female resident of estate given to press as cover. Public enquiry again failed to determine short-term causes.

Operational Status – closed (successful)

In addition to the above events and outside of the control of Operation Black Cloud there have been 18 serious public order situations in London since 1976, nine in the last 5 years. This does not include incidents of football hooliganism, which have been innumerable. Prior to that date, such occurrences were so infrequent as to be negligible.

Arrests for offences of violence have increased sharply since 1970.

It is the decision of Her Majesty's Office for Internal Affairs, recorded as per the date of this report, to begin the necessary steps to put the research phase of Operation Black Cloud into place. A suitable site for test premises has been located.

It is gravely feared that we may be approaching the critical period.

Part One

Sleeping

1

'Blaze like the sun!'

One eye half-opened and he sat up, blind in the twilight, face peeling off the pillow, membranes of dry saliva clinging to his lips. Breath came fast and hot, like a dying man.

A coarse blanket slipped off his lap and collected itself in a mound on the floor.

Zac had woken himself again. His ears echoed with his own voice: 'Blaze like the sun.'

Arnold turned to Margaret and shuddered. Something silent passed between them.

'Call Richter,' he said, emotion in his voice making the words hang for longer than they should have, polluting the sterile air.

Margaret swivelled and left, her solid shoes clacking the tiles, echoing around the giant room. The lab-door eased itself shut behind her.

Arnold's eyes remained fixed on the enclosure. He calculated. It was what he was best at. While he did so, he bit his lip.

Upstairs, Richter was oblivious: he hadn't concerned himself particularly with the goings-on in the lab. His morning had rotated instead through regular routines of e-mails and faxes and phone-calls. As Margaret hastened his way, climbing the steps two at a time, he was in mid conversation, but still heard her coming, the rhythm of her feet echoing up the stairwell.

'Another,' he was saying. 'Where this time?'

Margaret appeared in the doorway. She was slightly out of breath and tilted her head, trying to catch his eye. He leant against the far wall, by the window, one leg bent, the handset balanced on his shoulder. He was caressing the end of his goatee with the thumb and forefinger of his right hand.

'Lawrence,' she hissed. His forehead was grooved and creased. He waved her away.

'Really. Was it at rush hour?'

'Lawrence!' Her voice was dry.

Richter looked up. She glared at him. His face creased again.

'Something's come up,' he said. 'Send me a report.' As he turned to her he sensed something awry. His stomach tightened.

'Come down to the lab, Lawrence.' She was hoarse. 'It's urgent.'

Richter scrutinised her for a second, eyes narrow, then nodded. He followed her out of the office and they jogged down the two flights of stairs together. His mind churned possibilities.

As soon as they entered, Richter knew. It was instant and instinctive. No one was at their stations, the crew had loosely clustered together, as if for mutual protection, or at least reassurance, Arnold at their fore. Uneasy silence hung over their heads.

Quietly, with downcast eyes, the lab team parted to let them through.

'What is it?' Richter asked, as he brushed between them. His breathing became rapid and shallow. The anxiety of the group invaded him, despite his efforts to prevent it, to shut it out. It entered him organically, as if by skin-cell osmosis, or airborne spores through his sinuses.

Nobody answered his question. Eyes remained fixed. He followed their gaze through the toughened Plexiglas and beyond it.

Most of the subjects, including Ha-Ha, Brown-back, Pokey, and PG were already dead. Others were barely alive, crawling and gibbering. They lay scattered between the trees and bushes. Some of them were missing limbs. Several had suffered mortal injuries to their faces and heads.

Richter bowed his head, averting his eyes, then raised it again towards Arnold, hoping to find comfort in him, detachment, the computed rationality of the scientist.

But Arnold had watched the whole thing unfold and it had penetrated his surface, finding its way past the bright layers of positivism and objectivity and touching the dark, airless depths of him, where soft, jelly-like feelings, too translucent and fragile for exposure to light, were spawned and bred.

For the first time in ten minutes he turned away from the enclosure screen. Richter felt like he was looking at a stranger, or at least an actor, pretending to be Arnold and getting it slightly wrong. His eyes were blurry, his mouth tight, his cheeks hollow.

He didn't need to say a word.

2

Zac gave up on returning to sleep after ten minutes, rolled out of bed and made for the sink, where he ran some lukewarm water, splashed it onto his cheeks and forehead, then massaged a little into his armpits. He swilled some around his mouth and spat it into the plughole. It had a brownish tinge to it.

A brief scan of the single-room flat located his work-clothes, piled in a hillock of stained denim by the foot of the bed. After pulling on the dirty jeans, vest and boots, he snatched a jacket from the back of a chair and headed out into the North London morning.

It had the makings of a warm day and he walked quickly, as if marching, through freakishly quiet streets. Weary, willowy people with lifeless eyes waited at bus stops, a few skinny kids meandered in their uniforms. There was a feeling of space and openness, even on the roads. Occasional cars moved calmly, unhurried. Zac enjoyed the gentle sun. Its affections warmed his face and soothed the exposed areas of pitted, damaged, omelette-textured skin that wrapped itself up from his spine, down one arm and across his shoulders, stretching up above his collar.

His pace was quick, his walk long-strided, and in twenty minutes he had left the decaying rows of terraced houses and tower blocks behind and passed into a cleaner, neater zone. Extending from the middle distance, the glass and concrete towers of the City shot up, proud and vertical, while around him shops and banks, cafes and minor insurance companies hunkered together on the pavements. The few people around looked purposeful in their shirts and cotton blouses.

He stopped at a bakery and bought a toasted sandwich, which he finished in three large bites, tossing the paper wrapper into a bin, then licking bacon grease from his fingers as he walked, eventually arriving on-site early enough for a cup in the tea hut, a pre-fabricated, plasterboard rectangle by the gate. It was empty except for the scaffold crew and they presented him with a familiar gallery of shaved heads, tattoos and scars, yawning and joking, their raw, hairy-backed hands holding mugs and adding emphasis to conversation.

Football and the weather were discussed, opinions mixed with laughter.

'Best work in the world when the sun's shining,' Zac said, grinning, actually meaning it. They nodded and smiled their agreement.

He drained the last dregs of bitter tea from a chipped mug, removed his jacket slowly and placed it on a peg. He smiled again.

'I'm gonna make a start,' he said.

'Enjoy,' one replied.

'Don't work too hard,' said another.

He headed out, grabbed a pickaxe from the tool rack outside the tea-hut door and went straight over to the old walkway he had been ripping up all week. It was right in the middle of the site and gave him a view of all the new buildings. Two of them were near to completion. The other two were just foundation, steel supports and scaffold. They made angular metal shapes, like kids' Meccano models, stretching high into the blue.

He raised the pickaxe above his head and aimed it just in front of his feet, putting all his strength into one massive swing.

The point of the pick skidded across the surface, chipping two or three powdery inches off the side. He grunted as contact was made, expelling air. It jarred his shoulder slightly, but he swung again immediately. This time he caught the tip underneath the lip of the path, causing two large cracks. He was able to lever one of them with the axe and picked up a large, diamond-shaped slab of concrete, which he threw to one side.

3

Monuments, towers, temples, tombstones; the high rooftops of the square mile broke up the sky, greedily consuming morning light as if it were nutritious, casting shadows at ground level where buses rattled along old, grey streets, disgorging workers like waste. Underground stations spilt great retches of commuters to hurry and struggle. Shoulder knocked against shoulder. Every inch of space, every second was fought for.

Elliot sat on a middle storey, amongst it all, indirectly occupying half the building. Four floors, each the size of a football pitch, each filled with desks and chairs, phones and PCs, all of it the result of his vision, his will, his hunger.

'If by a man's works shall ye know him,' Elliot liked to say to friends, 'my legacy will be the hundreds of young men who have made their fortunes in my company.'

He leant back in his chair and brought a steaming Styrofoam cup to his lips. The first sip made him wince in disgust. He almost spat it out.

'Terrible bloody stuff.' He used a plastic spoon to encourage some of the remaining granules to dissolve, whirling it in the grey froth that sat on top of the drink before risking another taste and looking out, through the glass façade of his private office. The sight pleased him, although it didn't show on his face. His entire team had already arrived, early. They had absorbed his ethos, his focus and goals, settling behind their desks, waiting for his appearance.

As always, well presented, in a three-piece Saville Row number that rustled crisply over his doughy curves and a mauve silk tie bought in Milan, he rose from his chair and moved to the door to address the fourth floor at their weekly meeting. A tiny, one-sided smile dimpled his left cheek. The office chatter acquiesced to a hoarse accumulation of whispers as he emerged.

'Gentlemen!' he bellowed, striding across the front of the room, arms outstretched, expecting and receiving silence.

'It's time to celebrate success.'

He stopped still, front and centre, feeding on their attention, pausing to see their faces. They were utterly still, enraptured, like citizens at the Colosseum witnessing life and death. Each of them, with expressions of absorption, of absolute attention, played a game with him. He knew it and loved it. The game was, after all, his. When he spoke again, he spoke more quietly, as if about to share a secret.

'I can pull, you know!' he said. 'Oh yes, I can still pull! This lithe frame still attracts its fair share of totty!'

He massaged his tremendous, waistcoated paunch and a rumble of approval rose from the all-male room.

'It's because of this!' He smiled, eyes wide, at once appearing exultant and energised, holding a gold clip in the air. It contained £5,000 in fifties and the faces around him looked eager, there was even some applause. The money was in their eyes and it thrilled him. He had the lot of them by their collective balls.

'Yes...because of this,' he waggled the notes from side to side, 'I'm a bloody babe magnet!' More laughter.

He approached a young man in the front row with floppy blond hair and an open, expectant face.

'Hold that,' Elliot said, giving him a fifty from the clip. The young man took it.

'Smell it.' He smelt it.

'I bet you've never even seen one of those before.' Elliot

curled his lips into a mock snarl. Blondie shook his head, compliant and a little awestruck, his fringe bounced. Elliot snatched the fifty back and replaced it.

'This month's bonus is £5,000, enough for someone even on my inflated income to get mildly excited. The Junior Adviser who has taken on more new business than any other is...'

He allowed the anticipation to gather, steam-like around them and inhaled deeply, breathing it in, filling himself with it. A few of the boys fidgeted and adjusted their collars.

'...Antonio.'

A young man in the third row launched himself from his chair and punched the air. Others clapped as he walked towards the front, slim and strutting, dark blue suit, sleek and neat, black hair cut short and combed back. A huge, white smile split his face.

He reached the front and shook hands, briefly the focus of the whole office. Elliot pressed the money clip into the young executive's palm and from it, perhaps from the red ink on the bills, through his pores, adrenaline coursed up his arm, flooding his vascular system, making him hot and slightly light-headed.

'Words of wisdom?' Elliot asked.

Panic made a brief, unwelcome appearance on the youth's features, but disappeared as quickly as it came, replaced by a mask of charm. Antonio took his time, aware of the need to appear confident.

'Quality, not quantity,' he said. 'You need to find clients with money.'

Elliot shook his hand.

'Well done,' he said quietly. 'Back to your chair.' Antonio returned to his place. He felt taller.

'Success is based on strategy, gentlemen.' Elliot spoke to the room again.

'Antonio has a strategy. Go for middles and upper middles. So true! Don't waste your time with the working classes, they just don't earn enough.'

He smiled and paused, touching his chin with a thick finger.

'Bob the Builder may be a smashing bloke, although if he's anything like builders I've dealt with, he's probably just got out of Wormwood scrubs and his girlfriend's a crackhead! But the chances are he's on less than £300 a week. What's the commission going to be? Think about it. It may sound harsh, but these are the realities within which we work. Think higher. Although low earners are welcome to clean my house or shine my shoes, they're no bloody good as clients. Money makes money, okay?'

He paused and his face folded, furrowed, as if for a half-second he had been struck by inspiration, or come to terms with a previously unimagined deeper wisdom.

'Money makes money!' he repeated. 'Now hit the phones!'

As he turned and headed back to his office, head held too high, like a Wellington, or a Napoleon, his troops, in their polyester uniforms of navy and pinstripe, did exactly as they were told.

It was a special moment. They both knew it. In the seconds that followed there was the awkwardness in their feelings that special moments bring. Zac had dived and brought him down, out of danger, a fraction before the wooden palette crashed to the ground. Twenty large cement bags exploded. Dirty and breathing hard, they clambered to their feet amidst a cloud of white dust and walked slowly away together, towards a jagged, half built wall, the sun shining into their eyes.

'You alright, Darren?'

'Jesus, Zac.' Darren shook his head. He held his hands out in front of him as if checking that they were still attached.

'I saw it coming from over there,' Zac said, pointing at the area where he had been working. 'I heard the rope go. Dan must've lost his grip. I wasn't sure if I'd make it in time.'

'You alright down there?' a distant voice called from above.

They looked up through the thinning dust-cloud. A figure

peered over the edge of the scaffolding above them, five sto-
reys up.

'No one's hurt,' Zac shouted back, giving the thumbs up
sign.

'Listen Zac,' Darren said, appearing prematurely aged, with
white cement dust in his hair, eyebrows and lashes, shock quiv-
ering his voice. 'I'm gonna go sit down. Have a tea or something. I'm feeling a bit swervy.'

Zac grinned at him. 'See you later.'

He trudged back over to where he had been working before
the accident. It was a hot day, pretty much as hot as summer in
England ever gets. The burns on his left upper arm itched. He
rubbed them absent-mindedly for a few moments, then picked
up his pickaxe and swung it with primitive power.

4

Richter wanted to break the shocked silence, in fact needed to. It was beginning to get to him. He met Arnold's desperate, detached-from-reality gaze.

'Well?'

'I don't know...I don't know what to say about what we've just seen,' Arnold said.

Richter looked down towards the floor while Arnold continued speaking, words flowing, carried along like sediment in a current.

'I had always suspected such results were probable, but to see it first hand, so graphically, under test conditions. There can be no doubt over the validity of our method, the control sample showed none of the same signs and...'

'You're babbling!' Richter looked up sharply. He toyed with the end of his goatee with his thumb. Nothing was said again for a short time. Eventually he motioned to Arnold and Margaret and moved into a corner of the lab, away from the other technicians. He had made a decision, a small decision, but in that tiny moment, something began.

'For now, absolute silence. It is crucial that we keep this between the three of us.'

'But surely we have a duty...' Richter raised his right forefinger.

'No, not this time. Trust is needed here. I need you to trust me, and I need to know that I can trust you. Any leaks, from either of you, and I'll do my utmost to put you out of work permanently. Is that clear?'

Arnold and Margaret swapped a cowed look. 'Yes.'

'Now, organise someone to clean up,' Richter said. 'We've got to put this behind us and move on. I know it's been shocking, I know we weren't expecting it, but we're professionals, we're empiricists and we have very important work to do, so let's just forget and forge onwards. I've got some data to check so if one of you could pop up later to cross some T's and dot some I's, I'd be grateful.'

They watched him walk to the lab's circular door and waited for it to close behind him like a giant claw.

'Did any of them survive?' Margaret asked. Her eyes wandered randomly over the remains.

Arnold shook his head.

'As soon as the groups came into contact it exploded in there. It began with a couple of epsilons and a beta from the first community and two gammas from the second. In no time all of them were triggered. Three of them made it past the initial response phase, but they were so badly wounded that they didn't last much longer. There's been no life signs on any of the readings for the last five minutes.'

Margaret glanced over the bank of instruments underneath the huge observation screen. All the cardiographs showed straight, flat lines.

'So, we've had an affirmation of the power of tribal stimuli, which is something,' she said, 'but this is a much more powerful response than we were expecting, isn't it?'

'Yes. Predicted results suggested agitated behaviour, aggressive vocalisation, maybe pronounced demarcation of territorial boundaries, but not...'

Arnold waved a limp hand at the enclosure screen.

'Hmmm.' Margaret shook her head.

Arnold exhaled noisily.

'I can't imagine what Zoology are going to say.'

23

'Lyn's going to be very upset.'

'Well, maybe this will be a wake-up call for her. I'm not sure the attachments she builds up are such a good idea, bearing in mind the nature of the research.'

'I agree.' Margaret rubbed her eye lazily. Arnold thought she looked tired.

'We have to tell the Ministry, Margaret. You know that, don't you?' he said.

'But what about Richter?'

'I don't know what he's thinking. We can't keep secrets. It's my responsibility to write the report. What can I do?'

Margaret shrugged. For the first time since her promotion, she began to have second thoughts about the project.

'Write it, I guess,' she said.

5

With his back nestling against the soft leather of his swivel chair, Elliot let his eyes skip from point to point. Every face in his field of vision was intent and focused, every pair of hands, every mind, every soul busy accumulating, amassing, engaging in modern alchemy. Gold from base metals – money from hot air. He himself no longer dirtied his hands on the phones. Cold calling and appointment making were for the young bucks, with their testosterone and enthusiasm and desperation to prove themselves. He didn't need it. Elliot got richer by sitting still.

Since starting the company he had been able to buy a manor house just outside Potters Bar and his 'fun pad', a penthouse flat in the Docklands. It was all due to a system he had devised while playing golf in the Algarve while on a summer holiday from his former job in a leading merchant bank.

He recruited hopeful newcomers as 'Junior Advisers' and placed them initially on subsistence wages, on a two-week training programme. After the legal obstacles had been negotiated and the necessary certificates gained, these would-be millionaires were given a desk and a phone and asked to generate their own business, to book appointments with fifty clients of their own. For some, this was easy. Well-maintained filofaxes did the job. For others, whose instincts were less sociable, the last names on the list often belonged to obscure figures, retrieved from the depths of memory. Primary school classmates, even teachers commonly occupied the slots from forty onwards. Those whose ambition conquered their conscience then had to submit their friends and relatives to a full hour of carefully scripted hard sell, intended to put as much of their money in the hands of the company as possible.

'Desire!' he would tell them. 'How much do you want it?'

When, by using this method, a Junior Adviser had signed enough pension plans, equities packages, life assurance and savings schemes, he was promoted and deemed worthy of company business. It was, as Elliot often remarked, a 'sink or swim thing' and the high turnover of staff did not worry him at all.

'The trickle-down effect in reverse,' he called it. He sat at the top of a pyramid that comprised some nine hundred individuals and regardless of whether they were good or bad at what they did, whether they worked for him for a week, or a decade, he took a cut from each of them.

He stretched his hands above his head and the hem of his shirt pulled itself free of his waistband. He stood to tuck it back in and buzzed his PA.

'Suzy dear, send our new high-flyer into me, please. Let's see what he's made of.'

Outside, on the office floor, in his seat among the rank-and-file, Antonio checked his watch. It was approaching lunchtime. For the first time since the morning he allowed himself to reach into his breast pocket and remove the contents, letting his thumb furl the corners of the notes. The money was new and crackled to the touch, which inspired dreams of how it would be spent, which were interrupted by the ringing phone. A delicate and alluring voice spoke.

'Mr Rossley would like to see you in his office, now,' it said.

His heart jumped a little.

'I'll be right there.'

Antonio marched the length of the fourth floor, aware of the glances and under-the-breath comments of his colleagues. The boss's PA, an appealing redhead and the only female employed by the company outside of admin, sat at a desk just outside Elliot's office. He smiled and she nodded at him, as if to say, 'Go ahead.'

He knocked boldly and waited to be asked to enter.

'Yuh!'

Antonio stepped inside and allowed the door to close behind him. The office was small but impressive; a solid, mahogany desk stretched virtually the entire width of the room. Elliot sat symmetrically on the other side, with a bottle of wine and two glasses in front of his folded arms. An opulent oil painting hung behind his head, drawing the young man's attention for a second.

'*The Feast of the Gods*,' Elliot said, carefully observing Antonio's expression.

'Hmm?'

'Bellini.'

'Yes, it's…' Before Antonio could continue, Elliot cut him off.

'I like a painting that looks like what it's meant to be. I can't stand any modern, whimsical, abstract, wishy-washy nonsense, bloody cubism and what have you. I bought this from a private collector in the States.'

'It's nice.'

Elliot smiled.

'Take a seat.' He took a corkscrew from a desk drawer and opened the bottle deftly.

'Wine?'

'No thank you, I never drink during the day.'

'Very admirable.' Elliot poured himself a glass.

'In fact, I don't drink at all, Sunday to Thursday, it helps to keep my mind clear for work'

Elliot smiled approvingly and took an elegant sip.

'You can't beat a good Lanfeau,' he said.

'Sorry?'

'Chateau Lanfeau. It's a little known producer in the southern Bordeaux. Damn good. Do you like wine Antonio?'

'Yes, of course.'

'I love wine. Adore it. Can't get enough of it, which is unfortunate for my liver, but what the hell? For some it's property isn't it? For some it's Ferraris, for others it's bloody Versace suits, or antiques or even cocaine. For me it's wine. We're all individuals, aren't we? It's my passion. Do you know, last year I was in France with my wife, or was it my girlfriend? No, no, I think it was my wife. Anyway, I bought a bottle of 150-year-old claret.'

'Really?'

'Yes. Do you know how much it cost me?'

'No sir.'

Elliot laughed. 'Come on Antonio, you're not at school anymore. Call me Elliot.'

There was a short silence. Antonio ran a hand over his slick hair.

'Well, to put you out of your misery, it cost me £39,000.' He waited a moment before adding, 'What do you think of that?'

'That's a lot of money.'

'Too much, you think? Obscene?'

'I didn't say that.'

'But you thought it.'

Antonio smiled.

'Do you know why I spent £39,000 on a bottle of wine?'

The youngster thought for a while but no suitable answers offered themselves.

'Erm...No,' he said, apologetically.

Elliot paused for effect. He placed his hands flat on the surface of the desk, then leaned over it until he was inches from Antonio's face. For a moment the young man thought his boss was going to kiss him.

'Because I fucking can, that's why.'

Elliot settled his large frame back into his chair.

'Do you know what you look like to me?'

'No, Elliot.'

'A playboy.' He took another slug of wine. 'Do you like the ladies?'

Antonio tilted his head slyly. He didn't need to answer.

'Do you like fast cars?'

'Yes.'

'Do you like riverside penthouse apartments with private gym and pool? Do you like designer clothes and bespoke suits? Do you like fine restaurants? Do you want to be on the guest-list of every decent night club in this city?'

'Absolutely!' Antonio was grinning, swept along with Elliot's rising excitement.

'Well that, my young friend, is a millionaire lifestyle. Is that what you want?'

Antonio nodded eagerly.

'You've taken the first steps. You've got talent and something else. Something…different. I can see it in your eyes. My problem is that often I don't know what I'm seeing. It's a flaw of mine, I know, but one I've learnt to cope with. Sometimes, what I think is potential is just ignorance. Newcomers who seem confident often simply don't realise what hard work it is. Their confidence deserts them when things get tough. But if you focus and have the guts to do whatever it takes, *whatever* it takes, then nothing can stop you. About another fifteen clients and you'll make Junior Executive. Don't lose sight of your goal Antonio. Remember, clarity of vision is the key to…what?'

Antonio had been listening intently, head cocked slightly to one side. He was happy to play the game, particularly this private version between the two of them, that seemed to single him out, anoint him and raise him up before the others. Not every Junior Adviser got to have a one-on-one with Elliot Rossley and those that did often found themselves unemployed shortly afterwards. He knew that the other JAs would be watching, through the glass partition, envious, conspiring. Accomplishment brought jealousy with it.

'Success, Elliot. It's the key to success.'

'Good boy. Now go and make some money.'

As Antonio left, going back to his desk and phone, his boss took another sip, sucking the vintage through his teeth, over his tongue and onto his eager, receptive palate. He leaned back. He would watch the boy closely for the rest of the day, to see if he met the necessary requirements. He already had in mind a use for him.

'Success,' he said to himself, savouring the flavour.

'Success.'

6

Perched on a wooden stool in the corner, the tiny television flickered and whispered. He waved the aerial around and things came in and out of focus, never quite revealing themselves.

Zac was hungry. He dropped the twist of metal and contact with the floor made the screen crackle with angry interference. He padded barefoot across the boards to the cupboard over the sink. When he opened the door, a half-full tub of marmite greeted him in isolation.

'Shit.' He stretched his arms above his head and the mottled skin across his shoulders rippled. He felt a stroke of heat somewhere in his memory, somewhere that he didn't like to go and shook his head to banish the image from his mind before stepping into trainers and manoeuvring into a jacket. He then made for the door, catching the bony point of his right ankle on a loose dumbbell on the way. The ankle smarted as he jogged downstairs and checked his mailbox in the hallway, but he forgot about it briefly as he stepped outside.

It was a scene which he was used to. He had grown up with it, albeit in a different borough, but still it unsettled him. Instinct told him to be wary.

The sky was black and starless, fugged by the muggy haze of orange streetlights, glowing at regular intervals, competing for space with buzzing shop-signs and car headlamps. A steady breeze blew into his face and a crisp packet, caught by the draught, tumbled past, sticking briefly against the foot of a

31

'keep left' sign, before fluttering away.

The street itself was grey rather than black; dusky, not dark, indistinct figures loitered in shop doorways. As Zac walked, their forms became clear, their dress and manner marking them out as clearly as if they carried flags. Somalis with Somalis at the grocers, Turks with Turks at the kebab place, Kurds with Kurds at the green shop, Nigerians with Nigerians, Jamaicans with Jamaicans, Bosnians with Bosnians, Albanians with Albanians; the clans of the street, not gangs, not tribes, just people affiliated through common heritage and trust, the comfort of the familiar, each with their own language and norms of conduct. Sometimes Zac had seen them mingle, often sharing jokes and cigarettes, to buy or sell drugs or stolen mobile phones, but that would always be done as individuals. Once they gathered in their groups, the rules of their interactions changed. Cross-cultural contact and communication weren't sought. The factions were connected only by the heavy-lidded stares that linked them with tendrils of suspicion.

Despite his size, Zac felt conspicuous and vulnerable. He headed for the take-away, one block down, avoiding eye contact with those he was passing until two youths, crouching by the entrance to a piss-smelling alleyway, hoods pulled far over their faces, looked up as he went by.

'Ya wanna buy a draw?' one of them asked.

Zac turned his head. The eyes that met his were dark and ice-cold.

'I'm all right,' he said.

He went into the chicken shop and ordered his dinner, ankle still hurting. An argument, fuelled by alcohol or crack, was building between two yellow-eyed black men, one of them wearing an Arsenal shirt, in the corner of the table-area, by the window. It seemed to be over a newspaper article.

'The only reason why it's a big fuss is because it's up west. That shit happens round here all the time. Don't never get in the papers.'

'Nah, nah, nah, this is some different shit, blood. This ain't gangbangers and bad boys, this is some fat-wallet guy.'

'What sort of shit is that? People is people. Don't matter where they are. They gotta be judged the same way and if you don't agree with that you're stupider than you look, G.' He raised his hand in dismissal.

The other man was infuriated. 'Wha ya mean, *stupid*? Who ya talkin' to, blood?' He reached over and grabbed his friend's collar.

'Hey guys!' The chicken-shop man wasn't happy. 'You go outside now! I have customers!'

'Who was talkin' to you?' the gooner shouted. 'Shut up!'

'Your order, sir.' Zac turned to see the guy behind the counter offering him a brown paper bag. He handed over his last fiver and took the food.

'Enjoy your meal.'

As he left, one of the arguers took a swing at the other. He hurried out, not wishing to get involved.

Back in the street he felt cold and tired. The food was warm in his hand. Chicken fumes rose from the bag, teasing his nose with promises of greasy meat, making his walking pace quicken. His logic told him to slow down. The city's predators who, although not armed with the teeth of the great white shark, or the speed and savagery of the cheetah, could be just as ruthless and cunning, looked out for signs from the human traffic that passed through their territories, signs that indicated who was weak, who was slow, who, in other words, was prey. Walking quickly would suggest, if any of them were watching, that he was afraid and Zac knew enough about the area to know that would mark him out as a target. Unfortunately his own instincts, his own need to feed, drove him on. His belly ruled his head.

He walked back past the youths who had offered him weed. They were busy smoking and didn't bother to speak to him again. He hurried on. His ankle throbbed.

But when he passed the bus stop, not looking at the figures there, and reassurance in the form of his front door lay just ahead, he began to relax. He was close enough to see the four doorbells and the nameplate underneath each one. As he was about to start scrabbling for his key in the confines of the front pocket of his jeans, a voice came from over his shoulder. It was a lilting, soft whisper, gentle and calm.

'What have you got for me, bruv?'

Zac turned to see a tall man standing by the bus stop just behind him.

Flanking him, two others hovered, both shorter and stockier than the speaker.

'What?'

'What have you got for me? Me and my friends were wondering what you could give us.'

The man's voice was almost soothing. He maintained eye contact constantly.

'I don't want to hurt you,' he continued. 'Give me something I want and I'll go away.'

Zac felt another bite of pain from his ankle and resigned himself to the situation. With steady, careful hand movements he transferred his chicken from his right hand to his left.

'Now let me see…Have you got the time?'

The tall man hit the ground, coughing blood and teeth out of the side of his mouth and into the groove between two paving stones, his lips ballooning as he struggled to stay conscious, kicking his feet pathetically. Zac noticed that he wore a very expensive pair of trainers.

He had spoken and hit simultaneously. The word 'time' coinciding with a right hook, nearly full body power, straight in the mouth. It was a good tactic, tried and trusted. The idea being that the target is distracted by the words and won't see the fist until it's too late. He hadn't put everything behind the punch in case the other two stepped forward. He didn't want to be off balance. But he knew what he was doing. He had enough bodyweight and had moved his feet smartly to increase leverage.

One of the others did come at him and threw a lumbering blow at his head. Zac turned sideways, only a small movement, but just enough to allow the man's fist to swing narrowly off target, before moving his back foot and elbowing him hard on the nose. Bone met bone with a devastating crunch. He collapsed as if he had been shot.

The third mugger stayed back. It was clear that this big, white man was no pushover. Hell, he hadn't wanted to take him in the first place. He liked to stick to easy targets, women and the elderly. He pulled a knife and held it nervously in front of him, as if he didn't really know what to do with it.

Zac stood motionless, head down, watching the man's feet, waiting for movement. He had set his body to strike with full force if his assailant made any move in his direction. A few seconds passed, then the feet picked themselves up and ran down the road.

The tall man still lay on the ground, eyes half closed, gurgling through the swollen mélange of split lips, tooth-pieces and bloody gums that had been his mouth. The other had recovered sufficiently from Zac's elbow to be making his way unsteadily in the opposite direction, hands cupped over nose to try to stem the bleeding.

Zac stepped over his stricken assailant and headed indoors. Upstairs, he sat by the window and ate his chicken and chips. The pain in his ankle was lessening and he felt tired. He put the box in the bin.

Sleep came to him slowly. His burns were itching like crazy.

7

Elliot pressed 'Recline'. The easy chair hummed and began lowering his upper body gently downwards, while raising his feet. He was virtually horizontal when he twisted his neck around the headrest and called, 'Fetch another, will you, Janet?'

His wife tossed a limp sweep of blonde hair over one side of her head and tottered through to the kitchen, heels tip-tapping on the wood floor. She looked pale and waxy and a heavy line bisected her forehead, as if something troubled her deeply. Chewing at the inside of her cheek, she pulled a bottle from the wine rack next to the towering fridge-freezer and carried it into him. He stretched for the remote control, raising the volume on his wall-mounted, flat-screen TV.

'Look darling,' Elliot said. 'It's that press conference they were talking about, the one about terrorism.'

The screen showed the US President, a self-consciously grave expression on his face, speaking into a huddle of microphones before assembled ranks of journalists.

'In no way can we, should we, or will we give up our fight. We will not stop until those responsible are brought to justice. The situation is clear. You're either with us or against us. We make no distinction between the terrorists themselves and those who work with them or harbour them.'

Janet gave him the wine and he got up to open it, removing an elaborate ornamental corkscrew from a draw in the coffee table.

'It's a terrible business,' she said. The screen now showed

36

recorded footage of the World Trade Centre collapsing. He nodded in agreement.

'Yes, we can't have these buggers blowing up whatever they feel like. They'll return us all to the Stone Age if we let them.'

'I don't understand what they're trying to achieve.'

Elliot smiled.

'It's not a simple issue, darling.'

Janet stiffened visibly. She hated it when Elliot called her that.

'They have many aims,' he continued. 'On the one hand, there has been, shall we say, a rivalry between Muslim Arabs and Christian Westerners since the crusades. But there's also a feeling that America and, to a lesser extent, the UK, are taking over the world. We are slowly heading towards a global culture and that culture will be Western, darling, with English as its language and governed by Protestant morality and Capitalist ethics. The Muslim extremists don't like it and want to stop it from happening. They have limited resources and so resort to these amateurish acts of barbarism. They'll get what's coming to them sooner or later.'

The newsreader moved on to the next item.

Janet spoke suddenly, as if unexpectedly inspired. 'I really don't see why we don't just do something about the whole thing. I mean surely it's high time that somebody just…'

'Hold on,' he said, 'let's listen.'

'–the unrelated incident in Oxford Street today,' the news-reader finished.

'What was that about?' Janet asked.

Elliot glared at her and shook his head.

8

'Antonio, top man! Come over here and buy me a drink!'

Thin necks in unbuttoned collars and trousers with ties stuffed into back pockets crowded the bar. European bottled lagers were used for gesticulation. Through the bodies, Antonio saw two of his team sitting by the cigarette machine. He sidled his way over, steadily.

'Hey guys,' he said, when he reached them. 'What are you having?'

He bought some drinks and returned. He could tell by the tight-lipped expressions that he had been discussed while buying the round.

'I hear Rossley's got big plans for you, Antonio.'

'Is that right? And where did you hear that?'

'It's just a general rumour.'

'Well, listening to those creates far more problems than it solves. I'm just trying to earn as much as I can, as soon as I can.'

'Aren't we all?'

Antonio looked like he knew what was coming.

'How do you do it, Ant? What's the secret of your success?'

'Don't believe your own hype,' Antonio said, smirking.

'Come on, Antonio, we were on the training course together. We can help each other out a bit, can't we? Luke and I just want to know what we're doing wrong and what you're doing right. Help us out.'

'I don't know what to say, fellas. Just get out there, get sociable. Meet as many people as you can.'

'Everyone's a prospect?'

Antonio looked at him, one eyebrow raised.

'You see this bar? It's full of potential clients, each of them waiting to unload the contents of their bank account into yours. Don't see the business as a way of helping others, see it as a way that others can help you. Squeeze as much as possible from every situation.'

He paused for breath. 'Okay! Now let's talk about something else.'

'What are you going to spend your bonus on?' Luke asked.

'Now that,' Antonio said, 'is an interesting question.'

Two days later he was driving his bonus home. It was red and Japanese.

'Well!' he told his girlfriend, Sadie. 'It's not a Porsche 911, but it's a decent looking machine and I'm happy with it for now. I reckon it could do 150 with a nice bit of straight road.'

He grinned his big white grin and she kissed him, hard.

9

Richter removed a newspaper from under his desk and spread it out to read. Before he had managed to absorb a word, the computer flashed at him: *You have two incoming messages.* He massaged his temples for a few moments before checking them.

One message was labelled *High Priority.* Contrarily, he opened the other. It was from his partner, Tony.

Left without key this morning. Call me.

Richter raised his eyes.

'Brains in his anus,' he said to himself, clicking on the other icon. He thumbed his eyebrow as he read it.

Richter – Concerned by lack of communication – need update on population research. What were findings of Test Study One? Results needed urgently.

Instinctively, he picked up the phone and dialled Margaret's extension.

'Margaret, can you come up please?' Then, as an after-thought, 'And bring Arnold.'

It was ten minutes before they both arrived. They sat nervously. Arnold gnawed at the end of a cheap biro, and Richter thought it made him look slightly simian, like a Bonobo with a banana.

'Right,' Richter said. 'Here's the situation. The Ministry have grown impatient, as I suppose they were bound to. I have no choice than to make a report. We have two options.'

'I've written the report already,' Arnold said.

'I know.' Richter looked stern. 'It's very detailed. The problem that we have is that if we submit that report to the Ministry, this whole thing will explode in our faces. The research will almost certainly be taken out of our hands, we'll definitely lose the lab and our funding, meaning reassignment for the three of us.'

'Well there are other projects, Richter. Other commissions to win,' Margaret said.

'Of course there are, but let's look at the facts. We equipped these premises. We staffed this facility with hand-picked zoologists, toxicologists, psychologists, behaviourists and all the rest of them. We put this whole thing together! We put in the groundwork, not the bloody civil servants. Don't doubt it for a minute, they'll be more than happy to come in for the glory. In fact, it's probably what they want, but I want our names associated with the results of this study, not theirs. If we allowed that to happen it would be like winning a marathon and letting someone else pick up the medal. No one expected Test Study One to provide such definitive results, did they? None of the projections or pilots came close to predicting what we saw. Perhaps it was a mistake. We were supposed to be operational for at least another four years. We haven't even started human testing!'

Richter narrowed his eyes.

'I've invested the best years of my life in this and I for one am not in favour of passing it all over to someone else.'

'Try to put your pride away, Lawrence,' Margaret said.

'Now obviously,' Richter continued, 'as the other senior researchers here, you both have some say in determining what we do. I would like to remind you however that our achievements so far are relatively minor. I feel, and I know you both do too, that what we are trying to accomplish is a thing of great importance. We could mark our names in history.'

Margaret gave a wry smile. 'Still hoping for an MBE?'

'You've missed the point, Maggie. This could be huge. We

would be foolish to allow that to slip from our grasp. What if Test Study One was an anomaly? What if the subjects were reacting to some other stimuli?'

Arnold removed the biro from his mouth. He had chewed the pocket clip off the lid and turned the small piece of black plastic over his tongue.

'I don't think that's possible,' he said.

'We can't rule it out, Arnold. I think we owe it to ourselves to continue with TS2. At least then we can check for correlation. If the results match, then we go public.'

'What exactly are you suggesting?'

'I'm suggesting that we send the Ministry a different report.'

'A false one.'

'Not necessarily false, just incomplete. We won't include all the data.'

'I see.' Arnold looked sullen. He bowed his head. Light glinted from the skin on the top of his skull.

'What do you think?'

'I think you're asking me to lie to a government department because you want to take more credit than you deserve for the research you are supervising.'

Richter bridled momentarily, but spoke softly. He knew it would be foolish to allow the meeting to degenerate into argument.

'The lie would not be yours alone, Arnold.'

'But Test Study One was under my direction. They know that. The report is my responsibility.'

'It's a risk, I know. But it's a worthy one.'

'I can't do it, I'm sorry.' Arnold shook his head and put the biro back in his mouth. He made eye contact with both of the other two, waiting for them to say something. When several seconds passed and neither did, he got up from his chair and left. He didn't slam the door, but somehow it felt like he had.

Richter turned to Margaret.

'What are your feelings?'

'I can see both sides, Lawrence.'

'Do you think you can calm him down?'

'I don't know.' Margaret shook her head. Richter tried to read the expression on her face. She had half-closed her eyes and seemed to be weighing her thoughts carefully. He sat forwards slightly, lessening the distance between them.

'Maggie, will you talk to him please?'

She looked straight at him, unimpressed. Richter reached across the desk and grabbed her hand.

'Come on, Maggie,' he said, 'work with me.'

She glanced away for a few moments then turned back.

'Okay, I'll see what I can do.'

As she left, Richter realised that for the first time in a while he felt pleased with himself. He absent-mindedly went back to his newspaper, leafing through it until a headline caught his eye.

Trolley-Rage Incident at London Supermarket

Emergency services were called to a 24-hour supermarket in London's West-End last night when a serious disturbance occurred between two twilight shoppers. The men involved, whose identities have not been disclosed, are both in their mid-thirties and apparently have no criminal record. The incident was triggered when their trolleys collided by the dairy aisle, resulting in a fight, which caused both men to be admitted to hospital with serious injuries. The manager of the store described the night as 'eventful' but refused to close the store, even temporarily. 'We provide a valuable service to our customers and are fully committed to maintaining that service,' he said.

He took a pencil from his desk drawer and wrote on the margin of the newspaper.

> *Types of 'rage' mentioned in newspapers in last few*
> *years...*
> *Road rage*
> *Trolley rage*
> *Office rage (few cases)*
> *Underground rage*
> *Commuter rage*
> *Age rage*
> *Queue rage*
> *...any more?*

He tapped the tip of the pencil on the desk a few times and put it down. Thoughts sped in tight circles, always returning to the same point. Drumming his fingers, he wished desperately for the phone not to ring.

It did.

10

In truth, Elliot loved his work, although as middle age became late middle age, thoughts of retirement, maybe a farmhouse in Bordeaux, perhaps a villa in the Caribbean, a few years to wallow in the lavishness he had earned, seemed more appealing. Even so, there were no aspects of his day-to-day office life which he found particularly objectionable, feeling, as he did, that the role of leadership was one to which he was ideally suited.

'You have to be born with an aptitude for it,' he would say. 'Some people think it can be learnt or taught. Not true. If the spark's not there, you can't make a flame.'

But despite that, he felt obliged, when in social circles, to pretend that he didn't enjoy dismissals, which wasn't completely honest because on some days he enjoyed a good sacking more than anything else. There was something about the whole business of firing employees that people apparently found distasteful, so to protect their sensibilities and his own reputation, he would usually say, if asked, something like, 'An essential but odious task. It gives me no pleasure.'

In the real world, sorting success from failure was a key component in the machinery of the company, for as small as starting salaries were, it made no sense for him to throw money at individuals who gave him no return. Often, such failures left of their own accord, frustrated by the collapse of their dreams. On countless occasions he had seen young advisers simply pack up their stuff and walk out.

Weakness made them do it, weakness of character. To add to the humiliation, it was weakness of which they had been previously unaware, that had been spotlighted by their failure to convince people who knew them to buy a few financial products. *People who knew them, for God's sake!* If they couldn't convince their bloody family to do business, what good were they? The truth always showed through in the end. Those with desire and balls and that indefinable something made it. The rest went back to nine-to-five tedium and wage slavery.

Unfortunately, in some, their weakness was so engrained, so heavily scored into every thought and word that they couldn't even summon the courage to leave. They had to be told to. For such people, for young men who had so very few of the attributes on which Elliot placed importance, he reserved his deepest contempt.

'Terence Monahan, he's one of the newer Junior Advisers,' he told his secretary. 'He's not meeting targets and he hasn't settled in at all well. I think it's time for the "big chat". Will you send him in please?'

He twitched his mouth from side to side and stretched his fingers, making the knuckles crack, as he waited for the knock on the door.

'Come in,' he called, when it came.

Terence entered and sat.

'Terence,' Elliot said, briskly. 'How are you?'

'Fine, thanks.'

'I think we need to have a talk, Terence. I have one or two things to discuss with you.'

Terence shifted himself on the chair. It seemed a bit too small for him. His heavily set shoulders drooped down and in towards his chest.

'Firstly, you are not dressed appropriately for the office.'

'What? My suit?'

'Yes, not appropriate. Completely inappropriate, in fact.

You look like you're going to a wedding.'

'It's the only one I have right now.'

'Wrong colour. Not appropriate. You've been told about this before. Is that a Ben Sherman shirt you're wearing?'

'Yes.'

'Not appropriate. Your shoes are suede?'

'Yes.'

'Not appropriate.'

'But that's a £150 pair of shoes.'

'It doesn't matter, Terence. It's all about creating the right impression with the client. I could come to work in a Gorilla costume, couldn't I? And when people stop me and remark on it I could say, "But it's really expensive, it's the best Gorilla costume on the market!" The point is that I'm not supposed to be a Gorilla; I'm supposed to be a financial services professional. Therefore, wearing a Gorilla costume is inappropriate. Do you see what I mean?'

'I suppose so.'

'Right.' Elliot moved his shoulders up and down and pursed his lips momentarily, homing in now, ready for the kill.

'Secondly, you were told on the training course about the requirements for advancement?'

'Yes.'

'Did you make a hot list?'

'Yes.'

'Hundred names?'

'Yes.'

'And you know that you won't get any company business until you've got at least fifty clients of your own?'

'Yes.'

'Well, checking the sales sheets here, I see that in the two months you've been on the job, you've signed the grand total of one client.'

Terence nodded.

'And that was five and a half weeks ago.'

Terence nodded again and blew out a great exhalation of air. He began to look angry.

'Can you explain what's going wrong?'

'Look, I can sell, all right? I could sell ice to Eskimos.' Terence had raised his voice a few decibels. 'But this hot list just isn't bloody fair! If you come from London it's easy. You've got your friends and your family nearby. They'll all make appointments to do you a favour. I'm from Armagh for God's sake. The only person I know in London is my cousin Paul and he's the one client I managed to get.'

Elliot sat back in his chair and allowed his mouth to fall open. He looked at Terence with this expression for a couple of seconds.

'I have to say, young man, that I'm not keen on your tone, which brings me nicely to my last point. Apparently you've not settled into the team particularly well. I've had several reports of you being verbally aggressive towards others and I think I've had all the confirmation I need of that just now. We don't get our own way with aggression! Tenacious sales techniques certainly – we run a competitive office. The desire to outperform colleagues is advantageous, but aggression? We just can't have it.'

'They were taking the piss out of my accent.'

'Successful professionals rise above that sort of thing.'

'So, what's happening then?'

'I think it's time that you and Personal Financial Partners Ltd went their separate ways.'

'You're sacking me?'

'Yes. If I were you I wouldn't look on it as a sacking, more of a redirecting. I'm directing you out of my company. There's a big world out there Terence. Go and explore it.'

Terence stood up sharply.

'Go get fucked, you fat cunt.' His footsteps shook the furniture as he walked, slamming the door on his way out.

Elliot smiled and watched him go. He bounded through the

fourth floor, not even stopping at his desk to collect anything. Nobody looked his way. Elliot waited until he was out of sight and buzzed his secretary.

'Suzy, find out who recruited that thug and send him in to me please. Thanks.'

'Right away, Mr Rossley,' she said.

Zac sat in the tea-hut with Bernie, the site manager, a squat man who always seemed to have a half-inch of Rizla-rolled cigarette hanging from the corner of his mouth. Zac took a swig of water and stretched his hand out as far as it would go. The muscles in his right arm and shoulder were stiff and he waggled his fingers to try to ease some pressure.

'Is that a home-made tattoo?' Bernie stared at the blue-green lettering on Zac's lower right arm, which said '1 PARA'.

Zac frowned. 'Yeah, sort of. Some mates of mine did it for me once.'

'What? Like a gang thing?'

Zac frowned again.

'Regiment,' he said, simply.

Bernie nodded and made a little noise, as if the information given was to his complete satisfaction, there was no more he needed to know. He took a deep lug on his roll-up.

'Who's West Ham playing on Saturday?' he said.

11

Richter had been rushing around the building for ten minutes, spot-checking the different areas of the facility, ordering bewildered technicians to wipe surfaces and dispose of litter. He came across Margaret in the corner of the main lab, by the sealed door to the toxicology area and spoke to her in a half-whisper.

'How did you get on with Arnold? Is he on-side now?'

'Hard to say. He's in a bit of a state over the whole thing, really.'

'He's too scared of authority. He needs to see beyond the immediate consequences and focus long term.'

'He's finding that difficult to do,' she said.

'Well, you've got about another three hours to work on him. Two visitors from the Ministry are arriving at four for a meeting. They want to see all of us.'

From the moment he had been informed of the visit, Richter's morning had disappeared into a slough of semi-panic. They had been used to official visits at the beginning, during the construction and staffing of the premises but had been left alone for over two years, to the point where they'd pretty much forgotten that the project was actually a government commission and almost believed that it was their own cosy lab in which science was practised for the love of it. Unfortunately it seemed that now testing with live subjects had begun, the Ministry's interest had been reignited.

He had missed lunch because of the tightness in his stomach and when the officials arrived, there was a hint of the jungle, of the trapped animal in his eyes.

'Gentlemen!' he said, greeting them with a smile of crocodilian width as he met them at reception. 'Fifteen minutes early! How pleasant.'

The man standing closest to him, whose slender frame carried a slight stoop about the neck and shoulders, putting Richter in mind of a vulture, stepped forward.

'Dr Richter,' he said. 'Nice to meet you at last. My name's Richard Travis. We've conversed before by e-mail and fax. And this is my colleague, Francis Ripon.' The three of them shook hands, stiffly pressing palms, squeezing and releasing, forcing smiles.

'We were hoping to be able to look around your facility before the meeting, hence the early arrival.'

Travis' face had an evenness, a symmetry. His features seemed to open when he spoke, inviting trust and interaction. Ripon on the other hand was short and pinched. He moved his head in rapid, twitching movements, like a rodent. Richter saw accusation in his grey-blue eyes.

'Of course!' Richter said. 'An excellent idea! Would you like to follow me?'

He led the two men through a door set to the side of the reception desk. It took them onto a landing with two doors, above a downward flight of stairs.

'Downstairs are the laboratories and test areas,' Richter announced. 'We'll see those shortly. Firstly, if we head this way,' he pushed the landing door open and held it for the other two, 'we come to our data analysis department.'

Seven or eight young lab-assistants sat at computers tapping keys.

'Just here,' Richter continued, motioning towards a door on the right, 'is my office. Anyway, I know it's downstairs that you're most eager to see.'

The three of them left the data room.

'Will the research directors be there when we arrive?' Travis asked.

'Yes,' Richter confirmed. 'You'll be meeting both of them.'

'How is the project progressing?'

'Well, as you know Test Study One has just been completed – we'll discuss the results later with Dr Rustermeyer. Generally speaking, things are moving along as expected.'

They reached the bottom of the staircase and Arnold emerged from the toilet opposite the main lab door.

'Speak of the devil!' Richter tried to sound cheerful, but achieved something between panic and sarcasm.

'Arnold, this is Mr Travis and Mr Ripon, from the Ministry. They want to look around the labs.' Acknowledgements and handshakes passed between them.

Arnold smiled weakly.

'Shall we?' he said.

The group moved through the round, sealed door into the main lab area.

'We have three major laboratories here. Toxic Chemicals is through that door and Psychological Testing with Zoology is through there,' Arnold began. 'Our main lab with enclosure and observation screens is this one and will be used for all the test studies and behaviour surveillance involved in the research.'

The men walked forward together. The underground laboratory opened up before them, a cavernous, metallic, oppressive room.

Arnold began to speak again.

'The enclosure area, over here,' he pointed towards a huge transparent screen at one end, surrounded by dozens of TV monitors, 'is three square kilometres in size and has the latest climate control technology. Everything from temperature and humidity to brightness of daylight and even precipitation can be simulated at our discretion. It is a completely controlled environment.'

'It's very impressive,' Travis said. 'Is there anything in there at the moment?'

'No, we are waiting for the subject sample for Test Study Two to arrive.' Arnold fingered his ear uneasily.

'What happened to the subjects from Test Study One?'

Arnold looked blankly at the enclosure screen.

Richter stepped in. 'We returned them via the supplier. I think the stress of being under lab conditions was starting to show on a few of them, so bearing in mind that their role in the research was over, we thought it best to send them home.'

'But what about delayed development. Some of the subjects might start to show results. They should have...'

Richter cut him short.

'Gentlemen, let's adjourn upstairs. We'll discuss the whole thing in detail in my office.'

The meeting started without Margaret, who arrived five minutes late, pink-cheeked and with one collar of her lab coat torn.

Richter gestured at the men in suits. 'This is Margaret Hoffman, who supervises the two smaller labs. Margaret, this is Misters Travis and Ripon, from the Ministry.'

'I apologise for my lateness. We had a problem with one of the researchers in toxicology, McNally. I've just had to sedate him.'

Richter winced as if he had been hit in the stomach. Both Ripon and Travis appeared momentarily stunned.

'What happened?' Travis asked.

'Oh, nothing serious,' she backtracked, noticing Richter's reaction. 'He had a minor exposure to one of the chemicals we were testing and went a bit gaga. He'll be fine in a few hours.'

'Will he be able to resume work?'

Margaret looked down at the table.

'We'll have to wait and see.'

Ripon scribbled some notes in a pocket-diary.

'If not, he'll have to be replaced,' Travis said.

53

'We'll keep you informed,' Richter cut in. 'Anyway, on to business?'

'Yes,' Travis said. 'Test study One. I need feedback from you now and a report to take back to the department with me. Dr Rustermeyer, I believe this is your area of responsibility.'

All heads turned towards Arnold. Richter looked at him intensely.

'The results of Test Study One were inconclusive,' he said.

Richter couldn't help but smile slightly.

Arnold continued. 'We will obviously increase the number of subjects and also toxicity levels for Test Study Two, as per the research scheme. There is little else to say.'

He pushed a few sheets of paper across the table.

'My report.'

'Which timeframe were we working with in Test Study One?' asked Ripon. It was the first time he had spoken. His voice was sharp and nasal. He spoke briskly, as if pressed for time. Richter disliked him immediately.

'In what sense?' Arnold asked.

'The conditions of the test reflected which period?'

'Oh, I see. The test conditions, climactic, toxic, denseness of sample population etc were mimicking those expected of five years from now.'

'They were worse than current conditions?'

'Yes, I would say so. They allowed for increases in pollution levels and population concentrations of five years' time.'

'Hence the inconclusive results,' Ripon continued.

Arnold cleared his throat.

'Quite,' he said.

'The preliminary tests we were most interested in were always going to be those of test studies two and three. Remind me, Dr Rustermeyer, which projected period is Test Study Two examining?'

'About twelve years from now.'

'Yes.' Ripon stared hard, straight into Richter's eyes. 'That

54

should be most interesting.'

Richter tried to return his gaze but couldn't. He felt as if Ripon were assaulting him, searching his mind for secrets. He turned away, and settled right down into his chair, making himself smaller, less of a target. Five minutes of stilted conversation later, Travis and Ripon got up to leave.

Richter made the effort to smile and shake their hands.

'So, you'll be braving the gauntlet of the protestors again then, gentleman.'

Travis smirked crookedly.

'There's nothing they can do. We're in an armoured car.'

'I still wonder about the wisdom of leaking the vivisection story to the papers. It's making life pretty tough for us getting in and out of the place.'

Travis stopped smiling. 'You handle the research, Doctor. We'll handle everything else. The press leak occurred for very good reasons. Questions were being asked and it gave people the answer they needed.'

Richter nodded and looked down.

'Keep us posted,' Travis said. Ripon was already walking out. Margaret and Arnold stood up deferentially and the two officials left.

'Well done, Arnold,' Richter said. 'You did very well.'

'I can't help but think we're in way over our heads with this one.' Arnold looked a little traumatised.

'I'll cover you. Don't worry!' Richter was jubilant. 'People,' he continued. 'You can start to prepare for Test Study Two!'

Margaret smiled.

Eventually, so did Arnold.

12

'All right, Zac?' Andy from the gym asked, manoeuvring his twenty-two stone bulk over to the till, where he pushed buttons with cumbersome movements of huge arms which permanently rested at forty-five degree angles to his shoulders and upper back. Once a competition bodybuilder, middle age and a fondness for alcohol had robbed him of the muscle definition he had possessed when young. His upper body was still large and strong, but his waist had taken on similar proportions, as had his buttocks and thighs – or 'glutes' and 'quads' as he called them.

'Yeah, not bad. You?'

'Oh, you know, surviving!'

'Busy tonight?' Zac asked.

'Afraid so. It's all the summertime posers innit!' Andy picked his nose with his thumb, flicking the findings onto the floor behind him. 'Bit of sunshine, holiday booked in Ayia Napa and everyone panics and starts training. Give it two months and they'll all piss off again.'

Zac nodded. 'Until next year.'

'That's it. Puts money in my pocket though, dunnit! I wouldn't mind, but the little bleeders keep pestering me to put their CDs on. I have to sit here all night listening to fuckin' garage. What you doing?'

'Chest.'

'Give us a shout if you want a hand.'

56

'I probably will, I'm gonna do some heavy, today.'

'Yeah! Making rainbows again?'

Zac smiled warmly.

'That's it,' he said. 'Making rainbows.'

Twenty minutes later and Zac was lying on a bench with Andy standing over him. A bar loaded with 140kg wavered just above his nose. Andy's hands supported the weight from underneath while Zac pushed and strained, trying desperately to extend his arms.

'Lift it, Zac, *lift it!*' Andy urged.

A little movement and the bar rose an inch or so.

'Come on, Zac, push!'

Another small movement, Zac's face was deep crimson; thick veins bulged on his neck and arms.

Andy started to add his own strength, just enough to get the bar past the sticking point.

'It's all you,' he said softly, as Zac exhaled. 'All you.'

At last the bar returned to its stand with a deafening clank.

Zac sat up and breathed deeply. The large muscles in his chest and arms throbbed, engorged with oxygen-rich blood.

Andy slapped him on the back.

'Good set, Zac.'

Zac panted.

'Thanks,' he said, between gasps.

'One more?'

Zac nodded.

In Andy's gym the weights were colour coded. A 25kg weight was red and 20kg weight, blue. A 15kg weight was yellow, a 10kg green, a 5kg orange, a 2kg purple, and the 1kg weight was white. Zac liked to put them all on the bar, the full complement of colours, doubled up, a rainbow on each side. It made 156kg, the same weight as two largish men.

They gathered the necessary weights and started placing them on the bar. Some of the other punters noticed. Whispers trailed around the gym, hidden by the sound system. Weights were slid onto the bar in descending order of size and there was something satisfying, quasi-sexual, in the action. The 1kg fitted snugly onto the end. As Zac stretched and breathed, preparing himself for the strain, he realised that a circle of onlookers had gathered to watch.

13

Elliot called Suzy in to see him as he usually did at the smug end of the day, when business had run its course, when the score had been made. She listened as he spoke, noting 'action points' for the following morning.

'Lastly, remind me to check with the Regulators Office, we're due for an inspection during the next month and I need to make sure that all files are up-to-date.'

Suzy scratched in her diary.

'Right, Dinner!' Elliot got up, smiling. 'My treat!'

'I don't know. It's been a long day. I'm pretty tired.'

'No choice! I insist.' Elliot stood and Suzy did the same.

As usual, they had both arrived just after 8:00 am and spent ten minutes over coffee covering the day's action plan. The section managers and senior executives had arrived for the 8:15 strategy meeting before the Junior Advisers and executives rolled in between 8:30 and 9:00. The end of the day was something of a competition to see who could stay the latest in the office.

The Junior Advisers would be so keen to impress that some would hang around until eight or nine, desperately hoping that one of the management team would see them there and note it as a mark of excellence, of 'doing that bit extra.' On this occasion, Antonio was the last to leave, finally pushing the off button on his PC at 8:45. He rubbed his eyes, looked at his watch as he stood and pushed his hands through the sleeves of his jacket. Elliot and Suzy emerged from Elliot's office. He pretended not to notice them, but felt a jolt of excitement.

'The problem is not with the managers, Suzy, it's with the nature of the business. Ever since I started PFPL twenty-three years ago, we've always had this issue. Low salary, high-commission selling is highly competitive and naturally it sometimes attracts the wrong people.'

'So why don't we filter our applicants more carefully?'

'We could do that, but we'd inevitably lose money. The onus is on each team leader to recruit as many individuals as possible. Even if they only last a few weeks, it's money in the company's pocket.'

Suzy nodded daintily.

'The business has its own ways of sorting the wheat from the chaff. It's the law of the jungle, contemporary Darwinism, the survival of the fittest.'

The two of them reached Antonio's desk.

'And this is one young chap who's doing a damn good job of surviving!'

'Just on my way home, Elliot,' Antonio said.

'Really? Well, Suzy and I were just going for a bite to eat and a few drinks. Would you care to join us?'

Antonio didn't think about it for a second.

'Sure! Why not?'

He gathered a few papers and followed Elliot and Suzy to the lift.

'Where are we going?' he asked.

'Just a place I know. You'll like it. It's a nice place, isn't it, Suzanne?'

'Very nice. I like the seafood.'

A uniformed security guard smiled at them as they walked through the lobby and out into the night. It was threatening rain. Elliot hailed a cab and after a tortuous twenty-five minute crawl past the boutiques and designer eateries of mid-west London, they pulled up in front of a Spanish-Mexican place in

Notting Hill.

'I wouldn't have thought of this as being your kind of scene, Elliot,' Antonio said, as a pony-tailed waiter offered them menus.

'Why's that?' Elliot was smiling and leaning back in his chair. A colourful picture of a bullfighter hung on the wall behind him.

'I don't know, really. I suppose I expect a man of your wealth to be eating at Gordon Ramsay or that Marco-Pierre White place.'

'Well, I'm full of surprises, my boy.'

Elliot ordered a bottle and the waiter arrived with three glasses. He filled Suzy's and Elliot's.

'Oh, no.' Antonio put his hand over the top of his glass. 'Not for me.'

The waiter shrugged and walked away.

Elliot looked over the table at Antonio, nodding silently.

'This really is a smashing wine you know,' he said, after a time. He smacked his lips for emphasis.

'Don't you think so, Suzy?'

'You know me, E-R. I'm not exactly a connoisseur. It tastes fine, though.'

Elliot grinned broadly.

'Yes indeed. Fine! As grand a validation as one is likely to get from Suzy.'

Suzy smiled weakly, without feeling. She looked away.

'I really think you should try some, Antonio.'

'I promised myself no alcohol, Elliot, Sunday to Thursday.'

'I know, but a glass won't hurt. In fact, small amounts of alcohol are beneficial to health. It's a fact.'

'No, I really don't...'

Elliot picked up the bottle and examined it briefly, then filled Antonio's glass.

'Sorry, what were you saying?' he asked. He stared hard at Antonio, as if testing him.

'Nothing.' Antonio smiled and took a tiny sip.

The three of them studied their menus silently for a while.

'I think I'll be having the prawns,' Suzy said, eventually.

After the waiter took their order, Suzy excused herself to go the toilet. Both watched her as she walked.

Elliot leaned over the edge of the table. 'What do you think of Suzanne?' he asked, conspiratorially.

'She's friendly, seems very nice.'

'Nice! Bloody Nice!' Elliot laughed and slapped the table-top with his fingers. 'A sandwich can be nice! A cup of tea is nice! But I chose Suzanne to be my PA from over 150 applicants! She's got something special.'

He took a large swig from his wine glass and whispered, so quietly it was almost to himself, 'I think you know what I mean.'

A few minutes of silence followed. Antonio surveyed the restaurant, his gaze eventually settling on an effeminate-looking maitre-d who was helping some departing customers with their coats.

'*Buenos Noches*,' he said, with a lisp, his frilly-collared shirt open at the neck, revealing an upper triangle of black chest hair.

Suzy returned from the toilet, refreshed and talkative.

'So, what have you been telling our new superstar?'

Elliot smiled. 'Just the pros and cons of the business, Suzy. The perks and so on.'

Suzy smiled.

'There's a lot you have to learn, Antonio.'

'I just told him that.'

'He just told me that.'

The three of them giggled and sipped their drinks.

14

'Name?' The jobcentre clerk asked.

'Terence Monahan.'

'What's your usual line of work?'

'I don't really have one. I've been working in the city for the last couple of months.'

'Reason for leaving?'

Terence looked hard at the clerk.

'Sacked.'

'Why?'

'Failed to reach targets.'

'I see. Do you think there'd be a problem obtaining a reference from your previous employer?'

'Probably.'

'In that case it's going to be very hard for me to find work in that sector for you.'

'Right.'

'To be honest, Mr Monahan, we get very few vacancies for that sort of thing anyway. However I can scan the vacancies we do have and see if anything appeals.'

'Okay.'

'What sort of work would you consider?'

Terence ran a hand over his closely cropped head.

'Between you and me, pal, I need something quickly and I've had it up to here with offices. Just give me something outdoors.'

'Outdoors. Let me see. A building firm in North-Central London needs a window fitter's assistant.'

'I'll do it.'

'Involves heavy lifting and climbing ladders.'

'I'll do it.'

'£160 per week.'

'I'll do it.'

The clerk raised one eyebrow and started tapping out details on his keyboard.

'Well then, Mr Monahan,' he said eventually. 'You start tomorrow at 8:15. You need to report to Bernie Skeefe. I'll print you out an address sheet now.'

They interviewed the candidates in the conference room of a nearby hotel. So far none of them had met every requirement.

Richter looked back over the current applicant's CV while Margaret continued to press him.

'So what was the nature of the research that you were involved with previously?'

'It was concerned with conditions for workers on oil drilling platforms,' he said, repeating himself. Margaret wondered if she could sense irritation in his voice. It might just be his accent, she thought, although his eyes betrayed something too.

'How, exactly?'

'Testing levels of pollutants and toxins, examining psychological and physical effects on employees.'

'And this was in Saudi?'

'Yes.'

'And you say the research was used by…?'

'The international committee of OPEC.'

'Why did you leave that job?'

'I'm a contract worker, Mrs Hoffman, I …'

'Ms.'

'I'm sorry?'

'I'm not married. Ms Hoffman, please.'

The interviewee smiled and bowed his head slightly, maintaining eye contact.

'The position was a fixed term, non-renewable contract, expiring after eighteen months. When the work is finished, it is finished.'

'Well, I think that wraps it up. Thank you very much, Mr Walid.' She smiled politely.

'Have you anything to add, Dr Richter?'

Richter looked up from the CV.

'I don't think so,' he said. 'We'll let you know in a few days time.'

Richter stood up and the interviewee did the same. They shook hands.

'I'll take you to the door,' Margaret said.

'What did you think of him?' she asked, when she came back.

Richter shook his head.

'He's extremely well qualified.'

'Nationality?'

'Hmm. Could be a problem. It's a bad time to be an Arab applying for research work here.'

Margaret nodded in agreement.

'Shall we recommend him?'

'I don't see why not. I wouldn't have thought the Ministry would clear him though.'

'That's up to them, isn't it?'

'True.' he said.

15

Fut-fut-fut-fut. The dust cushioned the soles of his leather loaf-ers while behind him the sun slipped reluctantly below the horizon. His steps occasionally crunched through thirsty weeds and scrub. Olive trees cast shadows.

He walked steadily and softly, full of purpose, without fear, his dark suit neat, his black hair combed to a precise parting. A platinum lapel pin twinkled in the fading light. The car from which he had emerged, a long, black Mercedes, reversed and drove away, throwing up plumes of sand from its rear tyres. He didn't look back.

He headed towards a house. A flat-roofed house, with white walls and large windows, most of which were open. There was some kind of water-tank on the roof.

In the distance he heard the adhan *being called and tapped his forehead with his middle finger.*

As he approached the front door, it was opened from inside. The man that stood before him was dressed simply in a white robe and sandals. He smiled and lowered his head. They both entered and the door closed behind them.

Suzy found herself running on autopilot, which she often did during the semi-conscious mind sludge of early morning. The routine was so entrenched into her five-days-a-week con-sciousness that she reckoned she could get up, wash, dress and walk to the tube station unsighted.

She knew that her psyche had developed a special relation-
ship with her daily journey, as her dreams frequently featured
it, most recently in an apocalyptic nightmare in which the trains
filled with water and everyone had drowned. She had checked
it out in an interpretation book to find that night-visions involv-
ing water indicated sexual yearning, which she thought seemed
to completely miss the point.

Commuting, for her, began with boarding the Central Line
westbound from Epping Forest on which she would immerse
herself in a novel or a magazine until, roughly thirty-five minutes later she heard the recorded announcement say, '*Bank.
This is Bank. Change here for the District and Circle lines.
This is Bank.*'

Her hangover, which eased as she sipped from a small bottle of mineral water, had prevented her from making any kind
of reading material decision that morning and she had resorted
to collecting one of the freebie newspapers that they handed out
at the stations. She had left it, folded neatly on her lap for at
least five stops, while she closed her eyes and practised Yogic
breathing, which her instructor reliably informed her was a perfect cure for headaches. By the time she opened her eyes, headache free, the atmosphere in the carriage had changed.

A thin, Asian man in a business suit stood with his shin
pressed against her knee. He, in turn was pressed up against
five or six other passengers who in turn were pressed against
others. It was rush-hour tube travel as the human equivalent of
snake coiling or bee swarming; all had subdued their instinct
for personal space, the needs of the individual secondary to
those of the society, work and its implications dominating everything. The entire carriage was the same.

Suzy had a quick look around and noticed the same thing
that she noticed every day. No one on the crowded train seemed
to connect with reality. It was as if they withdrew within themselves, standing, eyes shifting to avoid others, many of them
listening to personal stereos, many others staring at the floor or

ceiling or an advertisement. Awkwardness rose from their skins and collected around the carriage, smearing the windows and dripping from the ceiling.

She picked the paper off her lap, opening it despite the restricted space, propping it almost against the Asian man's leg. The front page concerned itself with a number of London football clubs who potentially were going under due to unpaid TV royalties: *TV Foul Play Puts Clubs in Danger* it read. She flicked the page without reading and scanned the next few absently, half-reading an article about the dangers posed to cats from passive smoking and a short interview with an Olympic diver, who put his recent success down to 'stick-to-itiveness'. Reaching the middle pages, she glanced over the TV guide before she found an article that would hold her attention almost until the end of her journey.

London Workers Stress Levels at All-Time High,
Say Doctors

London workers are among the most stressed in the world. That is the worrying message of Dr Diprak Sharma of the Bethlem and Maudsley Hospital, Denmark Hill. 'Rising levels of mental illness are directly connected to the stress of living and working in London,' he said.

'In the last four to five years in particular, we have noticed an increase in certain kinds of psychological disorder. Mainly these are forms of depression, but we are also seeing increases in unrelated psychoses. Most notable of these are extreme forms of paranoia and attachment disorders which result in poor relationships with other people. This means that people are leading more solitary lives and are less in control of their emotions.'

Doctor Sharma went on to say that 'it has never

been more stressful to live in London. Overcrowding, poor public transport and the extremely high cost of living, combined with high-pressure working environments are creating a city populated by physically and psychologically unhealthy people.'

Dr. Sharma's report is based on a 10-year study, investigating working and living conditions in London and will be published in full, by the BMA, next week.

The results are no surprise to many of us, as our exclusive poll, conducted yesterday at a random selection of London tube stations, shows.

73% of passengers admitted to being 'less than happy' with their day-to-day life in the capital.

Use our questionnaire below to see if you show the symptoms of stress.

She read the article twice before she got off the train, leaving the paper on the small ledge behind her seat. The piece itself had worried her, but the questionnaire made her feel a little more positive.

She was able to answer 'Yes' to questions like 'Do you have satisfactory relationships with colleagues?' and 'Do you often eat food with high water content, such as celery?' and that helped to ease her mind.

16

While Suzy disembarked and joined a shuffling queue for the escalator, Antonio was dragging himself, shadow-eyed, out of bed. His mother's hammerings on the door increased the level of pain in his head. He had allowed Elliot to cajole him into drinking and had ended up having a skinful.

'Tony!' she called. 'You'd better get up, love! It's eight o'clock!'

'Hmm?'

There followed a frantic ten minutes of washing and dressing before he climbed into his Toyota, unshaven. He pulled out of the driveway and made his way carefully around the maze of suburban back streets that comprised his parents' neighbourhood. In no time he hit the North Circular Road and pushed up into fourth gear, motoring down the outside lane, passing a succession of slower cars and trade vans. Greyness pervaded everything. Drizzle pattered the roof and windows.

A white transit reared up in front of him and forced him to change down to third. He blasted his horn three times.

'Come on, dickhead.'

The van took ages to move, at last turning into the middle lane to allow him to pass. He stepped on the accelerator and changed back to fourth, as the motorway led him down into an underpass. In seconds he was out the other side and roaring past an articulated lorry. The twitching needle on his speedometer hovered around ninety.

Progress was short-lived. Soon he was forced to slow up once more, behind a pale-blue family saloon. The more he slowed, the closer he got and he realised grimly, seeing the line of vehicles stretching in front of him, that he was actually stopping altogether.

'Shit.'

He put the radio on and drummed on the steering wheel with his fingers.

Several hours passed before the door was opened again. The night had become oppressively dark. He stood on the top step and filled his lungs, while an orchestra of crickets sent out a rhythmic symphony, the sound coming from all directions, deafening and repetitive.

He walked back the way he had come, now clutching a small leather briefcase with a combination lock. His grip was solid, his knuckles tight with pressure, but his steps fell softly in the sand and gravel. One foot was placed before the other, gently, precisely, like a cat.

The Mercedes appeared again. He opened the back door and slipped inside. The tyres took a moment to grip the road, spinning in the dust.

17

Terence finished his first morning at the building site and went for a drink in the tea hut. He made himself a brew and sat down to drink it, inadvertently eavesdropping the conversation of two co-workers. The sound of their rough accents pleased him. He enjoyed the contrast it made with the office.

'They were mad days. Ninety of us'd be running like maniacs to the station. You'd make it to the train just before the doors shut and you'd all pile on, laughing and buzzing.'

'That's a big firm.'

'That weren't just our firm. On match days other firms would come to back us up. "The yellow firms" we called them, glamour-boys and ponces mostly – not serious hooligans, just lads who wanted to make a big noise and get a headline in the Sunday papers. The *News of the World* did a league table of hooligans once. They put us top, you know. We were fucking championship material.'

Darren nodded, a smile spreading on his face as he rolled a cigarette.

'That's the only time West Ham are gonna win the title,' he said.

Zac laughed.

'There was this one time at the Bridge: eight thousand West Ham and about thirty thousand Chelsea. My firm took the whole pitch. We charged it from our end and steamed the Shed. We fought our way to the fucking top. We had to battle through fists, elbows, knees, feet. They were flying in from all sides. About six of us made it to the top and we planted a West Ham flag on the top step. Course we didn't last long. We were only up there about a minute. Chelsea went crazy. In the end we were happy when the stewards got hold of us and kicked us out.'

'I've read about that before. That was you?'

Zac nodded.

'Come on.'

'It was,' he said, very seriously, staring straight ahead. 'Before I joined up. In a way, I suppose it was my first regiment. In some ways it prepared me for what I saw later.'

They sat in silence then. Terence considered introducing himself, but decided against it. The three of them drank their tea.

18

The new subjects for Test Study Two had been steadily arriving all morning, making throaty, glottal noises as they were led from the rig angled across the car park, to the back entrance of the enclosure.

'Have they all been checked?' Richter asked the delivery-man. 'Do you have the forms?'

In as disinterested a manner as he could possibly affect, the driver reached into the cab of the lorry and pulled out a sheet of paper. Richter took it from him and scrutinised it for a while, his finger and thumb twisting the end of his goatee into a point.

'What's this?' he asked, using his pen to indicate an area of the sheet that troubled him.

'I couldn't tell you, pal. You'll have to ring the centre.'

'You've brought me some juveniles.'

'Right.'

'I specifically said mature individuals only. We're not ready to start testing with juveniles.'

'I see.'

'I'm going to have to check this with my research director. Don't put those subjects inside yet, keep them here.'

Richter hurried indoors and found Arnold addressing one of the lab teams.

'From now on this team is working very closely with Toxicology. If Dr Hoffman asks you to adjust your settings or advance your timescale in any way that differs from the directions that I have given you then do it. We are still tweaking some aspects of the project and we have to make sure that we have all major research areas working empathically before the real studies begin next year. Don't be afraid to...'

'Sorry Dr Rustermeyer.' Richter interrupted. 'Can I speak to you for a moment?'

'Sure.'

They walked away from the group.

'The sample's arriving for TS2 this morning.'

'I know.'

'He's brought four juveniles.'

'What?'

'Four juveniles. Different ages, all below the required age we asked for.'

'What are we going to do with them?'

'I was going to ask you the same thing, what's your opinion? Shall I send them back?'

Arnold pursed his lips and wrinkled and unwrinkled his forehead. His bald scalp undulated with the movement.

'My initial reaction would be yes, send them back. From a professional point of view, they are not supposed to be here and they will obviously affect the predicted outcomes of the study.'

'That's what I thought,' Richter agreed.

'But from a personal and scientific point of view, it could be fascinating to have them here. We suspect that they will react to imposed conditions more readily than adults. We can see what they will do. As long as we are aware of the anomaly we can adjust the results accordingly. We will be testing with juveniles eventually, so why not now?'

'You think we should keep them?'

'Yes. Why not?'

'Okay.' Richter headed back outside and told the driver to continue what he had started. The deliveryman asked him to sign for the subjects and returned to the cab of his lorry.

Richter watched the line of chimpanzees being led into the

opened back door of the observation area, through which he caught a glimpse of the simulated environment. He often found himself marvelling at the skill of the people who created the study ecosystems. For this test, the conditions of sub-tropical Africa had been replicated. They had packed the huge room with four hundred different species of flora, towering trees and gigantic, impressive angiosperms. Luxuriant, broadleaved foliage stretched up to the high ceiling, creating a thick forest canopy. Standing at the doorway between the car park and the artificial jungle he felt caught between two worlds, like a man in the middle of something huge, a man with enormous responsibility.

The new arrivals babbled and grunted as they were led past him.

19

Antonio finally reached the office feeling tired and sick, but hurried to his desk, trying to look casual. When he got there he saw a note, stuck on the handset of his phone. It said simply, *Pop in and see me. E.* He took a moment to remove his coat and run a hand through his hair before heading over to Elliot's office.

Suzy busied herself at the filing cabinets just outside the door.

'Hey, superstar!' she said, eyes dancing with fun. 'Not feeling so super today, huh?'

Antonio smiled weakly, more of a grimace than a smile.

'I must admit I've felt better,' he said.

Suzy laughed. 'Elliot's been waiting to speak to you all morning.'

'Do you think he'll be upset I'm late?'

'Hard to say.' She spoke very quietly. 'It depends which Elliot you find in there. Yesterday you were like his favourite son. Today might not be the same. He changes his opinions of people frequently. He's done it with me enough times.'

Antonio frowned. She saw that she had worried him.

'I'd go in now if I was you, he's not busy.'

Antonio tried to smile, turned and knocked on the door.

'Antonio!' Elliot looked up from a document he was examining. 'How are you? You look like shit!'

'Thanks. Sorry I'm late in. The traffic was awf– '

'Stop!' Elliot held up the palm of his hand for added emphasis. 'I do not want to hear your excuses.'

'I just thought I should explain.'

'There's no need. We were together last night. I know what sort of state you were in. So you had a bit of trouble getting up. I used to be the same way. Not now. I'm used to my lifestyle. My constitution has adapted. But you're still a novice. Still mewling and puking, you'll grow out of it.'

He chuckled and slapped his stomach with his right hand. It made a heavy, dull sound, like a wet towel hitting the floor.

'You'll learn to deal with these things, okay? Don't worry about it.'

'Thanks.'

'And while I'm on the subject of growth and personal development, another tip. No matter how you're feeling, don't come in with a mouth full of excuses, looking like your mother's just died. Bright, alert, energetic, confident individuals sell financial products. Miserable losers with hangovers don't.'

Antonio nodded. Elliot smirked.

'I know what you're thinking. You're thinking "but I am miserable and hung over". Well, you have to overcome it Antonio. It's a form of strength, of bravery. You need to be confident and on the ball even if you don't feel you can be. Otherwise you can't do the job. This is the courage you need to succeed here. You don't have to fight or run or put your life in danger, but you have to do this. You have to do whatever it takes.'

'You mean fake it?'

'In a way, yes. Emotions and feelings are controlled by the mind. Strengthen your mind and you can conquer your feelings. All you need to do is decide that you have to do it.'

Antonio felt better already. He smiled. Elliot smiled back.

'Did you enjoy yourself last night?' Elliot asked, changing the subject.

'Yeah, it was fun. It's nice to see successful people in a social context. It helps you to understand them.'

'Suzy enjoyed your company, apparently.'

'She said so?'

'She didn't stop talking about you after you left. I almost found myself getting a bit jealous, which, of course is ridiculous.'

'She's an interesting one.'

'She certainly is,' Elliot agreed, oozing wisdom. 'Anyway, as we all had such a nice time, I'll tell you I'm having a party this weekend at my apartment in Wapping. I'd like you to come.'

'Thanks.' Antonio raised his eyebrows, widening his eyes. 'I'll be there.'

'So will Suzy.'

Antonio smirked and looked away.

'Anyway I'll get Suzy to leave a message with my address on it for you. Arrive at about nine, alone please.'

'Alone?'

'Yes, no girlfriends or chums. Just you, okay?'

'Guest list only, huh?'

'Go and hit the phones,' Elliot said, his manner changing. 'Twenty appointments today, please.'

'No problem.'

Elliot watched Antonio stride back over to his desk. He liked the way he walked.

His plans for the weekend were falling nicely into place.

20

The Mercedes moved through the dunes in long, sweeping arcs, leaving parabolic tracers on the landscape. He sat placidly in the back, feeling the welcome breath of the air-conditioner on his cheek.

His destination this time lay many miles away: a small village in the Hasa region, beyond the limit of local roads. Outside the car, a lively wind whipped sand into the air, making it dance in jerky circles. Two Bedouins struggled on their camels, their bodies bent into the storm, clothes billowing around them. He watched them impassively.

The driver asked him for permission to smoke and offered him one of his British cigarettes. He nodded, but declined to take one.

Instead, he took a gold plated cigarette lighter from the breast pocket of his jacket and lit a slim cigar. His briefcase lay on the seat beside him.

The three of them walked out of the main gates of the site and onto the high street. A days' hard work had rubbed itself into their faces and all over their clothes. Zac walked slightly in front of the other two. He winced a little as he turned to speak, and a muscle knot in his back tightened.

'We used to drink in here,' he said, to the Irishman. 'Before they did it up. It used to just be a regular pub. Most of the boys from the site went in there. They don't want us no more, though.'

'What d'you mean?' the Irishman asked. The three of them waited for a bus to pass and crossed the road.

'Look,' Zac said, pointing with his thumb. They walked past the pub. A sign in the window said *No work clothes or boots*.

'It's all bottles of Becks, now. Full of suits from the offices up the road. Anyway, there's another one up here.'

They walked in silence to the other pub and went inside. Darren and the Irishman found a table. Zac went to the bar. He returned with three pints, sat down, sipped the top off his Guinness and turned to the new guy.

'How was your first day then, mate? Terry, innit?'

'Yeah.'

'Zac.'

'Well, it wasn't too bad really, I quite enjoyed it in some ways.' He took a gulp of lager. 'Different from my last job, though.'

'What was that, then?'

'City.'

'Doing what?'

'Selling equities packages, life assurance and what-not.'

'There's some money in that, in't there?'

'Yeah, damn right. The boss of the office, big fat wanker that he was, was pulling in £950,000 a year. He said he didn't need the money any more. It was just a way of keeping score. He said when he got to £1,000,000 he was gonna retire.'

'Imagine that, Zac,' Darren said, from the other side of the table.

'£1,000,000 sovs a year. I think I could manage on that.'

'There's more to life than money, Darren,' Zac replied.

'Are you saying you wouldn't want that sort of wedge?'

'Not if it meant sitting in an office all day.'

'You could live in a palace, drive a fleet of luxury cars, have a summer home in Barbados and a supermodel girlfriend.

That's my dream life.'

'Have you met Darren?' Zac asked Terry.

'I have now.'

Darren and Terry acknowledged each other with gestures.

'He's not a bad guy. Dozy twat, but not a bad guy.'

Terry laughed.

'So why d'you leave?' Zac asked.

Terry laughed again and ran a hand over his cropped head.

'Do you want the short answer or the long answer?'

'Let's start with the long one.'

'Well,' he inhaled loudly through his nose and sipped some more lager. 'I couldn't stand the atmosphere in the place. Everyone was in competition with everyone else and there was a real nastiness about it. They were all backbiting and cheating to try to get one up on the next man. You know, like they'd be really nice to each other's face but be secretly planning to steal everyone else's clients. They'd sit around in cafes at lunchtime boasting about the dodgy schemes they had going. They're a bunch of crooks really, liars and thieves with suits on. Most of them were real snobs, too. They were public school, Oxbridge types, talking about vintage wines and rugby. They had a kind of in-crowd thing going on and I definitely wasn't in.'

Zac nodded in agreement. 'You see, Darren, that's why you don't need all that money; it's the sort of person you've got to be to get it. You're better off how you are.'

'You reckon?'

'Well, in your case, maybe not, actually.' Zac grinned and turned back to Terry.

'Carry on.'

'They started taking the piss out of me,' Terry continued. 'Because of my accent and everything. Real schoolyard stuff, you know. I was getting Paddy jokes every day and it started getting to me. One guy said he'd met my dad outside the tube station, drinking Super Brew and begging. I got angry and told him to fuck off. He reported me for it. But there were lots of issues, you know. My clothes weren't right, my accent, my face just didn't fit, I suppose. They've got a real long-hours thing going on as well. Most guys were doing twelve or more hours a day. I didn't want that. I've only been in London a few months. I want to go out, meet people and have fun. What's the point in having all that money if you spend all your time in an office? I tell ya, they may be rich but those guys don't have much quality of life. They don't know what living is, most of 'em.'

Zac took another gulp of Guinness.

'What's the short answer?' he asked, his face expressionless.

'I got the sack.'

Darren looked at Zac. They both looked at Terry.

The three of them exploded into laughter.

They laughed until tears began to form in the corners of their eyes, until the muscles in their jaws began to ache almost as much as those in their backs and arms. They laughed hard and deep. It wasn't that what had been said was particularly funny, but after a short time the laughter took on a life of its own. It didn't need a reason for existence. It was contagious and self-generating, like amoeba. It spread and grew inexorably. A long time passed before they stopped.

'Listen, though,' Zac said, eventually, light headed and elated. 'It sounds like they did you a favour.'

Darren spluttered into his pint. The other two managed to resist the urge to capitulate again.

'Building work's all right. It's got a bad name, but it's all right. You're outdoors in the fresh air, using your body. It helps keep you fit. You meet some decent people and some dodgy ones. The money's not great, but you can live on it.'

'Yeah. I'm not sure I'll be doing this for long, though.'

'You got something else lined up?'

'No, but I don't see this as a permanent job.'

'I used to be the same way a couple of years ago when I started. I did a few different things after I came out of the regiment but this was the only thing I could stand.'

'Regiment?'

'Yeah, First Airborne, I was a Paratrooper for five years.'

'Yeah?'

'Went in on my nineteenth birthday. I was a Sergeant before I left.'

Zac paused and finished his drink.

'Anyway, when I came out I was a bit clueless. I didn't know what to do. I had to move back in with my mum. So, this was something I could do to pay my own way. The way I see it, unless you're royalty or something, you've got to work. In the world we live in you need money or you're gonna end up sleeping in a cardboard box and eating out of dustbins. So, I'm in the building trade. I don't really enjoy it, but I don't hate it and it gives me enough to support myself. If something better comes along I'll jump right in, but until that happens…'

'So why did you leave the army?' Terry asked. Darren lit a cigarette.

'Para's not the army. I was a para.'

There was a short silence.

'I'm going to the bar,' Zac said, breaking it. 'What d'you want?'

21

From outside, the house seemed dark and quiet. Richter turned the key in his front door and breathed a long, somnolent sigh. The lights were off on the ground floor and the small hallway that led into the diner-through-lounge was tranquil. He almost went to the kitchen to make a snack, but fatigue guided him towards the stairs.

'Tony,' he called. 'Are you home?'

There was no reply. But a muffled rhythm came from the bedroom upstairs, some sort of house or garage music.

'Tony,' he called, heading up there, growing uneasy, paranoia building. 'I'm home!'

He pushed open the door of the bedroom and the music became deafening. He turned around and walked straight back out again.

Tony, his partner of three and a half years, was in bed with the pretty French guy he had met at Pilates. They were so intertwined in each other; they hadn't even noticed him come in.

In one sense, it was a good night for it to happen. Richter was too tired to get upset.

He went downstairs, flopped heavily on the sofa and fell asleep.

Elliot sidled up behind his wife. She stood at the kitchen counter, the outline of her full, heart-shaped buttocks sculpted by her linen trousers.

'What are you making, honey bunny?' he asked.

'Just a salad and some dips, Tanya's coming over to discuss what's happening this weekend.'

Elliot couldn't see that Janet raised her eyes upwards as she spoke.

'What do you mean?'

'I've invited Tanya to the party.'

'Oh for Christ's sake Janet! I'm trying to keep numbers down. You know how uncomfortable it can get in that apartment with too many people.'

'I know, but she's a long standing friend of ours and she'd be very offended if she found out that we had a party and didn't invite her.'

'But she's a terrible bore!'

'I don't care, Elliot, I've invited her now and that's the end of it.' Janet pursed her lips. Elliot didn't like it and looked away. He thought it made her look old.

'And she's got very saggy tits,' he whined, in desperation.

'For someone who's not exactly in peak physical condition you're very rude about the imperfections of others.'

'But you love me anyway.'

'Rude, coarse and vulgar.'

Elliot fiddled in the kitchen draw.

'Where's the corkscrew, darling?' he asked.

Antonio pushed Sadie's hand away. Her head dropped a little. A few strands of auburn hair fell across her face.

'I'm tired,' he said. 'Let me watch the film.'

Sadie let her arm fall onto the sofa.

'You're tired a lot lately, Tony.' She spoke the words very quietly, her head turned to the flickering screen.

'What?'

'You're tired a lot. And you're getting bad tempered. I think you're spending too much time at work.'

Antonio closed his eyes for a second and rubbed them.

'I'm trying to get rich Sadie. I want to be successful.' There was an edge to his voice. 'I've made a commitment to do this. It's important to me.'

'I know,' she said softly, nodding. 'Anyway, you can make it up to me on Saturday night. I fancy going for a meal in Chinatown. What's that place called that does the nice lobster?'

She went to kiss him but he moved his lips out of range.

'I'm a bit booked up for Saturday actually.'

'Booked up with who?'

'It's a business thing.'

'On Saturday night?'

'Yeah, you know, networking, meeting the right people. It's an important part of the job.'

Sadie crossed her legs and turned back to the movie. She nearly cried.

22

The Mercedes pulled up in the centre of a remote village in the Hasa. A group of elders assembled before the car, forming a line of long, grey beards and ancient, unknowable faces. They stood militarily, waiting, the wisdom of centuries of war and treachery in their squinting eyes.

He stepped out of the car and moved among them. He clasped their hands tenderly and kissed their grizzled cheeks. They warmed to him despite his expensive, western clothes and the trinkets he wore. He was invited to meet with the chief elder and he accepted graciously, knowing now that he would get what he wanted. The elder could make the necessary arrangements.

He walked calmly behind the elders as they led him to the house, a simple, wooden dwelling. When the chief emerged he took his hand and kissed it. They entered.

In his left hand, as ever, he gripped the handle of his briefcase.

He almost went outside.

Almost.

But it was just too hard.

He hadn't been out in daytime since...

He looked through the door crack with his one good eye. There was a group of kids in the street. One of them balanced on a skateboard, the rest tapped a ball between them. A fat woman in a vest-top sat behind them, on a low brick wall, half a cigarette hanging from her lips. She was the skateboarder's mother. He knew that. None of them noticed him looking.

He had spoken to the woman before, before it happened, nothing-words, shared between neighbours. Perhaps he could speak to her again. He wondered if she'd recognise him. In his mind he projected going out there and speaking, no heavy stuff, just hello, a word about the weather perhaps. And in his mind he saw the kids screaming, the fat woman turning away in disgust. He wasn't ready for that. No way.

Joel closed the door and went back down into the belly of his flat. At first he felt drawn towards the Bible, to lose himself in it for an hour, but he forced his unwilling body into the bathroom. He felt the need to speak to his reflection. Perhaps it would look better than the last time he had checked. Perhaps the healing process had accelerated. But...

'Oh God, no.'

He choked on the words.

No improvement at all, as far as he could tell. He still looked exactly as he had six months ago in the hospital, when they had removed the bandages and the nurse had held up a mirror.

'You were talking,' she had said to him, taking his hand in hers, as tears flowed down one side of his face.

'What do you mean?'

'When you were unconscious. You were talking.'

He had pushed the mirror away. She put it down on the bedside table.

'What was I saying?'

'A couple of things. You kept saying, "God has chosen me to live." And I knew when I heard it that you would pull through.'

He'd noticed the small cross around her neck and smiled, or at least tried to. His face felt so tight.

'What else?'

Mark Turley

'I didn't really understand, but it sounded like, "It ends with
the rainbow maker." Or something…'

'Oh.'

The words meant nothing to him. At least they hadn't then,
just the delirious chatter of sickness. But they repeated themselves, in his sleep, nearly every night. Each time they seemed
a little clearer, a little more specific. They were drawing him
towards something. Joel felt, for the first time in his life, that he
was subject to destiny, a calling from God. He didn't know
where it was taking him, but he couldn't stop it.

The phone rang and he left the bathroom to pick it up. It
was the employment agency.

'Are you still looking for work, sir?'

'Yes.'

The word just dropped from his mouth. He didn't let it go, it
fell. He had no time to check its weight or measure the depth of
its implications.

'Excellent. You start on Monday.'

23

The sun was only just starting to throw the first spears of light across the sky when Richter arrived at the lab. There were no protestors and he stopped his car by the security gate and swiped his pass card through the machine. The great steel panels eased themselves open and he drove in, stopping by the guarded barrier. Two security men acknowledged him and waved him through. Richter followed the asphalt round to the back of the facility and parked in his usual space. He picked his jacket off the back seat, locked the car and went inside.

He headed straight for his office and was pleasantly surprised to see Margaret at the end of the hallway, fumbling through a sheaf of papers.

'Margaret, you're in early,' he said, standing behind her. Margaret's back jerked itself erect. Her shoulders and head swivelled rapidly. Her face relaxed as she realised who was speaking.

'Lawrence!' she said. 'You scared me!'

'Sorry. What are you doing here at this time?'

'There's a lot my team need to do before we go live on Test Study Two at the weekend. I just thought I'd come and prepare a bit of groundwork.'

'Why don't you come to my office, have a coffee and we'll work it out together? I could use some company.'

'Is there something wrong?'

'Nothing you need to worry about, Maggie. Problems at

home. Let's focus on the project.' But his expression didn't endorse his words – he looked pale and harassed, wounded even. There was something of the hunted and haunted in his manner.

The two of them reached the office and Richter went over to the coffee machine by the window and switched it on. He pulled a drawstring to open the shutters and early morning sun, bright but timid, illuminated a small section of the office. He stayed there for a while, staring at the car park and the fields beyond. Neither of them spoke. Margaret studied the back of Richter's head, concern on her face. He looked a little dishevelled, as if he had slept in the clothes he was wearing. His hair was unkempt, sprouting in several directions from the crown. For Richter, that was very unusual. Eventually, the coffee was ready. Richter turned around, his face blank and unreadable.

'Black, no sugar?' he asked. Margaret nodded.

He passed her the cup and placed his own on the other side of the desk.

'Right,' he said. 'So what needs to be done?'

'Well, starting from the beginning, we in Toxicology obviously have most of the preparatory burden for this particular study.' She stopped, unsure if Richter was listening to her. He was staring morosely at his coffee.

'Lawrence?'

'A-ha, carry on.' He didn't look up.

'It is between us and the lab team that set up the environmental conditions to ensure that the active elements central to the testing are in place and controllable. We have a couple of small problems with regard to that, but I'm sure it's nothing that can't be overcome.'

'Problems?'

Abruptly, he snapped to life. It was as if his thoughts had scared him.

'It's not a Methane issue is it?'

'Well, no, but there is a problem with atmospheric composition. We are supposed to be mimicking projected conditions for twelve years from now. As we are all aware Methane levels are constantly rising…'

Margaret checked a paper on top of the pile she was holding.

'Up eleven per cent globally since '78. Sulphur and Ammonia are on the increase, too. But that doesn't pose us with any serious difficulties. We can introduce any of the active toxins involved in the project in precise quantities using the filter. Our main problem is actually with one of the inactive elements.'

'Yes?' He had relaxed again and was re-focusing on the shimmering surface of his drink.

'Oxygen. Oxygen levels are unusually high in the observation lab at the moment because of the plants and trees in there pumping it out all the time. It's very hard to put a lid on it.'

'I see.'

'You realise that the subjects are far less likely to respond to the controlled elements when surrounded by high levels of oxygen.'

'Mm… So if the problem persists we can disregard the study results?'

'I wouldn't say that exactly, no.' Margaret looked tense. She had wrinkled up her lips in a little, bloodless knot.

'What would you say?'

'That the test results will give us a picture nowhere near as serious as the biochemical reality. If you compare oxygen levels in there,' her thumb pointed vaguely in the direction of the observation lab, 'to a major conurbation like London, then clearly our subjects are under far less stressful conditions.'

Richter nodded slowly. His left forefinger flicked at his goatee.

'So what are you implying?'

'That perhaps, Lawrence, you ought to give very serious thought to contacting the Ministry. Perhaps the results of Test Study One should be documented, in case issues that arise from Test Study Two suggest that BCR may occur sooner than expected.'

Richter looked up momentarily.

'It's too late now,' he said. 'We've made our game-plan and we're sticking to it.'

They both sipped from their cups. After a while he spoke again.

'That new chap's starting today.'

'Walid?'

'Yeah, that's the one. He's in this evening, at seven-thirty. He'll have to get registered with security, so I imagine he'll be ready for a guided tour and a debrief at about half eight. Pick him up from my office then. He can do a couple of hours with the night shift and start properly tomorrow.'

Margaret nodded and got up to leave.

24

It was a cold evening and outside the snooker hall, Zac was starting to shiver in the wind that seemed to get trapped between the tall buildings of the High Road and then channelled along it. A piece of grit blew into his eye. He fingered it out and buried his hands as deeply as he could in the pockets of his flight jacket.

'Come on, Darren,' he said to himself. 'Where are you?'

There was tension in his body, borne from anxiety. At that hour of the evening, the streets crawled with noxious life and Zac felt exposed, standing alone at the corner. A stranger approached him, to his left.

'Gimme a pound.'

Zac turned to face the speaker. He was a fairly young black man, thin and scruffily dressed. He had a red tint to his eyes. He held out a bony hand.

'Gimme a pound,' he repeated.

Zac relaxed a little.

'If I give you a pound you're gonna buy food with it, right?'

'Yeah.'

Zac reached into his pocket.

'Here,' he said, placing the coin in the beggar's palm.

'Thanks.' The man pulled a dirty-toothed grin and walked away in the direction of a middle-aged Asian woman standing at a bus stop.

'Gimme a pound,' he said to her. She shook her head and he

walked on.

Zac checked his watch again. Still no sign of Darren. He looked left, then right. A steady stream of cars came from both directions. A long queue waited at the traffic lights, beneath the railway bridge, opposite him.

He exhaled loudly and stamped his feet on the ground, then bent his neck from side to side, then from back to front. He slowly tensed the muscles in his back, arms, chest and shoulders in turn and as he was trying to warm himself up the lights changed colour: red to amber, stillness to speed, calmness to chaos.

A black BMW screamed out from beneath the railway bridge, stereo pumping, wheels spinning on the road. It skidded over the tarmac, sliding as, too fast, it turned wildly onto the high street. The back end of the car swerved towards Zac. He responded intuitively, leaping out of the way, heart racing, respiration quick and shallow, only for the driver to seem to regain control and steer the car back into the correct line. But then, just as it started to straighten, the tyres caught the surface of the road and the vehicle leapt forwards, colliding with a red Datsun waiting outside a Chinese take-away. The sound of grinding metal and breaking glass punctuated the business of the High Road, everything and everyone stopped, heads turning to the direction of the noise. The entire front end caved inwards and the Datsun was pushed up onto the pavement, sending pedestrians scurrying in different directions. There was a second of shocked calm before the driver's side door of the BMW was flung open.

Six foot three of dark-haired white man with furious craggy features jumped out of the car, flinging a leather coat onto the ground behind him. In moments he was pulling at the door of the Datsun, screaming, making noises, not words, just sounds. It was vocalisation without thought, unconscious, instinctive use of the larynx. He grabbed the Datsun driver by the shoulders and dragged him out into the street, yelling unintelligible syllables in his face.

'Fuh, Brraaaaaaah!'

'Don't hurt me,' the smaller, older man pleaded, prostrating himself on the ground. 'Please don't hurt me.' His voice was shrill and quiet at the same time.

The BMW driver walked through his words, unhearing. His lips had rolled back, into thin, white strips, revealing both rows of teeth, his eyes huge and shining. Turgid, rope-like veins criss-crossed his neck. Bending down, he grabbed the other man by the hair. The Datsun driver started wailing like a baby. His cries were high-pitched and primal. They permeated the air and seemed so out of place in the depths of the city, where man has conquered, where nature has been beaten down. It was the sort of sound made by antelope, when dragged to its knees by the cheetahs' jaws.

With a sickening series of crunching thuds the big man slammed the smaller man's head onto the tarmac. Some of the observers standing by started screaming. After the third impact, the Datsun driver became silent. The left side of his head was shapeless and loose. His eyes were blank. Streams of bloody tissue seeped out of his ear onto the road.

It was already too late, but Zac moved in then, adeptly approaching the big man from behind and wrapping his arms around his chest and neck in such a way as to immobilise his entire upper body. The aggressor lost his grip on his victim's hair, allowing the man's head to collapse uselessly back onto the road like a punctured football.

He struggled and kicked at Zac's shins, grunting and snorting, bubbles bursting out of his nose. But the grip was too firm; there was nothing he could do.

'Call the police,' Zac shouted, at the Asian woman who still stood at the bus stop.

Her face was motionless, fixed in shock and terror.

'Call the fucking police!' Zac bawled, wriggling to stay in control of his captive. His arms were already beginning to ache from the strain.

She reached shakily into her handbag and pulled out a mobile phone.

25

'Taxi!' Antonio called, waving a forefinger at the street. The cab pulled up about fifteen metres away. He hurried to reach it.

'Where to, sir?' The driver was lean looking, of Mediterranean appearance. He had a slight accent.

'West Pier Village, Wapping, please.'

The driver motioned for Antonio to get in and smiled, an even, white smile, but with two teeth missing, one from the top row, one from the bottom. Antonio opened the back door and lowered himself onto the seat.

'Traffic's very bad tonight, sir.'

'Is that right?'

A figurine of the crucified Christ hung on the rear-view mirror on a beaded chain.

'Yes. There's been a big accident on Commercial Road. The police are down there with ambulances and paramedics; they've blocked the road off. There's diversions through Whitechapel.'

Antonio acknowledged the information by shaking his head and making a *tut, tut* noise with his tongue.

'There's been a death in Tottenham as well.' The driver made the sign of the cross and kissed his hand.

'Really?'

'Yeah, some sort of accident again. One of the drivers was so angry he beat the other to death.'

'Mm, you have to be careful where you go these days,' Antonio said. 'The dangerous areas seem to be getting worse.'

'London is full of trouble,' said the cabbie. 'Even the *nice* areas.'

He drew out the word 'nice' to emphasise it, rolling it over his lips.

'You know what the problem is here?' he asked.

'What do you mean?'

'What the problem is, why this is such a dangerous place to live.'

'Well I have my own opinions, like everybody else,' Antonio replied.

'Tell me what you think,' the cabbie said, shifting down a gear and pulling out onto a roundabout. 'That is, if you don't mind, sir.'

'Too much division between rich and poor. It leads to discontentment. There's a big gap between what most people aspire to and what they can actually achieve. Very few of us have what it takes to be really successful. That's a recipe for frustration. Frustration causes violence.'

'Well, very interesting,' the cabbie said. 'That may be true, sir, and I can tell you have thought about this before. But I think the problem is more simple.'

'Go on,' Antonio smiled patronisingly, the cabbie had his audience.

'Too many people, too many cars.'

Antonio waited, expecting more. The driver said nothing else. The cab accelerated through an amber traffic light before it had the chance to turn red.

'Right, well, I can't argue with that I suppose.' He checked his hair in the window. Half a minute passed.

'Fifth highest population density in the world,' he said, eventually.

'I'm sorry?'

'London, it has the fifth highest population density in the world.'

'I wasn't aware of that.'

'Well,' he said, 'imagine all those people living in this dirty filth-hole. Imagine what it's doing to them. It is no surprise they behave the way they do.'

Antonio looked a little shocked.

'And there's more arriving all the time.' He started to speak very slowly, emphasising every syllable. 'The population is rising constantly. Imagine that! If you think London is dirty and crowded now, you wait a few years.'

Antonio looked a little angry.

'Do you mind just driving for a while? I'm getting a headache,' he said.

'Sure,' the cabbie said softly, smiling again, showing the gaps in his teeth. 'Whatever you say, sir.'

They made the rest of the journey without speaking.

'West Pier Village,' the driver announced after about half an hour.

Antonio looked at the meter and rolled his eyes skywards. He took £25 from his breast pocket and leaned forward to give it to the driver, who put his hand through the gap in the plastic shield to take the money. He grabbed at the notes roughly, gripping two of Antonio's fingers in the process.

'The proud will not be allowed to stand in His presence,' he said.

Antonio tried to pull his fingers free but the driver's grip was strong, his face intense.

'And He reduced the cities of Sodom and Gomorrah to ashes and condemned them to ruin, making them an example to all who would be ungodly!'

He let go suddenly, grinning his gappy grin.

He took the money and gave Antonio a tiny amount of change. Antonio got out and watched the cab drive away.

'Nutbag,' he said, shaking his head.

The taxi had left him by a large iron security gate. He pressed one of the buzzers on the control panel next to it. He felt a little nervous. Opening line? he thought to himself. No possibilities leapt to mind.

The gate hummed at him and swung open smoothly, allowing him entry to a car park crammed with luxury automobiles. It was like an outdoor setting of the London motor show. Porsche, Ferrari, Aston Martin, even Bentley and Daimler; all were represented. Antonio thought briefly of his Toyota at home and was pleased that he'd left it there.

The door to Elliot's apartment block proved immovable. He pressed the intercom. When a voice from the other side said 'Hello?' he responded with a timid, 'My name's Antonio, I'm here for the party.'

There was a long pause. He stood in expectation, listening through the speaker to the music and the indecipherable rumble of a hundred muffled conversations for about thirty seconds before they buzzed him in. He jogged straight past the lift and climbed the stairs, seven flights, all the way to the top. Slightly out of breath, he rang the doorbell and Elliot opened it almost immediately, beaming.

'Antonio!' he said. 'Great to see you. What are you drinking?'

Antonio shook his hand and stepped inside.

26

Margaret frowned as Richter spoke. He had shaved off his goatee, and his dark brown hair, highlighted here and there by touches of grey, looked windblown and shapeless. He wore an open-necked shirt, the collars of which hung limply about his throat, revealing a lumpish Adam's apple. There was no tie or cravat as usual. His face seemed thin and creased, his eyes pinkish and twitchy.

For now, she focused her attention on the new man.

'You remember Dr Walid,' Richter said, forcing a bird-like smile.

'Please,' the other man said, holding up his hand. 'Call me Sahaal. I am not a formal person.'

Margaret noticed that the little finger on the hand he was holding up was missing from the first joint up. She smiled.

'This,' Richter said, his voice weak and insipid, 'is Dr Hoffman. You'll be part of her team, so for the rest of the evening, I'll leave you in her capable hands.'

Walid nodded and shook Margaret's hand. He made eye contact briefly and looked away.

'Follow me and we'll go down to toxicology,' she said. 'I'll introduce you to the rest of the team and you can see exactly where you'll be working.'

Before they both left, Margaret glanced back at Richter, hunched over his desk. He had screwed his eyes into tiny slits, as if battling a headache, or looking towards a bright light. Almost imperceptibly, his lips moved. He seemed to be talking to himself. They left his office and began descending the stairs.

'What has Dr Richter told you so far?'

'Not much, really. I've just been filling in forms and signing secrecy papers.' He spoke uncomfortably, his words slightly broken.

'Well, that has to be done,' Margaret said, slipping out of her concern for Richter and into her professional manner as easily as changing shoes. 'Now you are aware of the confidentiality we need here. This is an incredibly important project, funded and commissioned by the British Government.'

They reached the bottom step and Margaret ushered him towards the large sealed door to the main lab, punching the entry code into the keypad. Air whistled out of the door seal and it swirled open, the panels disappearing into the frame in a spiral, with a sucking sound, like a plunger being pulled from a sink. She showed him through.

'Okay, Sahaal. This is the main observation lab. It is the most advanced of its kind in the world. The various teams involved in the project can be found in smaller labs adjoining this one. We have zoology and behavioural psychology over there, environment simulation are in there and toxicology, which is us, is over there.'

Sahaal's eyes moved steadily, calmly, from place to place and Margaret examined him, trying to gauge his reaction. His face remained placid. There were no ripples of emotion or surprise, nothing on which she could base a judgement. He followed her through the main lab and into the toxicology section, where a few white-jacketed technicians worked behind safety glass, handling tubes and containers with thick gloves on. She took him through to a small area at the back of the lab. A couple of three-legged stools stood by a Formica work surface there and they both sat down.

'Right,' Margaret said. 'Let's start from the beginning.'

Sahaal stared straight at her, dark eyes oddly bright. Margaret had to look away before she started speaking.

'This project is known, rather unexcitingly, as the Population Research Project. It is part of a much larger, longer-term government undertaking, called The Black Cloud Operation, which I will explain shortly. In fact, the name does not do our work justice as, although analysis of population levels is a central part of our research, there is much more to it than simply that. Our primary concern is the development of aggressive behaviour in primates. We know, irrefutably, that aggressive behaviour, violence if you will, has been increasing in most major cities during the last fifty years. Here we are asking two questions. Why is it happening and where will it lead?

'Now, previous research on this matter has thrown up a bewildering plethora of theories, some plausible, some, frankly ludicrous. They range from the results of the study of Baldsubiramaniam Brain Surgery in 1972, which linked disorders of the limbic system, particularly the amygdala to aggressive behaviour, to studies of hormones and adrenaline levels, chromosomal imbalance, attention deficit disorder, right through to studies which suggested that violence was linked to certain physical characteristics, such as large noses.'

Sahaal chuckled a little and Margaret smiled too.

'I know,' she said, raising her eyebrows. 'Anyway, amongst all the dross, there has been some excellent work in this field. Darwin and other ethological theorists, like Desmond Morris, asserted that aggression was simply part of human nature and that ritual behaviours which may have been formed while we were still living as members of the animal kingdom resurface in times of stress. There has been great evidence for this in observing a variety of animal species and we will return to that later. Of major interest to us is the work of Powers and Kutash, who linked chemical poisons to violence, while the Sydney Allergy Unit, in 1991, showed behavioural changes were observable in individuals exposed to high concentrations of substances previously thought of as benign, such as chalk dust or

E301. This all leads us to the central tenet of our research here, which is the question of whether atmospheric conditions in our cities are leading to higher levels of violence. We have very high levels of pollutants in some areas, particularly Methane, Sulphur Dioxide and Carbon Monoxide, especially in localised atmospheres around conurbations. In the first instance therefore, our work is a study on the behaviour, particularly the aggressive behaviour, of human beings when stressed by pollution. Any questions so far?'

Margaret took a long breath and tried to read Sahaal's face.

'No,' he said.

'Right, well this is the important part. When faced with increasing population levels, which is another stress factor in modern cities, primates, that is monkeys, apes and, presumably, human beings have a breaking point. If the population becomes too dense, the animals lose complete control of themselves and enter a frenzied state, in which they attack others and even themselves. The higher functions of the brain close down and the animal simply becomes savage. When the population has been reduced to minimal levels, normal behaviour resumes after a period of time.

'The response to these kinds of stimuli has been observed in various ape species on several occasions. Early scientific attempts to analyse it, described it as being like a "mist" descending on the brain. For this reason it has become known, as "The Black Cloud Response." Okay?'

Sahaal squinted slightly. 'I have heard of this before,' he said.

'Anyway,' Margaret continued, anxious now to finish. 'We are trying to determine at exactly what point homo sapiens reaches the Black Cloud Response. It could be that with pollution levels as they are, that the reaction will be accelerated. Certain chemicals, in certain ratios, may trigger the response earlier than would otherwise be the case. There are fears in some sections of government that, if left unchecked, it could, particularly in London, occur en masse within the next fifty years. We are therefore conducting a series of experiments, initially using chimpanzees, with the aim of predicting exactly when, so that counteractive measures can be taken.'

Sahaal nodded slowly. 'Initially using chimpanzees?'

Margaret smiled.

'Yes. That's all you need to know for now. But obviously, this study is not only important for the British Government, but for the global community. Pollution and overcrowding are serious issues in many nations. We need to understand their consequences.'

She got up from her stool and walked back towards the door to the main lab, motioning for Sahaal to follow.

'Let's go for a walk around,' she said.

They toured around the test areas for ten minutes, eventually stopping by a slender operative, working at a computer.

'I'm going to leave you with Davis here for a while. You can watch what he's doing, familiarise yourself with the work.'

She introduced the two of them and went looking for Arnold. Margaret had noticed a difference in the lab during the build-up to Test Study Two. People moved about the building with a strange urgency, as if something pushed them to work faster and handle their preparatory tasks with haste. Teams of technicians hurried from room to room, ticking check-sheets and discussing their findings with grave faces. Even the chimps in the enclosure seemed to share the impending sense of commencement. They ate and babbled stoically, with no sense of play or freedom. The juveniles seemed particularly lifeless. Hanging limply from a low branch one moment, squatting on the artificial forest floor the next.

'I'm not really looking forward to this,' she said to Arnold, having found him by the observation screen. 'Hmm.' Arnold nodded. The strip lights glinted on his bald head. 'There's a fine line between anticipation and fear, isn't there?'

'It's not really that, actually. I don't see anything positive coming out of this. I'm fearing the worst.'

'I know what you mean. It's not as if TS1 was inconclusive.'

'Well, there's little we can do now, really. Hopefully TS1 was an anomaly.'

'We had our chance to do something earlier!' The volume of Arnold's voice began to climb. 'We've been bloody stupid to let Richter take this so far. Everything about this feels wrong.'

'Look, Arnold, if you're worried about losing your position, Lawrence said that should things fall down on us, he'll handle...'

'My position! It's not my bloody position I'm worried about.' Arnold was frowning so hard that a deep vertical groove appeared in his brow, stretching from where his hairline would have been to the top of his nose. 'This is rather more serious than that.'

Margaret shrugged, speechless.

She left Arnold and went back to the toxicology lab. Davis, the technician with whom she had left Sahaal, called her over.

'I have some good news,' he said.

'Really.' Margaret looked tired and strained. 'I could do with some.'

'We have made a small breakthrough with regard to the oxygen situation.'

'Go on.'

'Well, it's not so much of a breakthrough. More of a discovery, really. It seems that if the concentration of methane is increased, as it will be during the test, levels of hydroxyl ions decrease rapidly. There is, apparently, a direct correlation between the two.'

Margaret suddenly perked up.

'The reduction in hydroxyl ions will impair the micro-atmosphere's ability to cleanse itself, meaning lower oxygen levels,' she said, half-happy, anticipating his words.

Davis nodded. 'Sahaal actually noticed it. I'd like to take the credit but that wouldn't be fair.'

Margaret smiled at him.

'Thank you, Sahaal.'

'It's my job,' he said. 'You don't need to thank me.'

'Any other news to report?'

'Everything seems to be running smoothly.'

Margaret took a pen and a small notebook from her pocket and scratched a few words.

'I'm going up to see Dr Richter,' she said, hastening in the direction of the stairs, eager to share some positive news.

When she knocked on his door, the voice that reacted from the other side was thin and cracked.

'Who is it?'

'Lawrence? It's me. Margaret.'

'Come in.'

Margaret pushed the door and looked around its edge. 'Hello, Maggie,' he said, in a slightly off-putting, loose-lipped way.

'Lawrence, are you all right?'

'I'm fine,' he said. 'Why?'

'It's just that you look a little...'

Richter waited.

'Tired,' she said at last.

'Hmm. I've not been sleeping particularly well and it's been a bloody long day. I've been here over twelve hours you know.'

'Me too. What happened to your beard and hair?'

'I didn't have time for careful grooming this morning. I'm allowed that aren't I?' There was a sarcastic undercurrent to his words. 'As for the beard, I decided it was time for a change. A new Lawrence Richter. Besides, I think it makes me look younger.'

His chin seemed to wobble a bit as he spoke. Margaret realised that she had never noticed his chin before. It was a weak, pointy chin, imbalanced, with a slight lean to one side.

'Have you been crying?' she asked.

Richter looked away.

'We've known each other a long time, Lawrence. You can speak to me if you want.'

'Tony's sleeping with somebody else!' he said suddenly, almost shouting.

'He started going with this beautiful young French guy called Andre. He met him at Yoga. I caught them in bed at our place last week. They didn't even see me. I confronted him about it the next day and he was totally indifferent. He said if I wanted to leave him I could. I really don't know what to do, Maggie. I feel like such an idiot. It was never going to last was it? A pretty young party thing like that and a forty-something scientist like me...'

Margaret felt she should interrupt, to try to halt Richter's increasing hysteria.

'Obviously he's not good enough for you, Lawrence. Let it go.'

'But the balance of my life came from him. My excitement, my energy, it all comes from Tony. I'm scared Maggie. I'm scared that if I walk away I'll be half the man I was before.'

A couple of tears dribbled off his chin and splashed the edge of the desk. Margaret stammered, trying to find the appropriate words.

'I think the best thing for you at the moment would be to give all your energies to your work,' she said. 'We need everybody pulling their weight on this, Lawrence. We're going live tomorrow evening.'

'I know you're right Maggie,' he said, wiping his face. 'I know you're right.'

27

He made the journey without complaint, despite its length. The sun had set over the sand twice before he got out of the car. At last the end of the road was reached. Literally.

They had passed through a thousand miles of desert and jagged rock, but the Mercedes could go no further.

He stepped out of the car, suit slightly crumpled but hair still neat, sunglasses reflecting a bleak landscape in each lens. The vastness of the Hadhramaut valley stretched before him. He nodded and touched his temple with his middle finger. As arranged, two guides waited with camels. They greeted him warmly with squinting eyes. He treated them with respect. He knew who they were.

The driver said goodbye and offered his hand. He didn't take it. Their time together was finished.

The camels walked at steady pace, one behind the other, making a slow, unending descent. He rode between the other two, taking the middle position in the procession. No words passed between the men, only occasional glances and the considerate sharing of a water canteen.

The enormity of the valley opened up before them like an arid scar, a reminder of an ancient force that had ripped at the desert's heart, leaving a wound that had never healed. The mountains of Jabal an-Nabi Shuayb, huge and monolithic, stood tall in judgement and looked down with approval. He wiped the sweat from his eyebrows, where it seemed to collect

in volume. The sun too was unforgiving. It pursued them relent-
lessly.
   The camels had to fight for their footing amidst shingle and
rock. The valley would not allow its secrets to be obtained eas-
ily. Its steep sides gave no ground.
   'How much further?' he asked. The man in front turned
around, looking over his shoulder, his eyes just slits of dark-
ness beneath his headdress. He raised his hand and pointed
into the distance. They nodded at each other and continued on
their way.

Zac was allowed to leave the police station at about 2:30 am.
No lift home, no money for a taxi, just a polite, 'Thank you for
being so co-operative.' And a gentle push through the door.
   They had arrived at the scene of the incident with sixteen
officers in two vans, to find Zac still struggling to restrain the
big man. The police had pulled Zac away, wrestled him to the
ground and cuffed him. Zac was bundled into one van, the
BMW driver into the other. They read him his rights on the
way to the station and explained that he was being arrested for
disturbing the peace and on suspicion of actual bodily harm.
   Once inside the station he was taken first to a holding cell,
where they fingerprinted and strip-searched him, then to an interview room.
   'Wait here and the inspector will be with you shortly.' A
big, slack-jawed copper had said, before closing the door, leaving Zac alone to shut his eyes and focus on the rhythmic tides
of his breathing. When the inspector, a tall man with a lean face
and a neat moustache, accompanied by two constables, finally
entered the room, he had found Zac sleeping, head on desk.
   'Wake him up, Stanton,' the inspector said. The copper
nodded and walked over to Zac, shaking him roughly by the
shoulder. Zac snapped awake. His head jerked off the desk and
he grabbed the young constable by the wrist.
   'Blaze like the sun!' he screamed, bleary eyed. The other

two rushed across the room, but their panic was unnecessary. Zac let him go.

'Sorry,' he said mildly. 'I was having a bad dream.'

The interview began in an edgy manner. The inspector was obviously perturbed by what he had just seen. He switched on an archaic-looking tape recorder and after the opening preamble of personal details he said, 'Right then, Mr Tyler, why don't you tell us your version of today's events?'

Zac looked the inspector in the eye and began to relate his story. The inspector turned his head and Zac continued, staring at his ear. He told it exactly as he remembered it. When he finished he folded his hands on the desk and looked down at them.

'Thank you, Mr Tyler. A very full account.'

They took him from the interview room and put him back in the holding cell. He waited there for about three hours before one of the constables opened the door nervously.

'We've spoken to other witnesses. Your story checks out, Mr Tyler,' he said. 'We may be calling you to give evidence in court. Looks like being a manslaughter or murder case. The victim's dead. If you're happy to sign this statement, you can go.'

He handed Zac four sheets of paper, full of typewritten words. Zac couldn't be bothered to read them. He turned straight to the back page and signed his name.

He was then led out to the reception desk, given back the contents of his pockets and allowed to leave.

28

Antonio had a fairly good idea of what to expect at the party. He had gone with his father to a similar thing, two or three years before when at home on holiday from university and found it pleasant enough. Lots of forty- and fifty-odds with their partners, sipping drinks and starting conversations with lines like, 'So, what do you do?'

It had been, of course, very different to the kind of thing he had been used to at university, where gabba-techno and handfuls of ecstasy were more the scene, but he felt he had coped well enough, having spent most of the evening discussing financial careers with a stockbroker called Leonard. Elliot put a welcoming hand around him and led him from the front door to the kitchen.

'What do you think of my apartment?' He was brandishing a huge tulip-shaped glass of red wine in his hand. 'I bought it nine years ago as a present to myself when I took over the third floor. Only use it occasionally, really. I sometimes stay down here at weekends, or it can be useful if I have to stay late at the office, but more often than not we just use it for parties.'

The flat was a large, open-plan affair, its use of curves in arched stairwells and pillars in keeping with the fashions of modern interior design. Pretty much the whole place was white. It was the sort of thing, Antonio thought, he had seen on cable television on one of the style channels. He imagined a ridiculously coiffured fop, probably with a hint of an Irish accent, sauntering through the main room saying, 'Through its sense of air and space and bias towards light and circularity, giving an effervescent, invigorating effect, this home-space engenders the spirit of modernity while tipping its hat to the past. The quasi-Grecian pillars supporting the stairs and the Romanesque fittings are reminiscent of more classical, romantic periods, making the experience of being here not only stylish, but magical, timeless and thoroughly inspiring...' From the door through which he had just entered, marble tiles stretched to a gigantic plate glass window, set into the far wall, through which he could see the twinkling lights and angular edges of the London skyline. The high ceiling above the central room in which they stood was lit in bright triangles by a series of spotlights while, halfway up the walls, on both sides, pillars supported balconies, each with three doors. Marble steps led to their secrets.

'It's a nice place,' Antonio said, trying to be understated. His eye caught by an enormous fish tank, set into the east wall, beneath the balcony. 'To be honest, I've never seen anything quite like it.'

'I'm glad you find it to your taste.' Elliot had drained his glass. 'A young man with a taste for finer things will develop the will to succeed.'

He took Antonio to the kitchen area and opened the drinks cabinet door.

'Well?'

'I'll have a vodka mule, thanks.'

Elliot poured the drink dextrously and passed him the glass.

'Get that down your neck, now. I'll get you another and then I'll introduce you to a few people. Chin chin!'

Antonio knocked back the vodka.

'Excellent stuff!' Elliot slapped his belly. He refilled both their glasses and they headed back out to mingle, first approaching a group in the centre of the room, most of whom were bopping gently to the soft jazz-funk that seemed to come from everywhere. Elliot approached a tall, black woman in the centre of the group. She had an avalanche of red hair extensions tossed over one side of her head. He smiled and kissed her on both cheeks.

'Javene,' he said, grinning in that loose-jowled way of his. 'I'd like you to meet Antonio Merlin, a rising star of PFPL. This young man was the highest seller last month and he's only just started.' He held his hand out towards Antonio.

'Antonio, this is Javene Pascal, she's a Creative Director at Parker and Duffle. She was responsible for the "talking baby" ad campaign, you know, for some life assurance company or other. Do you remember it?'

'Absolutely!' Antonio replied, shaking her hand. 'It's hilarious.'

Javene laughed. 'So young and already a master of flattery! You'll go a long way.' She turned to Elliot and pursed her lips. 'You certainly know how to pick them!'

Elliot laughed and grabbed Antonio's arm.

'This,' he said, sidling up to a very thin man in a Lycra t-shirt which outlined his skeletal frame as markedly as if he'd been wrapped in cling film and whose heavily gelled, brown hair formed a kind of cowlick on the left side of his head, 'is Neville Kaufman. One of my first clients at PFPL and also one of the richest men in London, he was heavily involved in the telecommunications boom of the early nineties.'

Antonio smiled and stepped forward. The older man offered his hand limply.

'Enchanted,' he said, lightly squeezing Antonio's fingers.

Antonio withdrew on instinct, but spoke, not wishing to appear rude.

'So how did you meet Elliot?'

Kaufman leaned in, very close to Antonio's ear. 'We met playing squash in 1981. I beat him and he asked me for a few tips to improve his game.' He smiled a rather unsavoury, yellow-toothed smile. 'I think I showed him a thing or two.'

Elliot dragged Antonio away.

'Don't worry about Neville,' he said. 'He might be an old poof but he's a good client and I've known him for years.'

The introductions and handshakes continued for half an hour or so. Antonio's face began to ache from smiling.

'And here's somebody you know already,' Elliot said, having brought the youngster to a corner of the room in which a tall geometric sculpture leant against the wall. Standing next to it, smoking a cigarette, was Suzy.

'Hey, superstar!' she said, flicking her cigarette into a floor-standing ashtray.

Antonio smiled, genuinely this time. 'Have you got one of those for me?'

'Sure.' Suzy gave him a cigarette and helped him light it.

'I'll leave you two to it for a while,' Elliot said. 'I've just spotted someone I need to speak to.' He hurried off in the direction of the kitchen.

'I didn't know you smoked,' Suzy said.

'I don't, generally.'

'So why now?'

Antonio inhaled deeply. 'I'm a bit stressed.'

'Introductions?'

'Yeah, too many handshakes and too much grinning. Is there anyone here who isn't some kind of millionaire?'

'Other than me and you, probably not and in your case, I guess that's a temporary situation.'

Antonio couldn't help but notice what Suzy was wearing. Her dress was tight and shiny red. It exposed a lot of flesh. He let his eyes draw circles on her slender shoulders and the rise of her breasts.

'I think it'll be a while before I'm in this league,' he said.

'Well I never!'

'Huh?'

'I'm surprised.'

'At what?'

'At your lack of confidence, superstar! That's the first time

117

I've heard you say anything negative about yourself.'

'Hmm.'

'It's okay. You let your guard down. But so what? You're talking to me now, not one of them.' She waved an elegant arm towards the room. 'If you let your guard down out there, someone will take advantage. But I won't.'

Antonio pulled on the last of his cigarette and stubbed it.

'Come on!' Suzy said, grabbing his hand. 'I know just how to make you sparkle again!'

'You're not going to introduce me to someone are you?'

They both laughed.

She led him towards one of the steep marble staircases that rose to the balconies upstairs. He climbed behind her, watching her buttocks undulating against the sleek material of her dress. For one tiny moment, he caught a glimpse of pink underwear.

'This way,' she said, taking him towards the first of three doors. Antonio forgot his tiredness. Excitement began to grow inside him.

Suzy took him into a beautifully crafted Romanesque bathroom, mosaic tiles on every wall, complete with Jacuzzi and bidet. She locked the door.

'Sit there and close your eyes,' she said, pointing at the toilet seat. Antonio did exactly as he was told. Deprived of eyesight, he tried to figure out what she was doing.

At first he picked up the sound of a zip being unfastened, followed by rustling. Despite desperate efforts to control himself, his crotch began to swell and he shifted his sitting position to try to disguise it. Another tiny sound followed, a gentle tap-tapping that went on for some time.

'Okay there, superstar?'

He nodded, mouth too dry to speak.

'I'm going to put something on your lap,' she said. 'You must be careful to keep it steady. Don't open your eyes until I tell you.'

A light pressure exerted itself on his thighs.

'Okay, open up.'

Suzy stood before him smiling, still fully clothed. He looked down at his legs to see a shaving mirror with two fat lines of Coke carved out on it.

'Oh!' He hid his disappointment. 'Thanks.'

She gave him a note and he hoovered the bigger of the two lines up his right nostril. He then passed the mirror to Suzy who did the same with the other line.

'Do you think Elliot would mind?' Antonio asked.

'Mind! Are you fucking kidding me? He gave me the stuff in the first place. He's got tons of it. Everyone'll be doing it in an hour or so. These parties really get going later on.'

Antonio sniffed and felt the bitterness trickle down his throat. He found it hard to swallow.

'Really?' he said.

29

Four pints of Guinness and two scotch and gingers had slightly impaired Zac's judgement, but there was forty quid riding on the frame and he didn't want to blow it. Darren looked a little nervous. He stepped forward to offer support to his partner.

'It's not an easy shot, Zac,' he said. 'If you don't think you can slot it then just roll it up to the cushion, play it safe. There's no point taking any chances.'

Zac nodded in agreement. 'It's too tight, I think. I could cut it into the top left but if I miss it's gonna be stuck in the jaws and old cheeky chops over there'll be laughing.'

They both cast a disparaging glance at their opponents, two youngsters, dark haired and tanned, probably Turkish. They leant nonchalantly on their cues, smoking cigarettes, staring flatly at Zac. They had played a good game but were far too cocky. Zac desperately wanted to beat them.

'Fuck it,' Zac said. 'I'm taking it.'

'You sure?'

'Cometh the hour, cometh the man.'

Darren laughed. 'Go on then, big guy,' he said, stepping back. He took his pint off the shelf, sat next to Terry, who was there as a spectator, and drained it.

The Turkish boys exchanged a few words. Zac filled his lungs with air and bent over the table. He gripped the base of the cue firmly in his right hand, using his left to direct the shot. He didn't aim for long. His eyes locked on the target and he released the trigger.

The black ball shot into the top pocket and Zac stood up, leaving the cue ball to bounce around the table in isolation before coming to a stand-still just outside the 'D'.

Darren and Zac enjoyed their moment briefly and then went over to their opponents, shook their hands, took their money and left. Terry followed. Outside it was a dark, portentous night. The three of them raised collars and stuffed hands in pockets.

'Do you wanna come round for a bit?' Zac asked his companions. 'My flat's just up there, we'll have a drink and play some cards or something.'

'Yeah, why not,' Darren said.

'It's Saturday night, after all,' Terry agreed.

'I tell you what, though, boys. I wouldn't mind a bit of puff.' Darren pretended to smoke, by raising two fingers, held out in a victory salute, to his lips.

'Yeah?' Zac said. 'What about you, Terry?'

'I wouldn't say no, like.'

'All right then, gents, we'll stop off at the green shop on the way back.'

'The what?' Terry asked.

'The green shop. It's on the way home.'

The three of them walked away from the pool hall, discussing the evening's events and the match that had taken place. After five minutes walking and talking, Zac changed subject.

'Right,' he said, standing still. 'We're here. You coming in?'

He had stopped outside a blank-fronted shop. It was just a window with a plain green sign, no words, letters or pictures, just green. The other two both nodded. Zac led them through the door. Inside, the shop was virtually empty. A disused pool table stood in the middle of the floor, an ancient video game occupied one corner. Darren and Terry exchanged puzzled glances. Zac walked past the pool table to a counter at the far end of the store. He leant on the counter and waited.

Almost immediately a man appeared from the back room of the shop. He was short, wiry and dark, with a thick moustache and the kind of mullet haircut that was very fashionable in the mid eighties.

'Yes, my friend,' he said coldly.

'Weed,' Zac said.

The shopkeeper paused for a second. 'Skunk or Thai?'

Zac shrugged his shoulders. 'Thai.'

The shopkeeper put a small bag on the counter. 'Ten pounds.'

Zac took the bag and replaced it with a tenner. He thanked the man and left.

'I didn't know you were a smoker, Zac,' Darren said as they crossed the road outside the shop.

'I'm not. I never touch the stuff.'

'So how do you know about that place?'

'I live local. You get to hear about these things.'

At the flat they drank whisky and played cards for a while. Terry and Darren smoked. Before long, the effort became too much for them and they spread themselves out on the floor. The conversation began to wander.

Zac sat back on his chair, stretched his arms behind his head and yawned.

'What was it like in the Paras then, Zac?' Terry asked.

'Why, you thinking of joining up?'

'Nah, not now, but I thought about it as kid, when I left school. Not necessarily the Paras, but the army, you know. Didn't fancy it though, an Irish boy in the army. It's just asking for trouble, know what I mean?'

Zac nodded wisely. 'There's a big difference between the Paras and the army, Tel.'

'Yeeeaaaahhh.' Darren contributed to the discussion.

'The Paras are elite forces. Except for the SAS it's probably the toughest, most selective force in the world.'

'What about the Marines?'

Zac laughed. 'Are you winding me up?'

'Eh?'

'The British fucking Marines aren't a patch on the Paras. They like to think that they're our equals but they're not in the same league, bunch of public schoolboys. Most of 'em couldn't even handle the initial training that we do. I tell ya, the British Parachute Regiment as a group of men is probably the best-prepared unit out there. By the end of Para training you're fitter and stronger than an international athlete. You're mentally tuned, as well. You can spot dishonesty in someone a mile off.'

'What about after the training? What's the life like?'

'It's a good life for a young man, sometimes scary, sometimes calm. Depends where you're posted. I had a right mixture of postings in my time. But wherever you are, one rule's the same. Defend the honour of the regiment. Stick up for your mates. Don't let anyone take the piss.' Zac paused for a bit and then added, as an afterthought, 'You throw punches first and ask questions later.'

Terry's eyes widened slightly. 'I wish I'd done it now, you know. You make it sound kind of noble.'

Zac didn't answer for a long time. There was a great distance in his eyes. He had gone to a place deep within and had to shake himself out of it. Terry watched him scratch lazily at the burn scars on his upper arm. When eventually he answered it was in a very quiet voice.

'I'm not sure I'd call it that,' he said. 'But I know what you mean.'

30

Suzy and Antonio emerged from the bathroom, watery eyed and loose tongued.

'There was another time, when I was at uni, this friend of mine took so much speed, he was up for three nights. When he finally made it to bed he slept for twenty-five hours solid. He lost nearly two stone.'

'Yeah, someone I know did something similar with acid. I never liked it myself...'

'Too much of a head-doer.'

'Yeah, he was never quite the same again, really. He was always sort of nervous and twitchy.'

'I never do anything that messes with your head.'

'Do you do E?'

'Not any more.'

'It's too much of a false vibe. You feel like you love everyone and that you've finally released your true self but it's just the effects of the drug and when it wears off you're back to how you were to start with.'

'Yeah! Like you can be talking to someone all night and hugging them and telling them how wonderful they are and then suddenly at 3:00 am when you come down you just sit there, staring at the wall thinking, "Who's this stranger?"'

'That's why I like coke now. It gives you a little lift but you can still be real.'

'Mmm, things don't get out of hand, you feel on top. This

one time…'

They made their way back downstairs, swapping high-speed anecdotes and opinions.

Back in the main room the party seemed to be continuing in much the same vein as before. A few more people had arrived and the group in the middle had grown. Antonio noticed that Javene Pascal, who he had met earlier, was now moving quite freely and a loose group of enthusiastic dancers had formed around her. The music had changed slightly, as well. The subdued, jazzy tones of earlier had become a more vibrant, disco sound.

'I'm getting a drink,' he announced. 'You want one, Suzy?'

'Vodka and tonic.'

Antonio made his way across the room towards the kitchen, but a tap on his shoulder stopped him halfway.

'I've been looking for you, young man!' Elliot cried excitedly. 'There's one very important person here that you haven't met yet.'

Antonio groaned inwardly but gave a winning smile.

'Who's that?' he asked.

'This,' Elliot announced, with an air of grandeur that bordered on sarcasm, 'is my lovely wife, Janet.' He ushered Antonio towards an attractive, well-preserved, middle-aged woman, her blond hair chopped into an informal bob. She wore an expensive-looking, off-the-shoulder cocktail dress and elbow length gloves, one of which she extended towards Antonio in a rather regal manner. He wasn't sure if he was meant to kiss the hand or shake it. He opted for the latter.

Elliot leaned towards his ear. 'Keep her busy will you. There's someone I need to see. Use this if you have to.' He pressed a small wrap of paper into Antonio's hand. 'Good man.' Elliot slapped him appreciatively on the back, took a sip of wine and wandered off.

'It's delightful to meet you,' Janet said. 'Elliot has talked about you quite a lot. He thinks you've got great potential. I've never seen him so excited about a young exec.'

'That's nice to know.' Antonio smiled. He wondered how much Janet had drunk and whether she'd taken anything else yet. She was hazy-eyed and a little unsteady on her feet.

'So what do you do?' he asked, unsure of what else to say.

Janet laughed. 'I don't work if that's what you mean. I paint a little, I walk the dog, I play the piano. I have many interests, Antonio. I'm very good at keeping myself stimulated. Do you dance?' she asked.

'Well, you know, not professionally.' Janet laughed at the joke and grabbed his hand, leading him over to the group of people that had assembled around Javene Pascal. Javene was commanding the centre of the floor, moving her hips and waist elegantly in time to the music. She saw them approach and smiled a huge smile.

'Janet, you've been shark fishing again!' she said, winking at Antonio.

Janet laughed so hard she almost fell over. They began to dance and Antonio realised he was actually quite enjoying himself. The coke had relaxed him enough to get into the vibe and he swung himself around with decent rhythm. Janet too, seemed to need no help in letting herself go, gyrating, bouncing, sometimes throwing her hands up into the air, sometimes using them to point seductively. As one song finished and another started, she moved closer to him.

'Have you got anything to perk me up? I'm feeling a little needy.' As she spoke she ran one gloved hand through his hair. Antonio felt as if he could do with another line himself. Gently pushing her away, he nodded and said, 'Follow me,' leading her around the dancing group and towards the far staircase where he had left Suzy.

'Shit!' he said.

'Whatever is the matter, dear?' Janet asked.

'I was supposed to be getting a drink for Suzy when Elliot introduced me to you. I forgot all about her.'

'Suzy? Oh Suzanne, Elliot's PA?'

'Yeah.'

'Look, she's over there.' Janet pointed at Suzy, who was being engaged in conversation by an Asian man wearing jeans and a sport coat.

'Wait here,' Antonio said, heading over to Suzy, who seemed highly relieved to see him.

'Hey, superstar, what kept you?'

'I got introduced to Elliot's wife.'

Suzy peered over his shoulder and waved at Janet. They seemed to exchange a knowing look.

'What are you doing now?'

'We're heading upstairs, you want to come?' Antonio winked as he said 'upstairs'.

'Sounds good to me.'

Suzy turned to the Asian man. 'Excuse me,' she said.

The three of them climbed to the balcony and headed into the bathroom. Once inside, Antonio took hold of the shaving mirror and began to cut three chunky lines onto it. Suzy sat on the edge of the bath, while Janet began to run water into the Jacuzzi tub.

By the time Antonio had chopped out the coke, the tub was full. He turned around to offer the first blast to Janet, just in time to see her dress fall around her ankles. Her underwear followed shortly. Antonio tried not to look shocked and checked her out.

Loose skin around her neck and the texture of her hands showed her age, but her skin seemed smooth and tanned, her figure neat. She had clearly looked after herself well.

'I'll take mine in there,' she said, pointing at the Jacuzzi, before climbing in, wearing nothing except her gloves. Antonio looked at Suzy who smirked with wry amusement. She raised one eyebrow and shrugged.

'Don't try to look surprised, Suzanne,' Janet said. 'Antonio might not know you very well, but I do. Now why don't you stop play-acting and join me?'

Antonio stared, fixated, as Suzy stood up and undressed, her dress falling over the devastating curves of her hips and bum, she climbed naked into the Jacuzzi, sat down and smiled, the water frothing around her nipples.

Antonio took his line and passed the mirror to Janet who snorted hers in a millisecond. Dabbing at her nose, she passed the mirror to Suzy and said, 'Well, what are you waiting for my boy, a written invitation?'

Suzy did her line and put down the mirror. She smiled beautifully. 'Come on, superstar,' she said. 'Join us.'

Antonio thought about it for a second and then loosened his belt and kicked off his shoes.

Regardless of his reputation, the one he came to see had been reasonable and amicable. After all, they shared a common goal. He left after two or three hours, having enjoyed his host's hospitality, walking casually out of the cave entrance, no longer holding the briefcase. In his pocket he had something more valuable, an address on a scrap of paper. He looked up at a sky dotted with tiny clouds and smiled. His guides seemed surprised to see him and chattered excitedly in their dialect. All three climbed onto their camels and began their ascent.

Less than a day later, he was watching the clouds spread beneath him. The plane had taken off from the main airport just outside Sana'a in fine weather.

A stewardess, slender, olive skinned, with southern European rather than Arabic looks, offered him a drink. He took water and thanked her.

For the sake of reassurance he removed the address from his pocket and read it again: '17, Rue de St. Bernard, Montreuil, Paris, Peripherique de Sud'. He replaced the paper, folded his hands in his lap and let his head rest. Sleep overcame him quickly.

31

Guilt. That was Antonio's first feeling about what went on in the Jacuzzi. It was, after all, his boss' wife and PA. Two or three more lines of coke helped to ease his conscience and he decided, after an hour or so, to leave them to each other and go back to the party for a bit.

He felt smooth after his exertions, buoyant, full of confidence. He climbed out of the Jacuzzi and got dressed, taking extra care with his boxer shorts and flies, head buzzing as he left the bathroom, feeling like he was floating just above the ground. Emerging back onto the balcony, the discovery that the apartment's lights had been switched off dragged away his self-assurance as if it were weighted down. Huge shutters blacked out the window. Awkwardness overcame him. Here and there, shadowy shapes moved. Muffled voices could be heard over the music, which had reverted to its original, jazz-lounge mode.

Increasing disorientation made it difficult to descend the steep staircase in darkness and he moved slowly. Shapes on the floor below took on more form as he neared them, a pile of rags here, an arrangement of cushions there. As he eased himself off the bottom step, like a man testing the temperature of the sea with his toe, he leant forwards and examined one of them more closely. It was hard to delineate form in the blackness and giggles and lost syllables made their way to his ears from all corners of the room. The whole thing had a dreamlike ambience and Antonio half expected the lights to go back on and to find the room full of dancing penguins or that he was able to fly.

Reaching out a hand towards the pile, as the sense of unreality deepened within, he felt nervous and didn't know why. When he made contact, his fingers found cotton, which he gripped and held up close to his face. A shirt. He grabbed something else from the pile, examined it and dropped it immediately when he realised it was a pair of boxers.

Realisation began to flicker and he decided to make his way to the kitchen for a glass of water, having to step carefully over the pile of cushions he had seen from the stairs. As he did so it became clear that it wasn't a pile of cushions at all. It was Neville Kaufman, naked from the waist down, entwined with another figure. Antonio felt stabs of nausea as he made his way past several other couples. They squirmed around below him, like strange, multi-limbed aliens in the gloom.

He had almost made it to the kitchen when a hand wrapped itself around his ankle, nearly tipping him off balance. Looking down, he saw Elliot's face mooning up from the floor, leering and pale. He was naked, his bloated form prostrated on top of Javene Pascal, his white skin almost luminous. Antonio's eyes flicked up and down his boss's back, which was lumpy and scarred, the damaged tissue stretching from his shoulder blades to his wobbling buttocks. He was grunting and undulating, like a sea lion flopping up the beach.

'Enjoying the party?' He tilted his head to one side and the spare flesh on the top of his neck hung down loosely. He didn't even stop what he was doing, eyes wide and intense.

Repulsed, Antonio could do nothing other than nod. He broke free of Elliot's grip, leaving him humping and gasping, hurried to the kitchen and threw up in the sink.

The plane made a soft, cushioned landing and he remained in his seat until most of the passengers had left. When ready to move, he collected his belongings and walked up the aisle, thanking the stewardess on the way.

The queue for passport control was laborious. He made his way to the desk one step at a time. On arrival, a thin, rat-faced official in a blue jacket checked his passport with undisguised disinterest.

'Reason for visit?'

'Visiting relatives.'

The official stamped his passport vigorously and he walked through the airport terminal and out into the street, where he summoned a waiting taxi and climbed aboard.

As he headed for his penultimate destination, he felt flutterings of something that he had not sensed for many years. He had to think before he could pin it down.

When he eventually figured it out, he gave himself a little smile.

It was excitement.

The apartment at Rue de St Bernard was small and dark, located in a basement beneath a Lebanese kebab shop. On arrival, he was greeted warmly.

'Welcome, Khalifah,' they said, as a mark of respect.

The three men each kissed his hand and introduced themselves. They showed him into a small kitchen where they sat around a plain table. One, who had introduced himself as Adil, made four tiny cups of strong coffee.

'How was your journey, sir?' The man who spoke was bearded and light skinned, called Khashim.

'My journey was long and tiring,' he said. 'I feel as if I have been on my Hajj.'

'In some ways you have, sir,' Khashim replied. 'Doing the work of Allah is even more important than honouring him. We have all been praying for your safe arrival.'

Hasan spoke next. He was fatter and darker.

'Tell me how things are back home.' There was an undercurrent of sorrow in his voice. 'It is such a long time since I have been there.'

'I am sure there is little difference to what you remember.

People live in great fear. Every day we see the children turn away a little more. The great Satan is tightening his grip.'

'And the little Satan stands by his side,' Hasan said, in agreement.

He smiled and touched his forehead with his middle finger. 'Not for long,' he said. 'Not for long.'

They sipped at their bitter coffee and chatted for a while. They discussed life in Paris and the conflicts in Palestine. He tried to relax amongst them, to be their friend. It didn't come naturally, but he wanted it to be that way.

Adil, who had made the coffee, stayed silent as the other three conversed but after half an hour, he interrupted the conversation.

'Come with me, Khalifah,' he said, abruptly, getting up.

Doing as asked, he felt something that wasn't fear, but a close relative of it. He followed Adil out of the kitchen and towards the bedroom at the back of the flat. Khashim and Hasan stayed seated.

Adil opened the door and showed him inside.

'You see, sir,' he said. 'We have been preparing for your arrival.'

He nodded with approval. The bedroom had been equipped with a basic laboratory. A structure of chemical equipment sat on a plastic table.

'Would you like me to explain our work?'

He shook his head.

'I need not know the method, only the result.'

Adil stood next to the framework of conical flasks and u-tubes and pointed at a condenser, beneath which a greyish liquid had accumulated in a sealed Petri dish.

'You see this, sir?'

He nodded.

Adil smiled a little.

'So you know how it is used?'

'Of course.'

They both watched the liquid. Its still surface reflected the bare light bulb above.

Adil broke the silence.

'Sir, I know little of your past except that you are a man of courage. Here we are not suicide bombers or fanatical gunmen. Our work is planned. I like to know details. I hear you have an informer working at a secret laboratory in the UK.'

'You ask too many questions, my friend. You might cause suspicion.'

'I mean no offence, Khalifah.' Adil bowed his head.

He saw the man's response and wanted to speak, to tell him everything. In some ways, he desired that someone else should know, could share the burden of responsibility. But fear knotted his tongue. The wrong words and he would die.

'My informer has told me a great deal.'

He looked out of the flat's window, into a walled alleyway full of rubbish. His face was set, like a waxwork.

'What will you do, when it is done?' Adil asked.

'It is not important.'

'Stay here tonight,' Adil said, feathering the end of his black moustache with his finger. 'Tomorrow is your day.'

Part Two

Waking

32

It was the meekest of mornings. Night had not yet fully re-
treated and day was still contemplating its advance, only a pale
wash of grey on the lowest edge of the sky. Suburbia sat in its
tidy rows, silent and undisturbed.

The buzzer shattered the shell of Kostas' sleep like a hammer. He rasped his hands up through the dark, sandpaperish
stubble on his neck.

'Oh, that bloody alarm.' His wife's voice was thick with
sleep, her eyes still shut. He cast a glance her way, black hair
twisting over her forehead like wire.

'Go back to sleep, *gouri*,' he said, climbing from the bed.

A gap in the curtains allowed him a glimpse of an outside
world in which streetlamps still glowed, their orange lumines-
cence bolstering the dawn.

'You have to take the rough with the smooth. It's only one
Sunday in four, innit?'

'Why don't you call in sick?' She buried her chin into the
pillow, muffling her speech.

'Nah.'

Kostas liked to think he was a good employee, having
worked for Thames Water for seventeen years. He had organised the Christmas raffle for the last six.

'Your working life's what you make it,' he often told An-
dreas and Demetris, his overweight, over-parented sons. 'You
only get out what you put in.'

He washed and dressed methodically, went downstairs, tore a chunk off the loaf in the breadbasket, threw on a jacket and headed out to his car. While fumbling for the keys in his trousers, something made him turn and look back at his house and that same something inflated him with pride, despite the early hour.

The drive was quick and painless and in fifteen minutes he was pulling into his parking space and walking through the gate. Kostas mainly worked on the filtration pool that connected to the main reservoir. He had to take samples of water leaving the filter to ensure that what was being pumped back into London's domestic and industrial pipes was of the correct chemical consistency; a slight imbalance could result in millions of people being poisoned. They had told him that on his first day at work and it had made him feel significant, like a superhero, protecting the metropolis.

At first he had been nervous and had made more checks than required, each time anxiously examining the reading for any sign of irregularity. But the excitement soon evaporated. The fact of the matter was that the filtration system was very efficient. In seventeen years of daily checking he had never known the water to be even slightly contaminated. Not once.

He stood on the edge of the huge pool, his belly casting a shadow on the water. To his left the giant filters whirred and pumped. He lowered a long-arm scoop gently with his right hand, gathering a little water in the bottom and raised it, hooking the end over an angled pole.

In the old days the testing had all been manual. The water was treated with chemicals to see if it changed colour. But then electronic equipment arrived and made the job easier, if perhaps more boring. He took his hand-held tester from his pocket, inserted the nozzle and pressed the button. Moments passed and the tiny screen went green. 'Normal' it said. He tipped the sample back into the pool, walked away from the edge and looked up, towards the horizon. The sky was clear and the sun, while

while still struggling to drag itself clear of the horizon, was already hinting at becoming hot.

'Should be a nice day,' he said, to no one.

33

Lyn glanced over at Arnold, who sat, one leg crossed over the other, in front of the main enclosure screen. He smiled and sipped from a mug printed with the slogan, 'Scientists Do It Systematically!' He uncrossed his legs and placed a newspaper on his lap.

'Road Rage Killing is a Sign of the Times'

The banner headline on the front page was printed above a picture of some mangled car wreckage. Lyn raised her eyes from it and let them dawdle around Arnold's face. His skin seemed to be turning grey, which she put down to too much time spent indoors, and the pouches of loose flesh under his eyes were growing by the day. But the eyes themselves still had life, especially at certain times. She'd noticed that he seemed to be spending any free moments he had by the enclosure, poring over the monitors intently.

The chimps had organised themselves into two groups, as expected, each with its own social structure. Some of the females alternated between them, seeking affection from both sides, but the males, ready to hunt and fight, stayed loyal to their set. Each group had a dominant male who was followed in the hierarchy by subordinate males, females and of course, juveniles.

The lab crew had already named a few of them. The Alpha

males were given military titles. Major, the elder and larger, had assumed leadership without challenge. He had a few grey specks in his dark fur. Captain, a younger, darker, slimmer chimp, seemed initially to defer to Major, presenting his anus to him as a mark of respect, but as soon as the numbers in the enclosure had risen suitably, he had taken the opportunity to lead a few Beta males to the north-eastern corner and start his own faction.

'I reckon you picked the wrong field, Arn,' Lyn said, playing with the end of one of her hair braids.

Arnold smiled. He actually hated it when people abbreviated his name, but somehow, with Lyn's accent, it sounded quite agreeable.

'No, no,' he said. 'This is just idle curiosity.'

'Yeah,' Lyn replied, 'They're an interesting bunch.'

'They're nowhere near as active as the last sample though, are they? They don't even seem to have built nests yet.'

'No, I know,' she said. 'Even their grooming is half-hearted. Their behaviour is typical of captive chimps, those kept caged in zoos for example.'

'They should feel at home in there though, shouldn't they?' Arnold gestured at the enclosure with his eyes.

'Oh, of course. We know what we're doing. That's a faithful representation of the ecosystems found in Sierra Leone, Lake Tanganyika and the Congo Basin. This lab has the finest environment simulation systems that I've ever seen. In my opinion, there's no way that's the problem.'

'Well what is?'

'It's very hard to say. These are complicated creatures.'

Arnold nodded and sipped his coffee.

'I know,' he said. 'It's hard to understand their intelligence until you see them every day. I almost feel like I know them.'

Lyn's eyes widened, and sparkled. She stared right through Arnold as she spoke.

'Other than us, they're the most advanced land-dwellers on

141

the planet. They make and use simple tools and they can vocalise about thirty-two different sounds. They've been successfully taught to use sign language on several occasions. The results of some studies have even suggested that they use their own rudimentary form of conscious communication. Of course, that's been disputed by human supremacists and sceptics, but nonetheless they are incredibly sophisticated, in some ways more sophisticated than we are.'

Arnold put down his coffee cup and peered over his glasses at her.

'Lyn.' He wore an expression that he might have sported if talking to a child. 'Your passion for your field is truly admirable. But, although I can in no way claim to share your expertise in animal behaviour, I find your assertion that chimps are in any way superior to humans a little beyond the pail, frankly. Clearly human beings dominate the earth. Clearly therefore, of all animals, we are the pre-eminent species, the reason being our adaptability and intelligence. Chimps cannot compete with us on either of those characteristics. Hence their confinement to a few limited areas of the planet and their dwindling numbers.'

'I didn't say that chimps are more advanced than we are. I said that in *some ways* they are more sophisticated than us.'

'Explain yourself.'

'It's very simple. Chimps are still in touch with their instincts. We aren't.'

'Hmm.' Arnold thought about it. He turned the corners of his mouth down and bowed his head.

'Yes, I'd have to give you that. Our instincts are buried beneath routine. So, are you suggesting that the chimps sense that something is wrong?'

Lyn nodded smartly.

'It's like if there's going to be a hurricane or a tidal wave or an earthquake. The animals always know about it before we do. I think it's the same thing. They know something's going to happen. They can feel it.'

Arnold watched one of the juvenile males as he scratched disinterestedly at the bark of a tree.

'You seem to have a very high regard for chimps, Lyn.'

She smiled.

'Not just chimps, all apes. We're just like them.'

'Well, I suppose we are, yes. There's a physical resemblance. Bipedal, five digits, opposable thumbs and all the rest of it.'

'Not just that Arnold, their behaviour, their social structures, they're one of the few animals that show mercy or kindness.'

'Oh come on.'

'It's true.'

'Lyn, that sort of view was discredited years ago. You're attributing human emotions to animals. Even I know that.'

'Well maybe mercy and kindness aren't human emotions. Maybe they're part of something else.'

'Like what?'

'A natural law of behaviour, universal to all complex life-forms. We shouldn't think that we're so special.'

Arnold clicked his tongue.

'It's all to do with non-verbal communication,' Lyn continued.

'How?'

'Body language. Physical signs that are subconsciously interpreted.'

'So how do you explain occasions when apes have attacked humans?'

'A misunderstanding probably. The humans involved gave off the wrong signals, aggressive posture perhaps. Anyway, what about the times when humans have attacked apes?'

'But...'

'I'll tell you a story Arnold,' Lyn said. 'When I was twelve, my mum took me to Brisbane zoo. She left me by the gorilla pit and went off to buy drinks. This one gorilla was staring at me.

It was the strangest thing. It had climbed halfway up the wall of the pit and hung on with one arm, looking straight at me and it looked like it was smiling.'

'What?' Arnold shook his head.

'Hear me out, please... Anyway, being a dumb kid, I decided to get a closer look. There were no keepers nearby and I climbed to the top of the fence around the pit, so I could lean over and see better. I was leaning over the fence and me and this gorilla were talking.'

'I don't know what you've been taking Lyn, but if you've got any spare...'

'Well, not talking, communicating. You know, I'd make a noise, he'd make one back, like that. Unfortunately, when my mother reappeared and saw where I was, she started screaming. I tried to turn around to calm her down, lost my balance and fell into the pit.'

'Is this a joke or something?' Arnold finished his coffee and put the cup down.

'No, it happened.'

'Were you all right?'

'Well, I don't remember a thing about it. The fall knocked me unconscious and I broke my leg.'

'How did they get you out?'

'That's the interesting part, Arn. The gorilla saved me. It picked me up and carried me to the opening in the fence where the keepers put the food in. It waited there until someone came to get me. They had it on film, it made the national news and everything.'

Arnold studied the screen that showed Major. Undeniably he was an impressive animal, squatting on a branch, exhibiting strength and balance. Perhaps even, as he looked straight ahead, at nothing, there was arguably an abstraction in his gaze that suggested a depth beyond primal urges. But reflective, compassionate? It wasn't possible.

'Thanks, Lyn,' he said getting up. 'It was nice talking to

144

you.'

Margaret had assembled her team together in the centre of the toxicology section.

'Okay, people! As you are all too well aware we are rapidly nearing live status on Test Study Two. We have ten hours before the first environmental changes are made. I've mentioned the difficulties that we've had in preparation for this study to Dr Richter and he's been most impressed with the attitude and resourcefulness of members of this team. In fact he should be down soon to thank you all in person. So don't think your efforts are unappreciated.'

At exactly that moment, Richter walked through the door, looking more composed than the day before, although still naked and vulnerable without the goatee. His clothes were ironed and there was directness about his eyes, which suggested that he had slept well. He nodded and smiled at her and then spoke up.

'Dr Hoffman has made me aware of some of the problems faced by this team. I've been very pleased with what I've heard about how the Toxicology division has dealt with those problems and I have written a glowing report on your efforts, which will be passed on to the Ministry. As a result, I am sure that most of you will have no problem in obtaining work on other key projects once our initial testing is finished and our toxicity parameters established. Well done again and I look forward to seeing the fruits of your labour later.'

The team dissipated slowly, anxious chatter on their lips. Richter beckoned Margaret into a quiet corner. His eyes flitted left to right.

'Things are going to get serious,' he said.

'I'm fully aware of that, Lawrence. Ten hours and counting, we need to begin preliminaries…'

Richter dabbed at his eye with an elegant little finger and chuckled humourlessly.

145

'It's a bit more serious than that actually.'

'Go on,' she said.

'You remember Mr Travis, from the Ministry?'

'Of course.'

'He's paying us a visit shortly.'

'Really?'

'Yup! He's coming, so's the other goon, Ripon. Apparently there's a chance, if we're really lucky, that the minister himself may even show up.'

Margaret shrugged. 'There's nothing you can do, Lawrence. They were bound to want to see the testing at some point. It's probably for the best, anyway.'

'Maggie, explain to me how exactly this can be for the best?'

'Well…' Richter cut her off.

'If the results of TS2 are anything like those of TS1 then we're screwed. The likelihood is that the reaction will be far worse this time. If that takes place in front of ministry officials, there'll be no disguising anything. They'll make this whole project ultra high-level security with only Government personnel working on it. You'll be straight back to writing reports on factory emissions in Slough and I'll be overseeing some pathetic drug testing study at a university somewhere.'

'If that's what's meant to be, Lawrence, then let's accept it. Our involvement in these tests is not crucial to their outcome.'

Richter looked angry. 'Maybe not, but it's crucial for my career. I'm too old to start walking backwards.'

Margaret shook her head. 'I have things to do,' she said.

Richter nodded and walked away. Margaret watched him go with a mixture of admiration and disgust. Even after his recent traumas, part of her hoped that Richter's nightmare would come true. The thought of going back to her former post wasn't so bad. It certainly never involved the unbearable tension that ate at everybody in this place. She made a silent decision to hand in her notice after TS2. It was time to move on.

34

Steam filled the bathroom, sauna-style and Elliot sat on the toilet, dripping, a towel around his waist. The pendulous flesh of his upper arms and man-breasts jiggled as he perfumed himself with designer scent.

'Did you enjoy the party, darling?' He dabbed at his shoulders as Janet prepared to enter the shower he had just left.

'Yes, I did. I'm not sure it was the best ever but I had a good time. Your new youngster certainly is a find.'

'Who, Antonio? I'm not so sure. I've got my doubts about him, actually.'

'He seems absolutely perfect to me.'

Elliot smiled dryly.

'I'm not entirely surprised by that, sweetness. You seem to have taken a shine to most of the young execs that I've introduced you to over the years and not all of those made it in the business. I mean, sure he's just about the best newcomer in the office at the moment, but that doesn't guarantee anything. Let's see how he gets on in the next couple of months.'

'Why do you have to be so hard on these youngsters? Why don't you try to encourage them?'

'I know how to handle my team!' Elliot's eyes flashed. 'They don't need mothering. It's a competitive business and the man who succeeds is the man who is prepared to do what it takes to succeed. Do you remember Luke Boxley?'

'That chap you went to school with?'

'That's him. Now back in 1993, if I hadn't convinced his four most profitable clients to pass their funds and investments over to me, I never would have opened the third and fourth floors. Of course it meant that he lost his earnings and we haven't spoken since, but it's what had to be done at the time and I did it! Now I'm not sure that Antonio has that desire to win at all costs.'

'Why not?'

Elliot stood up and started drying his hair. 'I don't think his attitude is rock solid. I noticed a few cracks last night.'

'Why don't you try giving him another chance?'

'Why, was he a good lay?'

'I just think you're writing him off too hastily.'

'Well, we'll see how he comes in tomorrow morning. I'll be watching to see how he handles himself.'

Janet shook her head.

'Would you like me to rub some cream on your back?' she said.

Her husband's eyes became watery, gentle for a moment.

'Yes please. It'll get tight otherwise.'

He turned and bent over the basin while Janet opened the bathroom cabinet. She took a small, white tube off the shelf and squeezed some ointment onto her fingertips.

'I'll never forgive that bloody nanny.'

Janet rubbed the lotion into the mottled, uneven pink flesh that climbed up his spine from his waist to his shoulders.

'Don't start talking about it, you'll just get upset.' She spoke with well-rehearsed mildness. 'I'm sure she didn't know the bath was so hot.'

'Incompetent bitch,' Elliot spat.

Janet finished rubbing. He straightened himself and checked his face in the mirror.

Janet replaced the tube in the cabinet, switched the shower on and tested the water with her hand. Once satisfied with the temperature, she climbed inside.

When Antonio got home, marginally before his mother got up, he stumbled upstairs to his room and collapsed on his bed, fully clothed. Sleep never quite managed to overcome him. He lay still for a long time, twitching and sweating, occasionally peeling off an item of clothing until he lay naked. Still he couldn't sleep. His feelings were mixed about the party. On the one hand he had enjoyed the sex and drugs, but he had also been disgusted by the brazenness of it all. When he ran the events of the evening through his mind, despite himself, his memories aroused him. By the time he gave up on sleep and headed downstairs, hours later, it was with the same mixture of shame and excitement with which he had left the party. He dodged his mother's questions with the skill of an Olympic fencer, made a coffee and sat to watch a football match in his dressing gown.

Zac woke up first out of the three of them. He found himself lying diagonally across his bed, still dressed, boots hanging over the edge of the mattress. He aimed a gentle kick at Terry, who was within reach.

'Tel,' he said, 'time to go to church.'

Terry groaned loudly.

'Come on, Terry! Father O'Farrell will be angry.'

Terry opened one eye. 'Fuck off, Zac,' he said simply. 'What time is it?'

Zac checked his watch. 'Two.'

Terry nudged Darren, who lay beside him in a foetal position. 'Darren… Darren…'

Darren had dribbled down the side of his face.

Soon the three of them sat around Zac's tiny television, drinking hot, black tea, nursing their hangovers and watching the qualifying rounds of the Australian Grand Prix.

149

35

'Gentlemen!' Richter said, extending his hand towards Travis. 'Good to see you again! Can I get you a coffee?'

Travis shook his hand. Ripon joined in the formalities, but didn't so much shake as feel and retreat; he withdrew his hand sharply the instant contact was made, as if Richter carried a communicable skin disease. Once in the office, Travis and Ripon sat down, while Richter made a fuss of going to the coffee machine and switching it on. 'What can we anticipate seeing tonight, Dr Richter?' Travis asked. The question sounded friendly enough.

'Well.' Richter watched the coffee percolate. 'The subjects have been in place for over a week now. We've recorded the behaviour of each individual up to the present time.'

'Is it not hard to tell the difference between them?' Again, punctuated with a smile.

'Actually no... No, it isn't. I must admit I had the same concern, before the first group arrived, even though our zoological team assured me it would not be a problem. In fact, I know most of the subjects by sight now myself. They have very individual faces you know. Rather like us.'

Travis nodded agreeably and shared a vague sideways glance with Ripon.

The smaller man seemed to take it as a cue.

'The work of this lab is gaining greater resonance all the time, Doctor. You realise that don't you?' Ripon's voice was

thin and nasal but still carried a strange authority. Richter felt
as if he were back at school, facing the headmaster.

'I take it you mean the recent incidents that our press have
been reporting with such enthusiasm.'

Ripon nodded. There was no humour on his face.

'Concern is growing, Doctor, assurances are required.'

'Well, I can't promise that.'

'Why not?' Ripon spoke as if seizing an opportunity.

'Well, the study may not provide a positive result. We shall
have to see how things develop. Our conclusions may be
vague.'

Richter filled three cups with fresh coffee and put them, one
at a time, on the desk. He began to feel slightly sick, sat down
heavily in his chair and waited for the next question.

'Surely you have a very good idea of what we will be seeing later. Based on the results of the first study you should be
able to project some kind of a pattern.'

'Well yes, we're expecting –'

'That is, if the results of the first study are reliable.'

Richter was unsure of what to say. He turned to Travis,
hoping to see some sympathy, but Travis was staring over
Richter's shoulder and out of the window as if he had lost interest in the conversation.

'I don't know what you are suggesting, Mr Ripon. But I'm
not sure I like it.'

Ripon feigned shock. There was a victorious shift in his
tone.

'I didn't suggest anything, Doctor,' he said. 'And I don't
understand your sensitivity.'

Richter rubbed his temples. Travis and Ripon sipped their
coffee.

The clock continued its inexorable progress towards eight.

The sheet of figures fell from Arnold's hand, fluttering to the
desk. He sighed, toying again with the idea of leaving. He knew

exactly what was going to happen when the test commenced and didn't want to be held accountable. On several occasions he picked up the phone, intending to leave Richter a message on voice-mail. 'Lawrence, I've supported you thus far but the pressure has become too much,' or something similar. From time to time he took his car keys out of his pocket and jingled them in a shaky hand.

The part of him that still possessed some non-nervous energy, his subconscious, snapped hungrily at fantasies of the near future. Perhaps he'd buy a ticket to New York, hire a car and drive coast to coast. Perhaps he'd take up a new hobby, like scuba diving or Chinese calligraphy. Perhaps he'd give up everything and spend the rest of his life in contemplation. These thoughts gave lightness to his mood, lightness that was superficial, transparent and weak, but much needed.

The time to get up and go approached. It loomed for some time as he weighed his alternatives. It travelled slowly, so at first he was calm.

Then out of nowhere, it was upon him, tight and cloying. The time had come! The decision was too heavy. His shoulders sagged. The time passed.

He hadn't even got out of his chair.

By 19:30 the entire team had gathered in the main lab, semi-circled around the enclosure like a cinema audience. Richter sat before the central monitor, in line with the middle of the observation screen. Ripon and Travis flanked him.

'It's very interesting,' Travis said, 'to see the lab in a live situation. Are the subjects behaving normally now?'

Richter paused for a moment before answering.

'Normally enough. We do have one or two concerns, for example the absence of nest-building, but it's nothing that should affect the study.'

Margaret approached, doing her best to appear calm.

'Gentlemen,' she said.

'You remember Dr Hoffman?' asked Richter.

Ripon and Travis both nodded, smiled tightly and shook her hand.

'Everything ready?' Richter asked.

Margaret looked almost melodramatically positive.

'We've checked everything three times. If anything goes wrong it won't be the fault of toxicology.' She smiled.

Richter didn't.

36

'They're not doing much are they?' Fatigue and tedium had worn away the veneer of Travis' laconic charm. His features bore a blank, weary expression. Most of the chimps sat on the ground, looking glumly at each other.

'There's no response as yet. We're increasing methane levels at the moment. Other active toxins are being introduced gradually. It may be some time before a behavioural reaction is observable.' Richter fingered his chin.

Misty silence settled over them again, clinging to everything until breathing, the tiny scratchings of pencils on paper and the timorous echoes of footsteps were all that could be heard.

'Look at that one.' Travis fought against the increasingly oppressive soundlessness, pointing and sitting forwards, showing more animation than he had for hours. The small screen showed a young chimp picking absent-mindedly through a pile of faeces. 'Do they usually do that?'

'I'm not sure. We'll have to check with someone in zoology. It's not a response behaviour, anyway.'

Richter glanced over at Ripon, untrusting, nervous. The small man's eyes lingered nowhere for very long, jumping from screen to screen. Occasionally he scribbled a few notes in a small blue exercise book.

Richter checked his watch, levered himself from his chair and headed over to Margaret, who stood to the left of the main screen-bank, clipboard held cross-armed against her breast like some kind of holy relic.

'When are we expecting to reach peak toxic level?' He leaned towards her. She felt his breath on her cheek.

'Six hours or so. We're introducing all the active toxins in precise ratio. I've got Walid on the filter.'

Richter nodded jerkily. 'Good, good. But some of these subjects should be triggered by now, shouldn't they?'

Margaret's eyes met his for a second, then she shook her head.

'I'm not sure what's happening. It's strange.'

Richter paced back to his seat between Ripon and Travis and told them what Margaret had told him. Ripon scribbled in his book again. Travis removed his glasses and wiped them with a tissue.

Inside the enclosure, the chimps did nothing.

Kostas glanced up from his paper and checked his watch. It was time. He stood with considerable effort and advanced towards the edge of the water, the surface of which rippled and shone with speckled light. The dancing sparkles fascinated him, stopped him mid-stride. There was beauty in them, in their movement and effervescence, a graceful ballet of refraction. But the realisation bothered him. It was beauty he saw every day. Why should he notice it now, after seventeen years?

Eating dinner with his boys the previous night, he had told them how it was strange the way that fate or coincidence could affect someone.

'Sometimes things just happen,' he had said, waving his hands around to help make his point.

'There's no reason, you don't know why, they just do.'

He smiled as he took the scoop from its hook.

37

The chart was double-sided. One side bore a map of London, marked with a scrawled, red, felt-tip ring showing the location of his target, while the reverse was a plan of the water treatment plant itself. Adil had drawn an arrow for him, which indicated the precise spot to which he was heading. The briefing he had been given on the drive from Paris to Calais was very thorough. As a plan, it seemed simple and failsafe. It would be done on a Sunday, the quietest day, the day when the infidels prayed to their real Gods: sloth and self-indulgence.

'One man, with courage and determination, is impossible to stop as, unlike an army, he can go unnoticed, into the enemy's very heart,' Adil had told him.

Beneath the words, Adil's tone had been admiring, deferential. That gave him great pleasure.

The London morning was well established as he stepped onto the platform and walked through the station. The sky striped between the eaves was clear, blue and cloudless. Out of curiosity he took ten minutes to stroll around the area, eager to see if what he had been told was true.

His walk first took him past a parade of shops, some of them boarded up, where old men sat in doorways, chuckling and coughing, drinking from black and gold cans.

'Spare change?' one said, as he passed, one dirty hand on the rump of a dog that he held on a piece of string.

He shook his head and the old man reached out and

grabbed his trousers, just above his ankle.

'Come on sir, just a bit of jingle-jangle.'

In his mind's eye he pictured himself striking the beggar with his elbow, on the pressure point at the side of the temple and the beggar's eyes rolling up into their sockets, showing only white, as he lost consciousness. He pictured himself pushing the beggar away, watching him flop, like a sack of flour. Satisfaction lived in the thought. It would affirm his power over this filth, this product of western permissiveness and all its failure. But he couldn't. It might attract attention. It might obstruct the mission. And more than anything, he couldn't allow the assignment to be impeded. He had to be content with flicking his foot to free himself, jerking the beggar's wrist, making him drop his can, which spilt its noxious, sand-coloured fizz onto the road.

'No need for that, ya bastard!'

He sneered over his shoulder as he walked.

Past the shops and around a corner, he found himself on a road behind the station, where several women approached him, revealing clothes and desperate expressions, marking them out as unclean. Some of them carried scars on their arms, which told their own story.

If London's last hope was to convince him it did not deserve the fate he had planned, it failed. He headed for the tube, chin firm with new determination.

The underground was crowded and airless and it unsettled him. For much of the journey he found himself pressed against the soft backside of a white woman from whom the stench of sickly, rich perfume, rose and hung. The natural dark colour at the roots of her fair hair and the blemishes on her cheeks and neck, unsubtly disguised with make-up, added to his revulsion. After several stops, she and many of the other passengers disembarked. The creation of space around him felt like a release from prison.

By the time he arrived at his destination every cell of him hummed with anticipation. The area into which he embarked was very different to the other. It was more spacious, the buildings looked cleaner and trees lined the street.

The map was imprinted in his memory and negotiating the back streets around the station was a quick and easy task. Two and a half minutes after alighting from the train he found himself before a high wall, on which a placard read:

PRIVATE PROPERTY
THAMES WATER

He stopped for a few seconds, breathing deeply, drawing on his experience, filling his lungs and slowing his heart. The security gate and reception lay forty metres to his right. He headed left, walking another fifteen metres before satisfied with his position.

He stepped forwards to the wall and stretched his right hand as high as it would go, which left him still a few inches short of the top. Realising what had to be done, he took a quick look over both shoulders. The suburban location of the Treatment Plant suited his purpose, as the streets were empty. He took a few steps back, jogged forwards and leapt, grabbing the top of the wall with both hands and pulling his torso over.

From the full height of the wall he could see most of the plant laid out, exactly as it was in the plan. The only person in sight from this vantage point was the security guard by the gate, whose head and shoulders were visible through the window of the booth in which he sat. He swung his legs over the wall and landed softly, in a crouched position on the other side.

He found himself at the back of the main filtration pool, where the dirty water, fresh from the sewage system passed through the filters. About two hundred metres from where he knelt was the pool that connected to the primary reservoir.

A low concrete wall ran along the edge of the filtration pool. He scuttled along, keeping himself as low as possible, to

158

avoid drawing the attention of two workers, wearing white lab coats, standing by a boxed control panel. He passed closely enough behind them to hear snatches of their conversation.

'B Filter's only been operating at ninety-four per cent for the last few days. Management are talking about an overhaul of the whole system.'

'Can't see it happening myself. What they gonna do? Re-route the whole supply through Surrey? It just won't work.'

'They won't have to close the plant; they'll just do it piece by piece. Keep one filter going and repair the other.'

He crept past them unnoticed and continued, past the great, mechanical pumps and onto the area where the filtered water was collected. The clean water pool was large and yet, as far as he could see it was patrolled only by one man. The man was chubby and dark. He did not look English.

He crouched low behind the wall, watching carefully, waiting for exactly the right moment. The sun boiled above. Only one obstacle to the completion of his mission remained and it stood, about ten metres in front of him, facing the water. He hopped over the wall and padded up behind the employee.

When close enough to see the black hairs that spread up the back of the man's neck, he raised himself up, until his face was inches from white-coated shoulders. The worker smelt of sweat and cigarettes.

Focus, he thought to himself.

It was done in a second. His movement was sudden and smooth, reaching from behind his victim, grabbing his chin with one hand and his forehead with the other. Before the man could make a sound he pulled sharply and violently, snapping his neck as easily as twisting the lid off a jar. Kostas crumpled to the floor and was instantly forgotten. He stepped over the body, concentrating on the final part of his mission. But emotion interposed itself. For a moment, he stopped, the tiny vial in one hand, the other poised to remove the stopper. A waterfall of thoughts flooded his mind, almost dragging him down. He felt a

159

taste of the pain that he would inflict. But his hesitation shamed him; it was counterproductive to everything he had been trained for. Hot tears blurred his vision.

'It has to be done,' he said, encouraging himself. 'It has to be done.'

He removed the stopper and tilted the container slowly, deliberately. The grey liquid began to trickle towards the edge. He left the first drop hanging from the lip of the tube, where it grew pendulous and took a deep, calming breath. With his free hand he touched his temple with his forefinger.

The drop swung gently, biding its time, before gravity detached it, making it fall, opaque, glistening, towards the pool. As it struck the surface, causing a thousand tiny ripples, he smiled and cried, both at once, his chest shaking. The rest of it dribbled out of its container.

He flung the vial to one side and turned his head upwards. His knees were weak.

It was done!

The sun caressed his face and neck.

The grey liquid infiltrated the reservoir rapidly. Within seconds it had contaminated the entire pool. Some of it began to pass into the feeder pipes that would eventually provide water to every tap in the capital.

During the next few hours, the sun caused some of the pool to evaporate. The grey liquid molecules reacted to the heat in the same way as the water, becoming gaseous, mixing freely with its vapour, rising, floating, drifting, atoms mingling, towards heaven.

On reaching the cooler, higher air, they condensed and formed clouds, which, during the rest of the day and the night that followed, hung above the city, unnoticed, dark and menacing.

38

As Elliot's car twisted through the narrow streets around Black-friars, he reviewed the events of the previous seven days, digesting them and preparing himself for the week to come. He shared no words with his driver until he dropped him off at the corner of the square as requested.

'I'd like a short walk this morning,' Elliot told him. 'It'll be a nice way to start the week.'

'Are you sure?' the driver said. 'The weather's not looking too clever, sir.'

Elliot looked up at the sky. A massive storm front had spread from skyline to skyline.

'It's dry now. I'll be all right.'

He stepped out of the Bentley and put on his jacket. The wet smell of rain was in the air. The driver shrugged and pulled away.

He walked quickly, stopping at a newsagent to buy a paper. It took five minutes to cover the few blocks to the PFPL building.

On arrival, Elliot strode through the ground floor entrance and slapped his newspaper on the reception desk.

'Morning, Charlie,' he said.

The night-shift security guard smiled over his copy of *The Daily Star*. 'Morning, Mr Rossley.'

'Is the fourth floor open yet?'

'No sir, I'll come up with you now and unlock it.'

161

They rode up in the lift together and Charlie unlocked the door. Elliot acknowledged him with a wave and went inside. He flicked the light switch and strode past the rows of desks, computers, and telephones to his private office where, in accordance with years of routine, he sat and spread his newspaper out on the desk.

Violent Street Crime up 9% on Last Year

A spokesman for the Home Office addressed reporters today amidst growing concern over street safety. Fears that the capital is an increasingly dangerous place in which to work and live have been confirmed by the latest crime figures. Released this morning by the Metropolitan Police, they show that much of the increase in violent crime is centred in inner city areas. The junior minister's press statement said that the Home Secretary and his staff are 'taking all necessary steps to avoid further increases, whilst actively seeking feasible ways in which crime rates can be reduced.'

When asked to be more specific he told the press conference that, 'Research into the causes of this problem is presently ongoing. This government is no longer interested in avoiding the symptoms, but wishes to eradicate the disease.' He refused to be drawn on the nature of the research, saying that full details would be made public 'after analysis of the results.'

The shocking figures come in the light of recent panic among...

'Hi, Elliot!' Suzy placed two cups of coffee on the desk and grinned. Elliot looked up from his paper.

'Hello, Suzy.' He folded the paper and pushed it to one side.

'Is this one mine?' He took the lid off one of the polystyrene cups and peered inside. 'Bloody stuff gets worse every day. This is a cup of hot water with some kind of brown grit at the bottom. Get me a spoon will you.'

'There's one there.' Suzy nudged the plastic stirrer in his direction. Elliot toyed silently with his coffee for a short time. Then, when satisfied, he took a sip and said, 'Got your notepad?'

Suzy obliged him by taking a small green booklet out of her bag.

'Right,' he began. 'First things first. I've had a complaint from the regulator about Jasper, again. Apparently he's been forcing clients to take on pension schemes and savings plans they can't afford purely to gain higher commission. Worse still, he's been so bloody obvious about it that they've noticed. This could turn into something relatively serious. So I'm going to need to speak to him, first thing, soon as he arrives. Secondly, I've got one of the company's earliest and wealthiest clients, Mr Ly Thanh, the Malaysian electronics manufacturer, meeting me for lunch so I need you to book me a table at Les Pins.'

'When for?'

'Let's call it 1:30. As you know there's also a potential buyout on the cards from the USA. It's early days, but you need to tell the admin girls to be extra vigilant for the next couple of weeks. Any calls from the States come only to me. That's crucial. Okay?'

'Yup. Got it.' Suzy took a tiny sip of coffee. 'Anything else?'

'Yes, if you see I'm free at any point during the morning, get Antonio to pop in for five minutes. I'm a bit concerned about him.'

'In what way?'

'He didn't seem particularly on-form on Saturday night. I just want to have a man to man talk.'

Suzy gathered her things and left. Elliot drank the rest of his coffee alone, looking vaguely through the glass partition that formed one wall of his office. As usual, he felt good about the day ahead.

Zac arrived on site about ten minutes late. It was a grim day; pregnant skies threatened all below them.

'All right, Bernie?' he said, passing the supervisor on the way in.

'All right, Zac. Listen, I'm glad I've seen ya. I'm taking you off ground clearance this morning.'

'Why's that?'

'We need you over there.' Bernie aimed a fat finger at the newly erected block. 'They're hauling window frames up to all the floors. They need someone to give 'em a hand. It'll only take ya till lunchtime. All right?'

Zac shrugged.

'You have a good weekend?'

Zac smiled. 'Yeah. You?'

'Not really.' Bernie's broad face screwed itself into a collection of furrows. 'My wife got mugged on Saturday afternoon, behind the shopping centre in Wood Green. They done her over quite badly. Broke her nose and everything. Bunch of fuckin' kids it was. I tell ya what, if I could catch the fuckers….'

'Sorry to hear that, Bern.'

Bernie nodded and continued muttering as Zac walked away, towards the tea hut. He arrived and found it crowded with men from the site. Darren and Terry were among them. There seemed to be some sort of discussion taking place. All attention was focused on a young, thin, suntanned agency worker in the centre of the room.

'I'm not going out there if those conditions get any worse.' The speaker was South African. 'Where I come from we have a saying. Rain drops, work stops.'

A roar of laughter went up from the room.

'No one gives a toss about where you come from, Carl!' a

random voice called out.

'I'm bloody serious,' he went on. 'It's dangerous out there when it's wet. There must be some union regulations about this kind of thing.'

'Ah, tell it to immigration!' Another voice called. More laughter.

'If you refuse to work, they'll just give ya the heave-ho and get someone else in. Get out there and get on with it,' one of the brickies shouted. He made for the door as soon as he finished speaking. Others followed his lead.

'He's right, you know,' said another, on his way out.

His moment gone, Carl was left, dejected and unheeded, staring at the floor. After a few seconds he shrugged his shoulders and went back outside. Zac smiled and put his coat on a peg. He stretched out his shoulders, feeling a slight click from an old gym injury and walked over to the new block.

The site's first new building formed an uninspiring rectangle, cut into the sky in flat, red brick. He headed towards it quickly, the first drabs of rain spattering the back of his neck. Three men waited for him, sheltering in the overhanging doorway. Two of them he recognised immediately. Terence smiled as he approached and Connor, a Scotsman whom he knew just well enough to say hello to whenever they passed, nodded at him, while hunched over a cigarette lighter, shielding its weak flicker from the weather, a dirty looking roll-up in his lips. The other, a dark skinned black man, stood away from the other two. He wore a grey sweatshirt with a hood that he had pulled so far over his head that it hid his eyes. He said nothing. Zac had never seen him before.

'What's the plan then?' Zac asked.

Terence grinned. 'You're gonna love this.'

'Go on.'

'U-PVC window frames. Nine floors. About thirty frames for each floor. And I'm not talking portholes. These are for big double, treble, even bay windows. They're too big to go in the lift, so they gotta go up the stairs. And that's it.' Terence laughed and made a 'what ya gonna do?' gesture with his hands.

'Where are the frames?' Zac asked.

'End of the hall.'

Zac walked through the doorway and looked around. The lobby smelt like a new building; brick dust, fresh plaster and paint mingled in the air. He made his way over to where the huge stack of frames leant against a wall. He tested the weight of one in his hands, picking it up and then balancing it on his shoulder. It was about eight feet long and almost as tall as he was. It dug sharply against his collarbone.

'I'm making a start,' he called to the others, already heading for the stairs.

Reluctantly, they followed him in.

39

'Look at Major, screen twelve!' shouted one of the minor technicians. An entire room full of heads swivelled in unison. Richter jumped from his seat. The screen showed the dominant, grey-flecked male, surrounded by the four juveniles. The young chimps took it in turns to pick at the fur on his neck and around his genitals, chewing on their fingers in between.

Richter hurried over to Lyn, who stood by the left bank of screens.

'What're they doing?'

'Grooming. Standard behaviour, nothing unusual.'

Despite her answer, everyone assembled in the lab studied the screen eagerly, enjoying the fact that the chimps were actually doing something.

'But actually, thinking about it, there is something strange here...'

'Go on.' Richter gave her a sideways glance.

'Well, it's not normal for a dominant male to allow four subordinates so close to him, all at the same time. It puts him in a vulnerable position, should one of them decide to attack. In the wild, this just wouldn't happen.'

'Do you think an attack's likely?' The nerves in Richter's voice attracted Ripon's attention. The little civil servant leaned on the back of his chair, angling his head to eavesdrop the conversation better.

'Well, judging by the situation, I'd say yes. There's four of them, Major seems to be making no attempt to assert his ascendancy. They're not presenting to him, to show deference. In fact...' Lyn's eyes widened.

'What?' Richter prompted her.

'I've just realised something that makes this scene even more confusing. Three of those juveniles are actually from the other group. There's no way that this should be happening at all.'

'So this should be a confrontation?'

'All logic would suggest so. Chimps align themselves to their groups through grooming and mating and are intensely territorial. Like all primates, they have an instinctive distrust of "outsiders" or strangers. Individuals who cross into the territories of other groups are attacked and usually killed. These juveniles would normally be risking their lives. I don't understand this at all, to be honest.'

'So there's absolutely no sign of aggressive behaviour?'

Behind Richter's back, Ripon shared a fleeting, raised-eyebrow glance with Travis.

'Judging by body language and mannerisms, I'd say not. The opposite, in fact. Primates show their teeth when feeling hostile. It's a kind of visual warning. None of them are doing that. Their grooming and chattering looks slow and laboured. Almost as if they can't really be bothered. If I didn't know better, I'd say...'

Richter looked at her anxiously.

'What? What would you say?'

'You're gonna call me nuts.' She pulled her eyes from the screen and levelled them at his.

'This is a bad time for coyness, Lyn. Tell me.'

'It looks like we're being had.'

'What?'

'We're being had.'

'By who?'

'I don't know...'

'Wait a minute, Lyn. You're not suggesting...'

'I'm just offering an opinion...'

'These animals do not have the wit to control their own behaviour. To suggest otherwise is crazy.'

'I just think there's something funny going on.'

Richter stared hard at the young Australian zoologist. She didn't flinch. 'Anthropomorphism has been thoroughly discredited Lyn. We left the dark days of interpreting everything animals do in the context of human behaviour back in the seventies. Next you'll be suggesting that they're discussing politics or something.'

'Look at screens four, twenty-one, seventeen and ten,' Lyn said, her eyes darting from point to point.

Richter turned. He faced screen after screen of chimp indolence. They lay and leant and sat, muzzles and limbs slack and nonchalant.

'So you think the chimps are deliberately resisting stimuli?' He kept the volume of his voice low. 'You think I should tell the two representatives of the Ministry over there that the bloody chimpanzees have just decided not to play along today?'

'I just think it's a possibility, Doctor, that's all.'

'Fantasy,' he said, anger running through his voice. 'Fantasy, Lyn.' He had to restrain himself from shouting. The whispered words came out so hard that he spat on her.

'He,' he said, jabbing his finger at the screen that showed Major, 'is not some Machiavellian schemer. He's a fucking primate.' Rage flashed in his eyes.

Richter turned and headed back to his seat, trying to compose himself before speaking to Travis and Ripon.

'So are you,' said Lyn, smiling as he walked away. 'So are you.'

40

Marlon scanned the shop floor. It was unusually quiet. He leant on the wall behind the 'Film Soundtracks' section and tried to adjust the bottom of his trouser leg with his boot. It had got itself caught on the laces on his other foot and he had been walking around with it hitched up above his ankle, which he hated. It was bad enough having to wear the uniform, especially the hat. You just didn't need anything that made it look worse than it already was.

A bunch of Italian-looking tourists gathered at the rack and began leafing through the discs. Marlon decided to stay where he was and keep an eye on them.

His sartorial concerns were intensified by the fact that he was so 'on show'. That was the whole point of the job. He didn't actually have the authority to arrest or apprehend shoplifters, but provided a visual deterrent. For £4.45 an hour, he prowled around the ground floor looking mean. It was the easiest money he'd ever made.

During his two months of security guarding he had perfected the art of sleeping standing up and frequently killed ten or twenty minutes dozing against a pillar or a doorway.

Today Marlon didn't feel sleepy. In fact, he felt a bit edgy, twitchy. Something bothered him, but he couldn't figure out what it was.

The queue of cars had been waiting by the Great Cambridge

roundabout on the A406 for over an hour. After the first thirty minutes a policewoman had passed between the lines, asking drivers to switch off their engines and prepare for a long wait. She said a lorry had jack-knifed, creating a huge pile-up at the roundabout half a mile ahead. It would be some time before the road would be cleared.

Antonio flicked at his stereo, changing the track on the CD he was listening to, then craned forwards, to check himself in the rear-view mirror.

'Man, you look rough.'

He shook his head as he spoke, reached onto the passenger seat for the bottle of water he had filled before leaving the house and then thought better of it. Instead, he took a pot of styling wax from the glove compartment, smeared some onto his fingertips and began to massage it into his hair.

Zac had just carried the last of the first batch of frames to the top. Of the thirty window casings now stacked in the ninth floor corridor he counted twelve that he had brought up himself. He knew it was more than any of the others had managed. Probably double in fact. He began to trot back down the stairs, passing the agency worker by the landing to the sixth. His hood was still pulled down over his face.

'Ninth floor's done,' Zac said. 'Drop that one on the eighth.'

The black guy arched his neck upwards, angling his head so that one of his eyes was visible from beneath the fold of grey cotton. His lips moved, almost imperceptibly, but he said nothing.

Zac shrugged his shoulders and moved past him. He jogged down the remaining stairs to the hallway, where he found Terence and Connor busily rolling cigarettes.

'The hardest part's over,' Zac said.

'Eight more floors to go!' Connor looked up, sarcasm on his face.

'Come on! If we keep going we can have this done by one.'

'I'm not breaking my fucking back for anyone.' The Scotsman lifted the curled paper to his lips and licked the sticky edge. He then sealed it and spun it into the corner of his mouth in one flicking hand movement. 'I'm not paid enough to do that.'

Zac turned to Terry. 'Come on Tel, let's keep moving. Get it done.'

'Just a quick smoke, then I'm with ya.'

Zac made his way over to the stack of frames and began to manoeuvre one onto his shoulder. He stopped abruptly, as if he had thought better of it and turned back to the other two men.

'What's going on with that guy in the hood?' he asked.

'The black fella?' Terry had also finished rolling now and lit the end of his cigarette with a match.

'Yeah. Have you worked with him before?'

'Nah. He's agency. It's his first day today. He's a quiet one.'

'Hmm.' Zac showed his agreement with a nod. 'He's a bit too quiet for me. Seems a bit moody. But I s'pose as long as he does the work...'

'You say that, but you have to be careful. Darren told me about an agency guy that he worked with once. He turned out to be some kind of head case. They took him out of a home and put him on a site to give him experience of the real world. He was a strong fella, useful to have around, but one day he went nuts and tried to cave Darren's head in with a shovel. It took three guys to stop him.' Terry gestured with the smoking fold of paper in his hand, emphasising his words.

'Yeah, I remember that,' Zac said.

'A few hours with Darren and *I* feel like caving his head in with a shovel. That's no fucking surprise to me.' Connor blew a great, frothy plume of smoke out of his mouth.

Zac and Terry laughed.

'Serious, though,' Zac said. 'Just watch him, Terry's right, you never know where these agency guys are from.'

He turned back to the stack, hoisted the frame onto his shoulder and headed for the stairs, leaving Terry and Connor blowing grey clouds into the air. As he trudged up the stairs between the second and third floors he passed the hooded agency worker again. This time, he didn't even look at him.

41

Richter scratched at the stubbly point of his chin where his goatee had been. Ten hours into the second test study and few of the subjects had done anything other than sleep.

He noticed that Ripon and Travis had become twitchy, inquisitive, narrow eyed, like ferrets. They would sit for a few minutes, heads leaning towards each other, sharing whispers, jabbing pens at notes, then rise from their seats and wander around the lab, approaching technicians and asking questions. Richter sought out Arnold and found him sitting before the left bank of monitors on a chair that he had turned backwards. His arms were folded across the top of the backrest, his chin resting on his hands.

'What do you make of it?' Richter asked, his eyes following Ripon as he picked his way around the lab, weaving around tables, looking over shoulders.

'It's very hard to make any sense out of it, Lawrence. We both know what the real results of the first test study were.'

Richter flashed his eyes at him, in a 'Shut up!' gesture.

'Well, there's no way that what is happening here should be happening. All the stimuli have been increased. The population is denser, the two sub-groups have even come into contact and yet the results are non-existent. The circumstances were ideally suited to stimulating violence and yet this lot are actually showing less agitated behaviour than the control sample, which were kept under normal conditions. It's bizarre.'

'Is there any explanation, Arnold? Lyn Dickens in Zoology thinks the chimps are deliberately resisting.'

Arnold smiled wryly. 'I spoke to Lyn myself, earlier today. She has an interesting slant on things. She's spent most of her career working with apes and she seems to be very fond of them. I think she credits them with a little more intelligence than they actually have. I wouldn't worry too much about that.'

Richter looked left and right quickly, ensuring that no one was listening in.

'Well, if it's not that, what is it?'

'There's only one logical explanation,' Arnold said. Richter noticed that he seemed very tired.

'Which is?'

'Someone, somehow, is tampering with the levels of stimuli.'

'Sabotage? But Margaret's been checking the ratios going through the filter herself. There's no way anything could be wrong there.'

Arnold shrugged and opened his palms, as if to say 'it's only a guess'

'Okay, thanks.' Richter walked away slowly, towards where Ripon and Travis stood, examining an observation screen that showed two of the juvenile chimps sitting, virtually motionless.

Travis noticed him approach and nudged Ripon.

'Absolutely no reaction at all, then,' Travis said, over his shoulder. 'This isn't the outcome you were expecting is it?'

'Not really.' Richter opened his mouth as if he were about to elaborate, but then snapped it closed.

'We do, however, have to accept that this is good news,' Travis continued. 'If the population, climate and pollution levels of ten years from now don't produce the so-called "Black Cloud Response" then we have a bit of time to play with.' There was a moment of mutual, blank faced understanding between him and Ripon.

Richter nodded, smiling feebly

'I think we'll take our leave. I imagine that any response that would have taken place would have been observed by now. Should anything of interest occur during the rest of the study period, I would be grateful if you would inform us promptly.'

Richter nodded. His eyes were heavy and half-closed.

'Of course,' he said.

'We'll be expecting your report in the next few days.'

He shook hands with both of them and asked a technician to see them out. Not for the first time since he had taken on the project, his emotions were confused. He went up to his office, made a coffee and pressed the Tannoy button by his telephone.

'Doctors Rustermeyer and Hoffman to Dr Richter's office please. Doctors Rustermeyer and Hoffman.'

42

Elliot got up from behind his desk and stretched his arms above his head. With a heavy, cumbersome gait, he walked over to the glass partition that separated his office from the rest of the floor and surveyed his territory. He pursed his lips. His eyebrows crumpled towards his nose. Turning sharply to his left, he pushed his office door slightly ajar.

'Suzy,' he said. Suzy had her back to him, filing sales slips into the stainless steel cabinets that ran along the back wall of the floor. She turned.

'Uh-huh?'

'Am I finally going senile or do we seem to be missing a lot of the team today?'

Suzy flicked her eyes around at the scattered empty desks.

'It does look as if there's quite a few not in.'

'Is there something I'm unaware of?'

'I don't know.' She shrugged.

'Do me a favour will you? Pop down to admin and see if they can tell us anything. Maybe there's a flu-bug and everyone's called in sick. Have you had any calls for me yet?'

'No, nothing, the phones have been very quiet this morning.'

Elliot nodded and walked across the front of the office floor, looking around.

Antonio's desk was empty. Of the three floor managers, only Paul Long was in. Elliot stood in the middle of the office and counted heads.

'142 in, 62 missing,' he said to himself.

He walked over to Paul's desk.

'What's happening, Paul? Why so many empty chairs?'

The middle manager looked up from his screen, eyes slightly bloodshot.

'I've been wondering that myself, E-R. I heard that there were a few traffic problems this morning, but that doesn't explain this many absences.'

'Any illnesses going around that you know of? You don't look too great yourself.'

He shook his head.

Elliot puffed out his cheeks and exhaled noisily. He walked slowly over to the window and looked outside. Something out there held his attention. Concern grooved itself into the excess flesh on his face.

'Paul,' he said. 'Come and look at this.'

Outside, it was dark enough to be late evening. Rain attacked the ground mercilessly. Grey streams ran in the gutters.

Paul sidled over.

'A beautiful English summer's day!'

'I don't mean the bloody weather. Look outside. What do you notice?' It was several seconds before he responded.

'Not much,' he said. 'It's pretty quiet.'

'Do you not find that odd?'

'Not really.'

'You don't think it's strange that one of the major streets in the City of London, during a particularly active period in most major international stock markets, is virtually devoid of life or movement?'

'It's probably the weather, E-R. Wait until the storm finishes and everyone will reappear. Relax for an hour or two.'

Paul turned and went back to his desk.

Elliot stood pensively at the window, watching the rain. He began to feel uneasy.

43

'Come on, sweaty!' Zac laughed as Connor struggled to pick up an awkward three-pane frame.

'Eh, a bit less of that, if you don't mind.' Connor was smiling but there was a little edge to his words, as if there was some degree of genuine irritation. 'I won't have people taking the piss out of my nation.'

'Fair enough,' said Zac. 'I didn't think you'd know the slang.'

'Well I do.'

Zac held his hands up, body language indicating 'matter closed'.

'To tell you the truth,' Connor said. 'I'm feeling a little worse for wear.'

'Tired?'

'Aye, and I seem to be getting a headache.'

'Get some water,' Zac said. 'A lot of the time, if you're feeling a bit rough, it's dehydration. Go and have a little rest in the tea hut.'

Terence leapt off the bottom step, slapping down on the floor of the hallway, his heavy boots connecting with the concrete.

'All right, fellas?' he said.

Zac smiled. 'You've livened up a bit.'

'Yeah, second wind I guess. What are we now? About halfway through?'

Mark Turley

'Yeah, pretty much. Five floors left,' Zac said. 'But it's getting easier from now on. I reckon we'll be done in an hour.'

'What's the matter with you?' Terry moved over to Connor, who was now sitting on the floor, hands cupped over his eyes.

'Nothing,' Connor said, looking up. 'I'll be all right in a minute.'

As he spoke, he rose and stood for a second, eyes locked on something far away. Zac turned, following his gaze. There was nothing there. Connor swayed, then took a step, lurching, almost falling towards the door.

'Jesus!' Shocked by Connor's instability, Zac stepped forwards to help him. It looked like someone had taken a spanner and loosened all the joints in his body.

'Leave me alone!' The words were half-lost in the cracking of his voice. Zac stepped back instinctively, palms up, and watched him stumble across the lobby, out of the door and into the rain outside, heading for the tea hut.

'Was he drinking last night?' he asked Terry.

'Yeah, a little bit; nothing heavy though. He normally handles it better than that.'

'Next frame?'

'Next frame,' Terence agreed.

The two of them began their steady ascent to the fifth floor, each with a huge rectangle of UPVC balanced on their shoulder.

'You know, it's not the weight of these things, it's the awkwardness,' Terence said, wincing as the sharp edge of the plastic tried to cut a groove into his collarbone.

'You been changing shoulders?'

'Nah, my right's much stronger than my left.'

'Bad move,' Zac said. 'Tomorrow, you're gonna find burst blood vessels under the skin, where these things have been digging in. It's not dangerous, but it's better to balance them out by doing a bit on each side. Anyway, how're you ever gonna get your left side as strong as your right if you don't use it?

180

That don't make no sense.'

Zac stopped when he reached the third floor landing, giving Terence time to catch up. He turned his head to see the younger man edging up the last few steps.

'Have you seen that other bloke lately?'

'Who?'

'That agency guy.'

'Nah, not for about ten minutes. He must be taking a break somewhere.' Terence spoke a little breathlessly, his cheeks flushed with red.

'See you on the fifth,' Zac said and carried on.

Normally it would have taken Connor a couple of minutes to walk to the tea hut from the new block, but the swirling wind and punishing rain held him back. It was a battle to manage a few steps. From somewhere nearby he could hear raised voices. An argument was taking place, quite a serious one from the way it sounded, but he felt too rough to care.

Connor frowned deeply, almost closing his eyes. There was no strength in his body at all. His legs, in particular, felt weak and loose. Worse still, his headache grew, pounding and pulsing. Pain jabbed between his temples. When at last he pushed the thin, aluminium door open, his shirt was wet through, almost transparent. His face had turned the same shade of grey as the sky.

The tea hut was deserted and Connor moved over to the sink. A small collection of dirty mugs littered the draining board. He picked one at random and filled it from the tap. The water looked a little discoloured, but he didn't give it a second look. The temporary plumbing that served the tea hut meant that the water often looked, smelled and tasted a bit strange. He drained the mug in one swig, refilled it and drank again. Drinking seemed to temporarily ease the pressure in his head, so he drank a third cup, before sitting down heavily on one of the plastic chairs by the sink.

'Oh fuck,' he gasped, rubbing his forehead.
It was the last thing he did before the pain intensified.

Antonio had been asleep for about fifteen minutes when the line of cars that stretched into the distance began to move.

He jerked awake to the sound of horns blasting behind him, turned his ignition key and wiped at his foggy eyes. A dull headache emanated from his upper forehead and spread to the tops and sides of his skull. The weather outside was shocking. A deep, oppressive grey had attached itself around the skyline like a fitted carpet. Vicious rain stabbed the road, slashing at it in long, jagged streaks.

He maintained slow progress to the entry lane of the round-about, but his head thumped and pulsed. It felt as if his brain was expanding, becoming too big for his skull. The co-ordination between feet, hands and eyes required for driving seemed to be deserting him. It was an effort just to trickle along in first gear. He began to feel faraway and outside himself.

'Shit…' he massaged his temple with one hand as another jolt of pain jabbed at the area directly above his eyes.

The events of Elliot's party still troubled him. He had spoken to Sadie the night after.

'How was it?' she had asked him.

'Okay. A bit boring, really.'

'Shall I come over?'

'No, I've got some work to do. I'll catch up with you in the week.'

He had surprised himself with how guilty lying to her made him feel. Confused and desperate for reassurance, he had phoned Suzy.

'You know, it's funny,' he had told her. 'All your life you think you want something, you admire it and aspire towards it. But when you begin to actually get it, you don't want it anymore.'

'That's too deep for me right now,' Suzy had said, her

speech slow and weak. She had sounded exhausted, or possibly sedated.

'I mean money, flash cars and high-class parties. When you're looking in from somewhere else it all seems so glamorous and desirable. But when you get in there, when you start to get your own piece of it, it all just seems so...'

'So what?' Suzy slurred, her voice thick and dreamlike.

'Crap,' Antonio finished. It was the best word he could think of at the time.

'Listen,' Suzy had told him, the syllables coming in long, slow drags, like honey dripping from a spoon. 'You're just coming down after last night. We all get that. Try to get some sleep. I gotta go, I'll see you tomorrow.'

Antonio reached the roundabout at last. His vision was a little blurry and he strained his eyes to see through the sheeting rain and the poor light. Cars, some with headlights now on, paraded in front of him in a ceaseless rotation. He could not see well enough to judge distance or space. His head throbbed and pulsed. There were just so many of them. Everywhere he looked there were cars and lights, each car full of people.

'It's impossible, there's too many,' he whispered, into his chest. He was half-aware that outside some drivers had left their vehicles. Fights seemed to have broken out here and there.

Antonio shook his head, trying to banish any unwanted thoughts. The headache was starting to take him away. Dazed by the pain, he grabbed the water bottle from the passenger seat, twisted off the lid and drank half of it in a series of long, thirsty gulps. Once again, a cacophony of horns blasted the air from behind. There was an army of drivers back there, impatient and angry, desperate to get moving, to drive through and away from the bleakness; they buried Antonio beneath a deafening, crushing wall of sound.

Antonio cupped his hands over his ears as waves of pain crackled through the bone and tissue of his skull.

The noise was huge. Inside Antonio, the pressure continued

building. There was nothing he could do. It consumed and filled him. Somewhere, deep within himself, he let go. He let go of his job and his money. He let go of his car, his girlfriend and even his parents. He let go of the steering wheel, opened the door and stumbled out into the rain. It hit his face like tiny pellets of shot.

He slipped and staggered towards the back of his car, a strange blankness in his eyes. Something internal had snapped, exploded or imploded. Only primal instinct put one foot before the other.

Other cars now too sat empty. Drivers stumbled over slippery tarmac, some of them bleeding from the ears or nose. One by one, as they came into contact with each other, they tore and bit and struck and clawed. One by one they fell.

Six minutes of savagery and all was still.

Antonio lay on the hard shoulder, lifeless and limp, partially on top of the policewoman who had told him to switch off his engine earlier, and beside a delivery driver from a food company.

His body was twisted into a peculiar set of angles, like a Picasso portrait, or a discarded doll. One of his ears was missing. Here and there, the half dead and wounded shuffled and groaned, still trying, with any remaining strength, to destroy those near to them.

All around, the grey rain spattered and splashed.

44

The office in which they sat was small and plain, having none of the oak-panelled parliamentary grandeur to which they were accustomed. In keeping with the colour scheme of the rest of the complex, it had a white tiled floor, plain white walls and a white ceiling on which was mounted a pair of halogen spotlights.

The Protected Rooms, or PR's as they were known, had first been dug and sealed in a concrete shell during the sixties, as a cold war precaution. It had been felt by the Macmillan administration that the pre-existing government shelter, located in a secret tunnel adjoining the Victoria Line near Pimlico, was inadequate in the advent of nuclear war and so they had developed a new site. On several occasions during the forty years that followed, the cabinet and their aides had adjourned to the PRs for a day or two, while some international, diplomatic crisis ran its course.

But this time, it was not unsubstantiated fears over Russian foreign policy that had brought them here and they knew it. Even the most hardened among them showed signs of anxiety.

The Minister tapped something into his laptop, folded the lid over and looked up. He seemed detached, distracted by thoughts of distant events.

'It's begun,' he said.

'So Lawrence, what's next?' Exhaustion was drawn into every

line on Margaret's face.

'That is what I brought the pair of you up here to discuss.' Richter also looked fatigued, but seemed to possess a calmness that he hadn't shown for a long time. He had regained his old authority, his conviction.

'We can be pleased, I think, the three of us, that things have worked out as they have. We are still operational as a team and as a lab. The Ministry are satisfied, at least for now, that we have done nothing wrong. As far as they are concerned, the results correlate.'

Arnold cleared his throat noisily. His Adam's apple bobbed. He looked annoyed.

Richter continued speaking.

'We are left however, with one problem.'

Both Margaret and Arnold looked shattered, but met his gaze. They had a good idea of what he was about to say.

'We have a serious discrepancy between the results of the two test studies conducted thus far. This leads me, after conversations with both of you and various technicians, to surmise that there are two possible conclusions. The first, which I personally think is silly, is that the sample are deliberately affecting the outcomes.'

'That is silly,' Margaret agreed, rubbing her eye. 'You've been talking to Lyn Dickens haven't you?'

Richter smiled. 'How did you guess? The second possibility is that the studies have not been carried out correctly. Again, we can divide this into two possibilities. Either this is through some form of incompetence or...'

'It's deliberate,' Arnold said impatiently, finishing Richter's sentence for him.

Richter nodded. 'Everything all right, Arnold?'

'Fine.' Arnold's voice was blunt and hard.

Richter paused for a moment before continuing. 'What we, as the supervisory team of this project, have to do, is discover which of those it is and make sure that it doesn't happen again.'

'Right,' Margaret began. 'I think all three of us would agree that the chimps resisting stimuli is a non starter.'

Arnold and Richter both nodded.

'It suggests a level of cognisance that's just impossible from apes,' Richter said.

'So in that case, it's something in the lab. Something, somewhere, has gone wrong.'

'There was nothing wrong with the first study. I personally guarantee it.' Arnold spoke suddenly and sharply.

'Can you be sure, Arnold?' Margaret spoke softly, not wishing to start an argument.

'Listen, Test Study One was under my control and I took every possible care to ensure that all aspects were prepared and delivered with total accuracy and reliability. Toxicity was at base levels, so Margaret's team had a relatively light involvement. As the individual with ultimate responsibility for what takes place in the observation lab, I felt it was my duty to ensure that everything worked perfectly. I know that the results of TS1 were correct.'

Richter scratched his chin.

'Since we've been working together, Arnold, I've never had a reason to doubt you. If you say that Test Study One's results are reliable, I believe it.'

Arnold looked hard at Richter. Richter continued speaking.

'It will be interesting to see if the first human test next year supports those findings.'

'Next year might be cutting it a bit fine.'

'Yeah, but as I was – '

'Those results were only projecting four to five years into the future. The severity of them suggests that a reaction could very well occur before that time. If that's true and the country is unprepared, we will have that on our consciences.'

'Before we get too hasty Arnold,' the volume of Richter's voice began to climb, 'we need to remember that nothing is proven until it is tested on human beings in urban conditions.

These are chimps…'

'…ninety-seven per cent identical in terms of DNA!' Arnold was shouting now. Margaret tried to calm him by making a gentle waving motion with her hand.

'Chimps in the bloody jungle, Arnold! It does not prove anything!'

'Gentlemen,' Margaret cut in. 'I don't think we'll make too much progress like this. Let's try to focus on the original point of this conversation. Okay?'

The two male scientists looked a little ashamed.

'Sorry, Maggie,' Richter said, resting his cheek on his hand. 'I think we're all a bit tired.'

'So we've decided it's not the chimps and it's not Test Study One that's at fault. Therefore we can assume that our focus should be on Test Study Two. We need to discover what has happened in Test Study Two to change the outcome so dramatically.' Margaret kept her voice deliberately even, in an attempt to avoid any further conflict.

'That's really a question that you should provide an answer to, Margaret,' Arnold said. 'It was mainly your team involved in the specific preparations for TS2, mine were simply repeating the procedures from before.'

Margaret sucked in her cheeks and eyed Arnold seriously.

'So, you're suggesting that one of my team is responsible.'

'I think that's the logical conclusion to draw.'

'Well, I disagree, those technicians are as competent and reliable as any anywhere.'

Richter intervened.

'At this point, I think I'd agree that Arnold's conclusion is the likeliest. That's not to say it's certain, but it's the likeliest. Let's start with that.'

'I think we need to find the source of the problem and remove it,' Arnold said, coldly.

'You mean look for a scapegoat.' Margaret seemed unimpressed.

'Yes, if you like. If the person or people responsible for this are incompetent, they have no place working on a project of such importance. If they are deliberately sabotaging the research, then they clearly have to be removed. I would call it common sense rather than scapegoating, but let's not get involved in that discussion.'

Arnold's words, spoken impatiently, were the last at the table for about a minute. The three of them sat silently, each following their own train of thought.

'Where do we begin then?' Richter asked, at last.

'I think we should examine the practices and procedures of each of Margaret's team.' Arnold said.

Richter nodded and turned to Margaret. 'Is there anyone you feel may be letting us all down, Margaret? Any place where we should begin?'

'No, not at all.' Margaret looked despondent and harassed.

'What about the new chap?' Richter asked.

'Sahaal Walid?'

'Yes.'

'He's done an excellent job.'

'Nonetheless, I think we should start with him. He's someone who can be pinned down as a difference between the first and second studies.'

'I don't think you'll find a problem there.'

'We'll see,' said Richter.

Solemn faces ringed the table. Nobody looked at anybody else.

After a time, the Minister spoke again.

'Report and recommendations?' he said, to the two men directly opposite him.

Travis clasped his hands in his lap. Ripon took out his notebook.

'It's become a very convoluted situation, sir,' he said.

'We thought it might.' The Minister's voice was calm and low, honed by years of TV appearances.

189

'Fortunately we do have contingency plans in place. I don't think that there's anything to worry about. It's simply a question of choosing the correct course of action.'

Ripon's expression hadn't changed. His face looked tight and white.

'There've been two conflicting sets of results from the test studies conducted so far,' he said.

'And?'

'Well, naturally the staff are a little confused. They're trying to hide it, but I would imagine they'll soon be looking for the source of the problem.'

'Hmm.' The Minister scratched his ear. 'Has security been compromised?'

'Difficult to be sure, sir, but my inclination would be as yet, no, but potentially, yes.'

'Intervention needed, you think?'

Ripon nodded.

'Low level or high?'

'I think I'd go for the latter.'

The minister nodded slowly. His eyes shone with cold, clear understanding.

45

Zac crouched by the doorway, peering around the bottom edge, into the yard, witnessing the insanity, still trying to come to terms with what was going on.

'Calm,' he said to himself, deliberately breathing slowly and deeply.

He had just dropped a frame off to the fifth floor when he had first heard the noises from outside. People were screaming. And not just screaming: they were howling, like beasts.

Motionless, he had listened for a moment to the noises, standing still and quiet, instincts warning of danger. Recognition had stirred, somewhere within. Deep memory knew those sounds and subconsciously, he recalled a few occasions in his late teenage years, when he had found himself cornered outside The Den, or Elland Road, or Stamford Bridge. He also recollected other scenes that he had buried so far down, he had never spoken of them since they happened in North Kuwait in 1991. Finally, he recalled the recent incident in Tottenham, when he had acted too late to prevent death.

All of these sped through his head in the split seconds in which the brain works. By using the relevant chunks of his memory, in flash-frame, his thoughts had prepared him for what his eyes would see.

On reaching the hall he had moved to the doorway to investigate, walking tentatively, one foot placed deliberately before the other, each stride even. He carried his hands about his chest, as if holding a rifle. His eyes and mind had concentrated, ready to assess, and leaning around the edge of the doorframe, he had begun to survey the yard.

All over the site, man attacked man. Carl, the South African, who had been moaning about the weather in the morning, knelt on the ground next to a prostrate hod carrier, pounding his face with his fists. Others swung shovels and picks. Their faces bore the blankness of complete fear and complete anger, supreme emotion, sheer, urgent instinct, all rationality abandoned. Zac's breath became short, quick and hot. His heart raced. Adrenaline began to flood his veins.

Among the melee, he saw Darren, struggling with one of the other plasterers. They were on the third level of scaffolding around one of the newer blocks. Darren was no match for his attacker and was hurled, flailing from the boards. He hit the ground awkwardly and lay completely still.

A loud slap jolted Zac up. It had come from just behind him. He stood and span in one movement, blood surging, ready to strike.

It was the agency worker, grey hood still pulled over his eyes, just having jumped off the last few steps, his trainers smacking the floor.

'Stay there!' Zac shouted.

The black man took one step towards him.

Zac bunched the muscles in his right arm and upper back, ready.

'Don't fuckin' move!' Zac said, softer this time. 'Don't play fuckin' games with me.'

The other man stood perfectly still.

'Speak to me,' Zac said.

Nothing was said. They stood, several feet apart, the roars from outside filling the air.

'You hear that?' Zac said, calmly now. 'People are going crazy out there. I need to know that you're all right. If you can't talk, at least take your hood off so I can see your eyes.'

Terry appeared at the bottom of the stairs, looking strained after his efforts with the window frame. He screwed his eyes up into wrinkled slits. Zac saw him and held up his hand as if to say 'stay where you are.'

The black man still said and did nothing.

Nerves started to hum with fear. Zac readied himself, sensing the moment.

'If you don't show me that you're with me, I'll assume you're against me. Do something, make a move.'

A move was made.

The attack happened so suddenly and violently that even Zac didn't see it coming. One moment he was talking calmly, softly; the next he was buried under a barrage of blows. Punches, kicks, knees and elbows, flew against his legs, face and ribs. Nails clawed at his cheek and as he was pushed back, still reeling in shock and surprise, his assailant bared his teeth like a dog and bit savagely at his throat. Zac knew that the secret of fighting is to take the initiative, but by allowing himself to be taken by surprise, he had already lost that. He was in trouble and he knew it. He staggered back towards a plasterboard wall.

'Get the fuck off me!' Zac yelled, his voice shriller than usual.

His attacker just bellowed, growling, snorting. He had one hand on the other man's face, his thumb pressing against his upper lip, pushing against the top row of teeth as they gnashed. His other hand pressed on his throat, trying to cut off his assailant's supply of oxygen. It didn't seem to work. His foe fought with unbelievable savagery, biting, clawing, kicking and punching. It was all Zac could do to keep him away. He had not yet had a chance to strike back. An elbow dug into his ribs and a foot narrowly missed his groin. Zac pushed him off, the effort causing him to lose balance slightly and he went down awkwardly, on one knee. He knew that in this position he was vulnerable. His opponent came back at him quickly, sensing his advantage, going for the kill.

But then, the fight was over, as quickly as it had begun. The aggressor fell to the floor, wildness dying in his eyes, blood spraying from a deep neck wound. Zac had been lucky. He knew that. In those kinds of situations you have to stay open to all possibilities.

He had been so focused on the black man, that when Terence had run at him, teeth bared, he hadn't even seen him until it was too late. The agency worker had disappeared, leaving him to fight alone, but had returned some twenty seconds later with a small Phillips screwdriver, which he buried into one of the thick veins on Terry's neck.

'Are you all right?' the agency guy asked, from beneath his hood. He offered Zac his hand. His voice was low and soft. Zac used the hand to pull himself up and stepped away from Terry's dying movements.

'Yeah. I think so.'

Terry was flat on the floor. The flow of blood was weakening and his eyes were still and blank.

The black man made the sign of the cross.

'I don't know,' he said, turning to face Zac. 'I don't know what's happening.' The one eye that Zac could see beneath the hood was dark, but alive with fear.

'I was upstairs having a smoke. I saw this shit start from the top floor window. First one or two guys down by the tea hut started tearing into each other, then the whole damn site went nuts. People everywhere going crazy. Your friend lost it, too.'

They both looked down at Terry, a circle of red spreading around him, pooling on the concrete. His feet twitched.

'I think he would've killed you if I hadn't stepped in.'

Zac nodded, still shaken.

'Thanks,' he said.

Staying close, they moved together to the doorway.

The sweat poured off Zac's head.

It was already calmer outside. Many now lay on the ground.

'It's like…' The agency guy's voice trickled away.

Zac saw Connor, his checked shirt torn and hanging loosely from the sleeve, battering one of the scaffold crew with a hammer. They fought by the newly-laid foundations of the next block to be constructed, close to the entrance to the site, opposite the tea hut. He had caved in one of the man's cheeks, a froth of blood oozed from his mouth, but he still kept coming, howling and thrashing.

'That's the guy that started the whole thing,' the agency guy said.

'I was working with him earlier. The last time I saw him, he went to get a drink, that was like, ten minutes ago.'

'Was he okay then?'

'Yeah, he was fine. He said he had a headache, but nothing like…' Zac's words faded, too. They both sat in silence again.

After some time, Zac spoke.

'You got any idea...?' His voice was very quiet, almost child-like.

The agency guy nodded.

'My granddaddy always said this day would come.'

'What day?'

'And God said "They will fall down slain in Babylon, wounded and dying in the very streets of their sin."'

Zac looked across at him, still unable to see more than the tip of his nose and his mouth under the hood.

'Isaiah,' he said, with finality.

Zac said nothing. Again they were silent. Outside, only seven or eight men still stood and most of those were wounded. They prowled around in separate areas of the site, as if each were protecting a territory.

'What's your name?' Zac asked.

'Joel.'

'Listen, Joel, I think we need to get out of here.'

'I agree.'

'If we run for the gate, I think we can make it to that cement truck.' Zac pointed at a rusty van with a large cement mixer mounted on the back.

Joel turned his head sideways to face him, his eyes still covered by the hood.

'What about the keys?'

'There'll be in there. Bernie always keeps the keys in company vehicles when they're on site.'

'You sure?'

Zac nodded.

'If the keys aren't there we're fucked.'

'If we stay here we're gonna get caught up in it.'

Joel looked again, eye shining from the shadow under his hood. He nodded.

'Then let's go.'

'Ready?'

'Ready.'

Synchronized by panic, they leapt simultaneously from under the covered doorway, sprinting across the yard, knees and arms pumping frantically. Two of the remaining builders saw them and gave chase, shrieking and growling, one of them carrying a shovel.

Zac reached the truck first and yanked open the driver's side door

'Get in!' he shouted. Joel bundled into the passenger's side of the truck and slammed the door just as Carl, who no longer seemed to care about the weather, lunged at him, snarling.

Joel fumbled desperately for the lock and closed it, as Carl pounded the window with his fist, teeth clenched, a dribble of spit hanging from his chin.

'He's gonna break the fucking glass man, get out of here!' His voice was high, close to cracking.

The other builder closed in. Zac recognised him as one of the bricklayers, a broad shouldered, tattooed, shaven-headed man, whose usually genial face was twisted and feral, his eyes blank. A deep wound ran down the side of his head and across one cheek.

Zac went to turn the key. It wasn't there.

The window by Joel was vibrating from the power of Carl's blows. Carl was snorting and grunting, blowing trails of mucus out of his nose.

'The key's not here.'

'What?'

'The fucking key's not here.'

The bricklayer reached the truck, tilted his head backwards and bellowed at the sky, as if to warn the world of his intentions. He put one booted foot on the front bumper and stepped up on to the bonnet, raising the shovel above his head as he did so.

Zac frantically checked the dashboard, his hands flickering over the dials and switches.

Joel put his head between his knees and looked on the floor, hands scampering over the foot-mats, then raised himself slightly to check the glove compartment.

The shovel came crashing down through the windscreen, glass exploding into the truck. The angle of the shovel blade caught the passenger side headrest and tore through, sending clusters of upholstery stuffing cascading onto the dashboard.

'It's here!' Joel found the key at the back of the glove box, behind a map-book. He pressed it desperately into Zac's outstretched hand as the bricklayer started to climb through into the cab of the truck.

Zac gunned the engine, and pressed down heavily on the accelerator, shifting his head quickly to one side to avoid a powerful boot aimed at his face. The tyres slipped momentarily on the wet ground, before catching grip. The truck shot forward and the bricklayer flew off the bonnet, landing in a heap on Zac's side. Carl too was left reeling, clutching frantically at nothing. In the rear view mirror, Zac saw the two builders turn their attentions to each other as he pulled out of the gate.

The truck powered out of the entrance to the site and onto

the road outside.

'Shit,' Zac said, as the carnage on the street unfolded before him. 'Take a fuckin' look at this.'

46

'Admin haven't heard anything from any of the missing personnel,' Suzy said. 'The phone lines are down for some reason.'

Elliot rested his chin on a podgy fist.

'This just gets weirder the longer the morning drags on. It's 10:45 and I've got twenty-eight missing here. It's the same story on the other floors too, right through the company. What on earth could be preventing something like a quarter of my bloody staff turning up for work?'

'Is there a tube strike?'

'Not that I know of.' Suzy paused. 'Check the Internet,' she suggested.

Elliot touched the power button on his PC and reached for the mouse.

'The server's down,' he said, the corners of his mouth drooping after his last word. 'Have we got a radio?'

'Yeah, I think Vincent in Paul's team brought one in to listen to the rugby on Saturday. I'll check if it's there.'

Suzy wandered off, meandering around the desks and chairs, returning moments later with a tiny, hand-held receiver.

'Good.' Elliot motioned to her to put it on the desk. 'Let's get some news on.'

She turned the dial from one end to the other, but found nothing.

'Just interference,' she said, shrugging her shoulders.

Elliot looked down at the desk.

'This isn't looking good,' he said.

Suzy nodded.

'Yeah, it's quite strange.'

'It could be worse than bloody strange, Suzy, and I don't think I'm being paranoid. What if there's a bomb or something?'

'We'd be warned, the police would evacuate, surely?'

'I'm not so sure. To be honest I'm getting quite a bad feeling. I've worked in central London all my life and I've never known anything like this. It just feels wrong.'

'Wrong?'

Elliot nodded. Suzy suddenly felt a bit disorientated. She had never seen him with anything other than controlled confidence on his face. His eyes were watery, full of confusion.

'Have you got an umbrella?'

Suzy shook her head. 'Why?'

'I think we should go outside, see what we can find out. I don't want to sit here in ignorance. Come on, put your coat on.'

'Where are we going?'

'We'll start with the tube station.'

47

Elliot motioned Suzy out of the office and the two of them hurried out. In their haste, they left the radio buzzing and humming on the desk. By the entrance to the lift, they passed two of the admin girls coming up with the morning coffee trolley. They disembarked on the ground floor, stopping by the reception desk. George was nowhere to be seen. His copy of the Daily Star lay spread over the top of the counter.

For a moment they stood and waited. Elliot leant on the doorframe and caught his breath. They both looked out at the great, grey blankets of rain, hurtling down on the tarmac.

'Why's it so quiet?' Suzy asked.

'This is what I mean, I don't know. You wouldn't expect to have too many people out walking, but cars, buses, taxis, where are they?'

'There's some cars over there.' Suzy pointed at the lights, which changed from red to green, commanding non-existent traffic. Two small lines of cars, maybe ten or twelve on each side had stopped, nose to nose, in the middle of the crossroads. On some, the doors hung open.

Elliot sucked in some more air, his chest heaved.

'Let's head for the tube station. There should be someone there who can tell us what's going on.'

Suzy nodded.

'Ready?' he asked.

Suzy looked pensive. She had lost all the colour from her

201

face and her lips were pressed together. She nodded jerkily and winced and rubbed her forehead. Elliot grabbed her hand and they ran out into the street.

The rain hammered at the pair of them as they trotted through the city. It flew into their faces and stabbed continuously at any exposed flesh, making them feel raw and vulnerable.

Despite the conditions, after thirty metres or so, Elliot felt hot. His breath juddered out of him heavily and slowly. He had to gasp to be able to take in any oxygen at all. His heart thundered out of control.

Slowing to a shuffling walk, he turned to Suzy, 'Go on ahead,' he said. 'I'll catch you up.'

He was so pre-occupied with filling his failing muscles with oxygen, that he didn't notice how bad Suzy looked. The greyness of the sky and rain seemed to have imprinted themselves on her features and she screwed them up as if she were in terrible pain. He watched her jog on.

Left alone, he felt more aware, as if his mind knew that he had become self-dependent for survival and woken itself up. For a few seconds he stood and absorbed details of his surroundings. Abandoned cars sat silently, dotted across the roads. He felt exposed, afraid. Something in him warned him of danger. The need to keep moving reasserted itself.

The first body he saw wore a blue suit. It lay across the bonnet of a Ford, big purple welts covering its face. Blank eyes stared blindly at the sky, the rain filling them with pools of tears.

Elliot stopped and gazed, unable to move. Other corpses lay here and there. His stomach tightened. There were a lot of them. It seemed that everywhere he looked, his eyes met death. He stopped, looking around. A couple of metres in front of him, a middle-aged man in a raincoat sat propped against a lamppost, blood running from his nose and ears, the rain washing it off his chin. Elliot didn't check if he was alive and began to half-walk, half trot. Suzy was out of sight and he gathered up his collar, heading for the station, white-faced, looking at nothing.

By the time he arrived, his shirt and suit were heavy with water. He trudged into the ticket hall, sodden shoes making a wet, plopping noise on the floor.

The foyer was deserted and dank. Elliot wiped as much water from his face as he could and looked around.

'Suzy,' he called, his voice thin and small. The ticket booths were empty. The safety glass on one of them had been smashed and lay in glinting shards on the floor. He didn't dare to go and look inside.

A small newsagents store stood at the rear of the ticket hall, door open. He walked towards it slowly, ignoring the smeared red stains on the station wall that bore a poster.

Had enough of crowds, noise and traffic?
GET AWAY FOR THE DAY!
Ask here about our day-trip specials.

He reached the door of the shop and looked inside. Much of the stock had been pulled off the shelves. The floor was littered with magazines and chocolate bars. A thick, cloying smell hung in the air.

'Hello?'

No response.

'Hello?'

No sound other than the relentless beating of the rain outside. He edged inside the shop.

'Is anyone here?' He placed both hands on the counter and leaned forwards. His belly rested on the surface and he craned his neck until he could just about see over to the other side.

An Asian man lay crumpled against the foot of the cigarette display case, behind the counter, coiled intestines glistening in his lap.

'Oh Jesus!' Elliot jumped back, slipped on a magazine and slid backwards out of the shop on his backside.

For a short time he didn't move. He lay on his back, on the concourse, staring at the ceiling.

'They're all dead,' he said to himself.

He rubbed his eyes and blinked, raising himself to a seated position. He found his mind blank, mental synapses dulled with shock. As he got to his feet, Suzy appeared, on the other side of the ticket barrier.

'Suzanne! Have you found anyone?'.

Suzy said nothing.

'I don't like this at all, you know, there's no one around, there's dead people everywhere and I'm thinking I'm going to go and get the car and go home. I think you should join me.'

Suzy placed one hand on the ticket barrier and leapt over it.

'What do you want to do?' Elliot asked again, increasingly unnerved.

Suzy walked towards him silently. As she got closer, a trickle of blood ran from her nose. Fear started to rise in his chest.

'For Christ's sake, Suzanne! I know we're all getting a bit stressed but this is hardly the time or the place for that sort of thing! Didn't you have enough on Saturday? You're unbelievable!'

Suzy shrieked and threw herself at him, her perfectly manicured nails digging into his throat. Elliot managed to push her away, but she came straight back, clawing at his eyes and hissing like a snake. Elliot slapped her hard across the face. Her cheek flared pink and she grabbed his hand and bit it, hard, drawing blood and tearing off a small triangle of flesh.

'Fuck!' Elliot howled in pain and punched her, with all his remaining strength, full in the face. He felt her nose burst beneath his fist and she went down sharply.

Elliot staggered backwards, legs wobbling. His breath came in short, desperate gasps.

'Stay away from me!' he screamed at her, panting. She got up and charged, blood pouring from her nose and dripping over her lips. Elliot backed off, soon finding himself up against the wall with the smashed ticket booth behind his head.

'Please, Suzy!' His voice trembled. 'Please.'

He sank to his knees as she approached, whimpering. She grabbed his hair, pulled his head up and dragged her nails across his cheek, leaving four deep wounds, running from ear to chin. He was sobbing. She began to kick and thrash with her arms. Elliot felt himself sinking further as the blows struck into his legs, chest and the soft, doughy flesh around his midriff. He just wanted it to end. His hand pressed on the floor and found the edge of one of the shards of glass there, cutting his fingers in the process. He shut his eyes, and tears pressed through the lashes. Somehow, almost involuntarily, he grasped the piece and drove its point into her side. Suzy howled and went down, mewling on the ground.

Elliot sat, shaking and gibbering, watching the life flow slowly out of her.

From outside, he heard the rumble of an engine.

On the fourth floor, the scene was chaotic. Tables and chairs had been turned over in the frantic rush to annihilate. Smashed computers lay here and there. One man remained alive, walking and circling. On Elliot's desk, the radio finally crackled into life.

'Do not attempt to leave London!' it said. 'A state of emergency has been declared in the Greater London area. An army roadblock has been enforced around the M25. No one will be allowed to leave or enter the city until further notice. Do not attempt to leave London!'

48

Richter felt refreshed after his brief sleep and headed straight for his office. His computer beeped intermittently. *You have one incoming message,* the screen said.

He clicked on the icon. It was from the Ministry:

Black Cloud Response in all areas of Greater London. City closed down. State of Emergency. How can this have happened? Respond please.

Richter read the message three times before he even half believed it. He sat for a few minutes, elbows on his desk, his face resting on his hands.

He had no idea what to do.

He rose from his chair and rushed from the office, heading through reception and out of the front door of the building.

'Dr Richter!' the receptionist called. 'Is everything all right?'

In the distance, roughly in the direction of London, a storm fogged the sky. Some part of him sensed the truth. He ruffled his hair with one hand and stared.

'This can't be happening,' he whispered. 'No way.'

He tried to imagine what was taking place in the busy commercial areas, remembering the results from Test Study One and magnifying them, conjuring images of Trafalgar Square, or Piccadilly Circus and somewhere, beneath the layers of sheer horror, the feeling that it was his fault gnawed and nagged.

Marlon scratched at his head. The weather was bad and business in the store seemed a little slow. There was still a reasonable number of customers, but by the standards of HMV Oxford Street, it was a quiet day. He stopped for a couple of minutes to chat to David, his manager. They talked briefly about the heavyweight championship fight at the weekend and then went their separate ways.

Marlon couldn't quite find the state of relaxation that he often allowed himself to lapse into when on patrol. He was peculiarly alert. He noted that the management had moved the Hip-Hop rack, which had swapped places with the 60s rack. He guessed this was so that Hip-Hop would be closer to Soul to encourage people to buy from both racks at once. He saw a CD on the floor and picked it up – Shania Twain. Where the hell does that go? he thought. He couldn't bring to mind what it sounded like and so settled for returning it to one of the cash desks.

Marlon headed for the main desk, on which four separate tills were placed, each with a cashier. It ran down the whole length of one side of the store. There was a lovely girl working there on till seven and this would be the ideal excuse to speak to her.

As he approached he saw that Sinesha, the girl in question, was engaged in a conflict with an angry customer. The guy was yelling, leaning over the counter towards her. Marlon neared and saw beads of sweat forming on the man's head. He was very pale and the perspiration had stuck his thin, ginger hair to his scalp. Marlon was vaguely aware that his head had begun to hurt.

'I don't want a credit note, I want a fucking refund,' the man said.

Sinesha sighed, blinked a few times and said, 'I think you'll have to speak to a manager, sir.'

'I don't want to speak to the fucking manager. Just give me my fucking money! I bought this in good faith and…'

The ginger man rubbed at his eyebrows with the flat of his hand. The sweat was dripping off him, some of it collecting on the surface of the counter.

'You don't have a receipt, sir. We don't give refunds without a receipt.'

Sinesha had a weird look in her eyes, Marlon thought.

'Dammit!' He was feeling a bit light-headed himself. It sounded as if some sort of riot had started in the street outside.

The customer hurled his bag onto the counter, the CD case inside cracking on the glass.

Marlon began to feel particularly angry. What right did this guy have to behave like that? The pain in his head increased as he stretched forwards, grabbing the customer around the throat. The last thing he could remember doing was lifting him up by his neck. The man's feet kicked pathetically as he gasped for breath. Marlon held him there for a good minute and a half, until he stopped moving. When satisfied, he simply let go, allowing him to fall to the floor. He then turned around, climbed over the counter and attacked Sinesha.

49

'Maybe you're right,' Zac said, turning to Joel. 'Babylon is falling.'

All he could see of Joel was his mouth hanging open beneath the hood.

'Just drive!' Joel shouted.

The street was full of shoppers. Or at least, they had been shoppers. Many of them now lay still, decorating the rain-drenched tarmac with vivid pools of red. Those that still stood were lashing and biting, punching, kicking, doing anything they could to destroy each other.

'The world's gone fuckin' mad,' Zac said.

'Just drive, man,' Joel repeated, his voice suddenly more urgent. 'Just drive.'

On instinct Zac decided to turn north, back to his flat. It would be somewhere safe to hole up.

He turned into the street and pressed down hard on the gas, pushing the speedo up to fifty-five. Some of the mad crowd lunged at the truck as he passed. Zac had to swerve to avoid hitting a young woman wearing a business suit, her face drawn back into a snarl. He winced as the truck bumped and crunched over a body.

Overturned bins had spilt their loads onto the street and many shop-fronts had been smashed.

Zac pressed on north, continuing up the high street, away from the shops and the crowds. The truck left the savage masses behind, howling as if the world were ending.

Once out of the shopping centre, the street emptied out. The occasional body lay twisted on the tarmac, abandoned cars zigzagging here and there. Those still living prowled and snarled, but safe in the truck, Zac was able to relax a little.

'What d'you think's going on?' he asked.

Joel let the breath escape through his teeth with a soft whistle.

'Like I said before. It's Judgement Day.'

'You really think so?'

'What else could it be?'

Zac looked right. A brutish youth sidled along the pavement, bleeding from the crown of his head, dragging one foot behind him as he walked. He turned to face the van and roared.

'Eeeaaahhh!'

Zac could see right down his throat.

'I don't know,' he said, quietly.

They made steady progress north for five minutes or so, snaking along the road to avoid abandoned cars and bodies.

'Fuck it.' Zac slammed the brakes on.

'What?'

Zac pointed up ahead. Joel followed the line of his finger to the intersection of the North Circular. Just before the junction, stretching from one side of the road to the other, a jack-knifed articulated lorry completely blocked their path.

'There's no way around it.'

'So what now?'

'We have to go back.'

Zac turned the truck around and they headed back the way they had come. Soon they were where they had started, on the high street, outside the entrance to the building site. The street and shops were still and silent, the ground a lawn of corpses.

'What now?' Joel asked.

'South, I guess.'

'As good a way as any.'

South took them through the inner city, past tower blocks and houses with boarded up windows. Some streets were quiet and empty. Others were littered with the dead and dying. Occasionally they saw someone standing, often horribly injured, sometimes shambling around, as if on patrol. All of the living that they saw had the insanity in their eyes.

Going south eventually brought them out of the poor, residential zones and into the City itself.

'It's quieter here,' Zac said to Joel, who sat with his feet up on the dash.

'Why do you think that is?'

'Maybe they're all inside. Who knows what's going on inside those buildings.'

They saw the fat man curled up, chin on knees, just inside the doorway of Bank tube station. His clothes were torn and he sat amidst a mosaic of blood and broken glass. A female body, face down and motionless, lay beside him and he looked up as they neared. Unlike the other survivors they had seen, his face bore expression, chubby, red features contorted with fear and sorrow. He was crying.

'Slow down,' Joel said. 'Let's get a good look at him.' Zac eased off the accelerator and shifted down to first. He stopped the truck as close to the man as he could.

Zac leaned out of his side of the truck.

'You all right, mate?' he called.

No answer.

'Leave him,' Joel said. 'If he wanted help, he would have asked for it. I don't wanna take no risks.'

Zac leant out from his side.

'If you don't answer, we're out of here,' he called.

Slowly, the fat man opened his mouth. Tears ran down the loose skin on his cheeks, eventually hanging off his jowls.

'Help me,' he said simply.

'He's okay,' Zac said, climbing out of the truck. He took a quick look up and down the road and then hurried over to where he sat.

'Come on, mate,' he said, offering the fat man his hand. 'Get up. This don't look like a safe place to be sitting.'

Elliot grabbed the big, blond man's hand and pulled himself up. They walked over to the truck together. Joel moved over to the centre of the seat to allow Elliot to sit down. Zac helped him in.

'You all right there, mister?' Joel asked.

Elliot was shaking. He tried to nod but it wasn't really discernible from the other spasms in his body.

'He's in shock,' Zac said. 'He'll be all right in a while.'

Joel put his hands up to check his hood, ensuring that his eyes were still covered.

'Where are we going, anyway?' he asked.

Zac shrugged.

'Away,' he said.

50

The phone rang on Richter's desk and he picked it up. He had lost a great deal of colour from his face and again looked haggard.

'Lawrence Richter.'

'Richter, it's Ripon.'

'Ah, Mr Ripon, I'm pleased you...'

'Don't flannel me, Richter.' Ripon's voice was calm. 'I don't have the time or the patience to listen to lies. Do you have any idea what's been happening?'

'I received a message. It said the Black Cloud Response had already happened. I don't know any more than that at the moment.'

'That's right, Richter, all over London. We have bodies lining the roads. This is a bloody holocaust, Richter. Do you understand?' Ripon spoke so evenly and without emotion that Richter half-wondered if it was a recording.

'Is there anything I can do?' he asked, feeling pathetic.

'You can try to offer me an explanation.'

'Mr Ripon, I think there is only one possible explanation. I think our testing has been sabotaged.'

'Why?'

'Several hours after yourself and Mr Travis left, yesterday I had an emergency meeting with Drs Rustermeyer and Hoffman to discuss this very matter. We have noticed, unfortunately, some inconsistencies in our findings that are very difficult to

213

explain. The inconsistencies seem to have arisen since a new technician was taken on.'

'Really?'

Richter felt encouraged.

'Yes, a foreign national. He's Bahrainian. To be honest I'm surprised the Ministry approved him in the first place. In the present international climate and bearing in mind the sensitivity of our research – '

'Richter,' Ripon cut in.

'Yes?'

'Stick to the point.' Ripon's words rang with contempt.

'The point is,' Richter began to sound a little shrill, 'that there were no problems at all until this man, Sahaal Walid, joined the team. I'm certain there's something going on.'

'Richter.'

'Yes?'

'Listen very carefully. I'm sending a car for you. It will be there in about forty-five minutes, a black Mercedes. The driver will have instructions to bring you and this Walid to us. I want you waiting, with him, in your office. Is that clear?'

'Yes.'

'In the meantime, I want you to behave completely normally, as if nothing has happened. Do not speak of this to anybody at your facility.'

'But...'

The line clicked and hummed. Ripon had hung up.

51

Zac continued driving south, passing around Trafalgar Square on his way to the river. The rain had begun to subside, leaving pinkish rivulets running into drains. Corpses littered every square foot of concrete, with piles of them clustered around the feet of the stone lions and Nelson's Column. No-one in the van spoke. The sight that confronted their eyes defied words. Overhead, pigeons swooped beneath lightening cloud. A couple pitched and dived, landing, flapping, then picking their way among the dead.

Above the north corner of the square, the giant Coca-Cola sign had been smashed. A double-decker bus sat in its wreckage, the driver's body lolling from the window, hair hanging in bloody scrags. Still-glinting chunks of red neon dangled in long strips. Much of the sign lay scattered on the street, jewel-like, a coating of rubies over bodies and empty cars.

Joel was the first of them to speak for several minutes. It was little more than a murmur, but it jolted Zac and Elliot as much as if they had been asleep and he had screamed in their ears.

'Babylon has fallen and the images of its gods lie shattered on the ground,' he said.

Zac turned to look at him, wary.

'Isaiah again?'

Joel's reply was an almost imperceptible nod of hooded head.

Zac drove carefully, managing to pick his way through the wreckage towards Parliament Square, past pavements swathed in dead tourists, through streets dotted with empty vehicles. A guardsman lay outside his watch-station at the Palace, red uniform torn from his back, bearskin hat horizontal, wet, like a dead animal, its white plume identifying him as a Grenadier. Zac wondered what the soldier had thought as the madness had taken hold, wondered if he had tried to do anything, remaining calm as his training would have dictated, or whether he had been one of the first to succumb, savagely attacking those around him as they stood with their cameras and children.

He pressed on. The Houses of Parliament stood tall, untouched. Big Ben chimed, a booming funeral gong for the cradle of democracy, the mother of the free world. The sound echoed around lifeless streets. Three heads in the van turned. Wordlessly, they shared thoughts. The triumphant, classical architecture, beautiful, intricate, a symbol of national endeavour, seemed only cold now, uncaring, oblivious to the clusters of corpses scattered on the lawns.

Then they were there, the river, a destination of sorts. Zac slipped down into first gear. It stretched before them, flowing left to right, a dirty monument to a dead city. The rain had eased further, spotting here and there on the surface of the water rather than throwing down great blankets of grey as it had before. He pulled up, stopped on the north side of Westminster Bridge and turned to the other two men. It occurred to him that they hadn't seen anyone alive for a long time.

'Where are we gonna go?' he asked, looking out over the bricks and concrete.

Joel shrugged and made a 'Psssshhhh' noise through his lips.

'I have an apartment,' the fat man said in a tiny, fragile voice.

Zac and Joel both turned their heads to face him. It was the first time he had spoken since they'd picked him up.

'Where?' Zac asked very softly, not wishing to upset him.

Elliot raised his hand, still bleeding steadily from the triangular wound Suzy had given him. He directed them towards Canary Wharf tower, its pyramid roof pointing like an accusing finger at the sky.

'Near there.'

Zac shifted back into first and began moving, chicaning along the embankment through the debris of cars and corpses.

'It's only my weekend place, you know,' Elliot said, timidly. He seemed to be talking more to himself than his companions. 'I bought it when I expanded the business. I don't use it that often.' He stared, unblinking, straight ahead as he spoke. 'We can go there. We'll be safe.'

Zac gave him a sideways glance.

'Alright, stay calm. You give me directions when we get to the area.'

Elliot's eyes remained blank.

It took thirty minutes for the cement truck to meander its way to West Pier Village. The three of them had made the journey in complete silence. Zac pulled up in front of the tall, iron gates.

'This is it?'

Elliot nodded.

The car park was half empty. Zac peered through the windscreen. There didn't seem to be any signs of movement.

'How do we get in?' he asked.

Elliot looked at him wide-eyed, white-faced, like a disturbed child.

'Pass-code,' he said simply.

'Yeah?'

'PH9Z6.'

Zac left the engine running and stepped out of the truck. Drops of rain splashed his face and hands. He walked quickly over to the entry keypad, staying alert, on his toes, quickly checking left and right every few seconds. Joel watched from beneath his hood, his mouth and chin set and motionless.

After the last digit was pressed, the gate hummed and swung open. Zac trotted back to the truck and climbed inside. He manoeuvred the vehicle deftly, passing through the gate and parked near the front door of the building, between a large black BMW and an Aston Martin. The three men climbed out one by one, leaving the truck, with its dirty, steel mixer mounted on the back like a gigantic seashell, incongruously sitting among the luxury automobiles.

The three of them stood by the entrance to the building.

'Right,' Zac said. 'Which floor?'

'Top,' Elliot choked the word out.

Zac winced, as if it were bad news.

'Okay,' he said. 'I'm going in first. Joel, you go last. We need to remember that there might be people in there and if there are, we don't know what they're gonna do.'

Elliot whimpered softly.

Zac felt like slapping him, but resisted the temptation.

'Single file, in order. If you see anything, you shout. Let's go.'

Zac pushed the door gingerly and it squeaked open. He edged into the smallish hallway. Two apartment doors were set in the wall to the left. One of them was slightly open. Halfway down the hall, a solid-looking wooden staircase rose to the next floor. The area behind the staircase was black with shadow. Something shifted and scratched down there.

Zac was already halfway up the stairs before he heard it. It was too late to react. Elliot was close behind him and let out a stifled scream. It was Joel who bore the full brunt of the attack.

The cat leapt out from behind the stairs and attached itself to Joel's leg. He cried out, startled and kicked at it with his other foot. It let go and backed away, hissing and showing its fangs. When it came at him again he was ready. His right foot connected hard with its belly, sending it two feet into the air and making a sickening crunching sound. The cat landed flat and lay, twitching its paws, its breath rattling from its mouth.

They climbed the first two flights of stairs without further incident, walking in close single file. Elliot's laboured breathing was the only sound, but as they approached the landing to the third floor, Zac stopped abruptly. He had already put one foot on the top step when he extended his right arm, straight out from the shoulder, as a signal to the other two. Elliot peered through the gaps on the stair riser. He had to stand on tiptoes to see over the edge of the floor. Just visible from his position was a pair of women's shoes, fairly plain, with a slight heel. They lay on their sides, with the soles facing him. Beyond the shoes, legs in black tights extended to where they crossed at the knees. He couldn't see anything past that point.

'Zac, what is it?' Joel asked, half-whispering.

Zac waved his hand jerkily behind his back and took a small step forwards. Joel moved up to Elliot's shoulder. He leaned in to his ear.

'Stay here,' he said, and moved up four steps to join Zac.

Elliot ignored Joel's advice and took a couple of steps himself. Both of them could now see exactly what Zac was looking at.

'She's still alive, man,' Joel said, looking down.

Zac nodded.

A middle-aged woman, thin and tanned, lay on the third floor landing, a small leather handbag by her side. She stared at the ceiling. Her eyes neither moved nor blinked. The only thing that indicated that she wasn't dead was the fact that she was breathing, very faintly. Her breath was quick – in, out, in, out – and her chest expanded and contracted rapidly. She seemed to be concentrating, as if it required a great deal of effort to stay alive.

'It's Loretta,' Elliot said.

Zac looked over his shoulder. 'What?'

'Loretta Young, she's a friend of my wife.'

The woman's blouse had been ripped almost completely

off, revealing a white bra, stained crimson. A gaping, zigzagging wound ran down her right side, as if her abdomen had been unzipped. Five of her ribs lay exposed. They shone, like an ivory glockenspiel, beneath the landing light. Blood soaked the carpet in a semi-circle around her body.

Joel pursed his lips. 'Jus' leave her man. We can't do nothing.' He had to fight back a gag in his throat to speak.

Zac thought for a second, weighing options.

'I agree,' he said, putting his hand over his nose and mouth. 'Let's go.'

One by one, they stepped over her and made for the next set of stairs. She didn't acknowledge them or attempt to move or speak. Elliot looked back at his dying neighbour as he began to climb. She coughed up a bubble of blood before he disappeared from view.

A couple of minutes of cautious stair climbing and they reached the top floor. Elliot fumbled clumsily in his pocket and was relieved to find that he still had his keys. He opened the door and pressed the light switch on the wall to the right. The other two followed him in.

'Fuck me,' Joel said, as he passed through the doorway. 'You live here?'

Elliot looked sheepish. 'No, I live in Potters Bar, this is my London apartment.' Joel kissed his teeth. 'You're rich, huh?'

Elliot nodded awkwardly.

'So what now?' Joel had turned to Zac. 'What do we do, big guy?'

'Now we sit down and think about it. At least we've bought some time.' He motioned to Elliot. 'Lock the door, please.'

Elliot did as he was asked and ushered them onto his leather suite.

'I need a drink,' he said. 'Can I get you anything?'

'Water,' Joel said. Zac nodded. 'That'll do for me as well.'

Elliot shambled to the kitchen, rattled around in a few cupboards and returned quickly with a bottle of red wine, a bottle of mineral water and three glasses. He poured the drinks and passed them with well-practiced cordiality.

'Let's start this from the beginning,' Zac said. 'What the hell happened out there?' He used his thumb to point in the direction of the huge window at the far end of the apartment.

'I told you before man. I was on the top floor of the new block. I heard strange noises outside and everyone was just going fucking nuts. Knocking the shit out of each other.'

'What about you?' Zac looked at Elliot. His wine glass was already half empty. The drink seemed to have revived him.

'Look,' he said. 'Firstly, I don't even know your names.' He was staring at the tattoo on Zac's forearm.

Zac smiled a little. 'Zac and Joel,' he said. 'What about you?'

'I'm Elliot. The second thing I want to do is thank you. I was in a pretty bad way when you found me. I owe you both one.'

Zac nodded.

'It was good to find someone else unaffected. You were the only other person we saw who wasn't going nuts.'

'So what happened to you?' Joel asked.

'I was at work. Strange bloody morning. Hardly anyone there. The streets outside were quiet as anything. I tried to check what was happening, on the Internet, on the radio. Everything was dead. I decided to check outside to see if anyone could tell me what was going on. I thought there may have been a bomb or something. Anyway, we made it to the tube station, I found a dead man in the shop there and then Suzy tried to kill me.'

'That was the girl lying next to you?'

'Yes.' Elliot's chin wobbled a little. 'She was my PA.'

'And she just switched, just like that?' Joel asked.

Elliot nodded.

'There's a lot I don't understand about this,' Zac said.

'You're telling me,' Joel shook his head. 'Number one, why

221

did everyone start going crazy and killing each other? Number two, why are we still okay when everyone else isn't?'

'I was thinking that myself,' Zac said. 'And the last question, which is the most important, is what do we do now?'

'If you don't mind, I think I'll call my wife.' Elliot's colour had mostly returned.

He reached over and picked up a cordless phone from the coffee table. He put it to his ear and pulled it away again instantly.

'The line's dead,' he said, throwing the handset down in disgust.

'But maybe…' Elliot was talking to himself. He reached underneath the tabletop and pulled out a well-disguised drawer, from which he picked a small, blue mobile and tried again.

52

Janet was semi-reclined on the sofa, wearing a pink, silk night-dress with Chinese lettering on the left collar when her mobile rang. She looked at it bemused for a moment and then picked it up. Her jaw dropped, forming her mouth into a lipstick-perfect 'O' when she heard the voice on the other end.

'Is that you, darling?'

The line was a bit crackly.

'Janet, it's me. I'm in London.'

'But I thought you were…'

'Yes, yes, nothing to fear at the moment. I'm all right. Do you know what's going on?'

'They announced it just now,' she said. 'There's been a terrorist attack. The water's been poisoned with something that's made everyone go mad. They've had to blockade the M25. They said there were no survivors.'

'Well there are. I'm at the penthouse with two other people. Our phone lines are down, we've got no radio or TV or anything. It's been madness.'

'I'll make some calls,' she said, emotion causing her voice to crack. 'I'll get someone there for you, hang on.'

She put the phone down and doubled up over her knees, sobbing violently. She clutched at her hair with her hands.

A young, handsome, dark-haired man stepped out of the kitchen door. He was wearing Elliot's dressing gown. It was too small for him and the sleeves exposed his thick, hairy wrists.

'What's the matter?' he asked.

'He's still alive!' she wailed, make-up running down her face. 'He's still fucking alive!'

He put down the drink he was mixing and crossed the room to comfort her.

'Oh my God,' Elliot said. His chin wobbled. He switched his mobile off and put it down.

'What is it?' Zac asked.

'Terrorists.'

'What?'

'Terrorists. A chemical attack of some kind. That's the cause. Everyone's killing each other because of poisoned water. They thought there were no survivors.'

Zac and Joel both looked at their glasses.

'Don't worry,' Elliot said. 'Bottled.'

'But there are survivors,' Joel said.

Zac nodded. 'I would imagine that if we've made it this far, there must be some others.'

They all looked down at the floor.

'So anyone drinking or washing from the London system gets poisoned?' Joel said.

'It would seem so.' Elliot poured himself some more wine. 'Perhaps, if whatever chemical it is got into the water cycle, it could even be brought on by the rain.'

'That would explain a few things,' Zac said. 'It seemed that everything went off after the storm started. People got caught in the rain and went crazy.'

'How many people in London?' Joel asked.

Elliot answered. 'About eight million.'

'The attack's just in London, though, right?'

'I didn't ask, but Janet sounded all right.'

'So let's get in the truck and get out. We'll drive into the country somewhere.'

Elliot shook his head. 'The army have blockaded the M25. No one's going in or out. We're stuck until they come to get us.'

'They're coming to get us?

'My wife's going to arrange something.'

Joel rubbed his hand roughly across his mouth. 'Sooner rather than later, I hope,' he said.

'If your mobile's working, you can call yourself.' Zac eyes were firmly trained on Elliot's.

Elliot felt compelled to do as he was told. 'True.'

He dialled '999' and received a recorded message.

'Due to national emergency, the Metropolitan Police are unable to take your call at the moment. If you are ringing with regard to the terrorist strike please call the following number....'

He dialled the number and waited.

A male voice answered the phone.

'Look,' Elliot said. 'We're stranded in the middle of London. It's an apartment block in Wapping called West Pier Village. There're three of us in the penthouse. Can you send someone down here?'

'Someone will call you back, sir,' the voice said.

'When?'

There was no answer.

'Bastards hung up on me,' Elliot said. 'They're calling back soon.'

53

The car arrived for Richter at exactly the time he was told it would. He was sitting in his office, trying to make small talk with Walid, when the noise of tyres on tarmac caused him to turn his head and look out at the car park. A long, black Mercedes pulled up by the security gate. He watched as the passenger-side front window scrolled downwards. A hand emerged and signalled to the guard. Words were said. The gate opened and the car rolled in. Richter turned back to Sahaal.

'Would you like another coffee?' he said.

Sahaal shook his head. 'No thanks. If you don't mind, Doctor, I'd like to get back to the lab.'

Richter's eyes widened.

'No, look, there's something I need to talk to you about. It's very serious. I'll be back in two minutes. Wait here.'

Richter sidled out of the door and stood on the landing at the top of the staircase. He watched the door from the reception area and waited for it to open. He didn't have to wait long. Perhaps a minute and a half had passed before Ripon, his face cold and tight, walked through the door, a broad-shouldered, unfamiliar man by his side.

'I told you to wait in the office,' he said.

Richter said nothing.

'Is Walid in there?'

Richter nodded.

'Get him out here.'

Richter turned to go back to his office. He opened the door.

'Sahaal, can you step out here, please?'

Sahaal did as he was told.

'Gentlemen, come with me,' Ripon said. He turned to the big man next to him and looked at him. The man nodded and walked past Richter and Sahaal into the office.

'Don't worry about Robinson,' Ripon said. 'We're going down to the car. He's going to make a few quick security checks. He'll be joining us shortly.'

Ripon led the way. Richter and Sahaal followed him. Richter looked over his shoulder and wondered what Robinson was doing in his office.

Ripon thanked the receptionist on the way out of the building and led the other two men to the Mercedes, which sat, engine still running, at the mouth of the car park.

Ripon opened the back door.

'Get in,' he said.

Ripon himself got into the front passenger seat.

'Where are we going?' Richter asked.

'Can't tell you that.'

Richter began to feel very uneasy. He looked over at Sahaal, who sat loosely, hands resting, palms up, on his lap. There were no signs of tension or distress on his face.

Three or four minutes passed and Robinson came striding out of the front door to the facility, the back of his jacket flapping behind him. Richter saw something that shot fear through his chest. An angle of black metal, pressed against a white shirt. Robinson was carrying a gun, tucked into his waistband.

Robinson opened the door to the back seat.

'Move,' he said to Richter. There was urgency in his voice. Richter shuffled along to allow him to sit down. Immediately, the Mercedes pulled out of the car park and roared away, the fields and trees dissolving into a blur through its darkened windows.

54

Zac stood by the huge window at the far end of Elliot's apartment. There was a remarkable calmness about London. He looked out over miles and miles of bricks, chimneys, concrete and tarmac and could see no movement. Everything sat still and silent. Even from his elevated position, Zac could make out areas where bodies covered the ground like a carpet. He found himself wondering when they would start to smell.

He didn't like that train of thought. When he had guaranteed his own survival he would think about those who had not been so lucky. He turned around and faced the others, who sat in the middle of the apartment on the leather suite, looking weary and strained.

'You got a great view from here,' he said. 'You must be able to see half of London.'

'Yes.' Sitting down with a glass of wine had relaxed Elliot considerably. 'A good few miles on a clear day. That was one of the reasons I bought this place.'

'What did you do?' Zac asked. 'Before all this. If you don't mind me asking, I mean, you must be some sort of millionaire, right?'

'Well, yes. I'm in financial sales. Life assurance, pensions, equities packages, that sort of thing.'

'I had a friend who did that,' Zac said. 'He got sacked. To be honest he said he hated it anyway. But that's life I suppose, horses for courses, innit?'

Elliot nodded. There was faint amusement on his face.

'Horses for courses,' he said. 'Yes, indeed. So what about yourselves?'

'Building.'

Elliot nodded. There was a short silence. Zac walked over to the middle of the room and sat down with the other two.

'What's that on your arm?' Elliot asked. He was looking at Zac's tattoo.

'I was a para.'

Elliot put his wine down. 'Really? My father was a Captain in the Royal Fusiliers. Did you see any action?'

Zac scratched his nose. 'Yeah. '91. Kuwait.'

'Gulf War?'

Zac nodded.

'You musta seen some evil shit,' Joel said, slouched on the sofa, his hood still pulled over his head. 'You wouldn't get me fighting in no army. I've had enough problems sticking up for myself. That's where you got those scars huh?'

Zac looked down at his burns. It was only the scars on his arm that were visible. At least three times as much covered his chest, shoulders and back. He had forgotten about them for the first time in a long time.

'I don't like talking about it,' he said.

Joel sat up. 'Come on, man. We're sitting here waiting to be picked up. We don't know how long it's gonna be. We may as well talk. What you scared of? You think we're gonna tell everyone? There's no one left to fuckin' tell.'

'Why do you wear that hood like that all the time?' Zac asked.

'Trust me, you don't wanna know.'

'See?' Zac said. 'Same thing.'

'So if I show you what's under the hood, you'll tell us about your scars.'

Zac looked at Joel fiercely, but he couldn't meet his eyes, covered, as they were by grey cotton. 'Okay,' he said.

229

Mark Turley

Joel put his hands up to his head and wrapped his fingers around the edges of the material. Elliot took a swig of wine. Both he and Zac watched, suddenly captivated by the moment. With a whip of his wrists Joel flung the hood back over his head.

'Da da!' he said, grinning.

Elliot spat wine all over himself and turned away. 'Jesus Christ!' he said, dribbles of red spit hanging from his chin.

Zac looked straight at Joel, not flinching, looking him in the eye for the first time.

'What happened to you?' he asked softly.

'I was a bit of a player, bruv. I liked to mess around. A little bit here, a little bit there, you know how it is. But I started playing with the wrong girl. It weren't no big deal to me. But it was to her man. He was some proper Jamaican bad man. He lost face because of me. Them boys, they don't give a fuck man, I'm just some English nigger to them, they don't even recognise you as a real black man.'

'So what'd he do to you?'

'Acid in the face. He wanted to teach me a lesson. Stop me being a player. He done it, too. Ain't been with a woman since.'

Neither Zac nor Elliot spoke.

'I was lucky, in a way. He only got me from the top of the nose up and it only went in one eye. At least I ain't blind. I'm just never gonna win any beauty contests, that's all.'

Joel's right eye was stuck, half closed. From underneath the partial lid, a milky, greyish ball occupied the socket sightlessly. He had no hair in front up until the very top of his head and half of the right side of his head was bald too. His right eyebrow was missing, as was the top third of his right ear. His forehead and the exposed skin on the top and the right side of his head had a mottled and uneven texture. The dark flesh was lumpy in places and almost transparently thin in others.

'Believe it or not,' Joel said, 'I looked a lot worse just after

230

it happened. It took a lot of hospital time to get me to this stage.'

He replaced his hood and drank some water. 'So what's your story?' he asked Zac.

'My story?'

'Your burns.'

'It happened in the Gulf War,' Zac started and then stopped. Elliot had looked up from the floor now. He seemed relieved that Joel had covered himself again. He said, 'I'm interested to hear about the war as well. The only way to know what really happens in those situations is to hear from someone who was there.'

Zac scratched his scars, acutely aware of them again. He looked at both Joel and Elliot. He had never told anyone about this. Somehow, the extremity of the day's events and the uniqueness of his situation, sitting there, with two strangers, with whom he had shared so much in such a short time, seemed to make what he was about to say less important. For the first time he felt able to talk about it. He took a long breath through his nose and then began.

'I'd been in the Paras for three years when the Gulf War started. Most British regiments that went were used as ground forces. We were no different. The air war was short, the Iraqis had no chance against the US Airforce with back up from Britain, Saudi and all the rest of the coalition, but we hadn't won until we defeated the Iraqis on the ground.

'First of all that meant the Iraqi infantry, who'd dug themselves in on the Saudi-Kuwaiti border. The Saudis were shitting themselves because they thought if the Iraqis were allowed to stay there, they'd use it as the base for an invasion. So that was the first job. It was intense. The fucking heat burning your neck and your hands, losing pints of water through sweat. Heat rash, sweat rash, the lot. The fighting was easy, though. Shooting down Iraqis like fuckin' coconuts at the fair. They weren't a good force. Badly trained, they didn't have our discipline, or

231

our firepower.

'We didn't have the right kit, really. The British military isn't equipped for fighting in the desert. But we stuck it out. We defeated them quickly. Two days. Loads of casualties on their side. Bodies all over the place. A lot of 'em kids, teenagers. Operation Desert Sabre they called it. Not many people have heard of that.'

'I thought it was Desert Storm,' Elliot said.

'That's what I'm saying. There was more than one operation. Desert Storm was the name for the air strikes. Desert Sabre is less known but was more important. We had to cut through the ground troops as quickly as possible.

'Anyway, the Iraqi infantry weren't that good and we defeated them quickly. But then it was straight on to Northern Kuwait where the last Iraqi forces were. The Elite Republican Guard, they were called, 125,000 of them. This lot weren't just a bunch of kids and shopkeepers with rifles in their hands. They were real soldiers, like us. Properly trained, properly equipped. They meant business. It took us a week to finish them off. We had the numbers on them and much better weapons but they were well organised and they fought with passion. Like they really believed in what they were doing. They had that on us. We were just following orders, doing our job. They had their hearts in it. They had a cause. You had to admire them really.

'Anyway, we killed most of them, took a few as prisoners and went back into Kuwait to our base at Ar Rawdatayn. They kept the prisoners there in a few small barracks blocks and each unit in turn got detailed to guard them, two days at a time.

'I enjoyed it when it was my turn. I didn't think I would, but the prisoners were friendly. They mostly spoke English.

'We started our first night, sat by the door of the barracks, feeling nervy. But this prisoner introduced himself as Salim and asked me for a cigarette. I gave him one and he said "*shukram*". I asked him what it meant and he told me it means "thank you" in Arabic. So I asked him to teach me some other words. "*Iss me* Zac", that means "my name is Zac". "*Yalla habebe*" means "let's go, my lovely".'

Zac smiled as he remembered.

'He told me that he was from a town called Tuz and his family had a business growing olives or something. He was going to take it over after he left the army. He wanted to know all about London and he said he wanted to visit one day. Anyway we played cards a bit and talked a lot and it was all right. In fact, it was just about the best evening I had while I was over there. It was good to speak to someone from the other side. It makes you realise that they're human. I went away looking forward to guarding prisoners again the next day.

'So, when the next evening comes, my platoon go back on guard detail and this American SEAL, off duty, comes to join us for a card game. Anyway, Salim didn't want to play with the Yank. He just refused. "*Gella Americano*," he kept saying. There was no talking him round. So him and the other prisoners sat on their bunks. The fucking yank kept insulting them, making fun that they'd allowed themselves to be captured, what shame they were bringing to their mothers and everything. It was childish stuff but they seemed really wound up by it. I should have stepped in and said something, but I guess I wanted to avoid trouble. He really got to them. One of them started fucking crying, it was so weird.

'Anyway, the American had one of those Zippo lighters; they give 'em out as standard issue in the US army. Halfway through the game, Salim comes over to the table and asks for a light and this Yank gives him the Zippo. It's not working. So the Yank gives him a bottle of lighter fuel and tells him to fill it. It was a fuckin' stupid thing to do. But none of us stopped him. Salim turned to me and said something, I didn't really listen, I was too busy playing cards.

'He took the fuel and the Zippo and used them to set fire to the yank's hair. Just a little bit, you know. All the prisoners were fucking pissing themselves laughing. Even I had a

233

chuckle, to be honest. But the SEAL went crazy, he put the flames out with his hands and grabbed Salim, pushed him down on the floor. He had his boot on his chest, holding him down and he was swearing and calling him a "fuckin' heathen bastard" and stuff. Anyway, the yank covers his clothes in lighter fuel and sets him on fire. I couldn't believe it. Shit like that never got reported in the papers, but it happened. Salim was rolling around on the floor, screaming, and I remember noticing that the flames seemed to be on his face, not just his clothes and I shat myself, I mean, the poor guy was being fuckin' burnt alive. And then he shouted, in English, so we would understand. "The glory of Allah shall blaze like a sun." I'll never fuckin' forget it.

'I ran over to him and he was on the floor, the flames were just eating him up. It smelt like fuckin' roast pork. I didn't have anything on me to smother him, so I just dived on top of him. I was only wearing a vest. His skin was bubbling and dissolving and he was screaming like an animal. I managed to put the fire out in the end, but it was no good, he was fried.

'The other prisoners were going nuts, so the SEAL shot one of them in the foot to shut them up. Then he just shrugged it all off and said they deserved it. I lost it and chinned him, broke his jaw. We all got disciplined for failure to follow orders and all my enthusiasm for the regiment went. I didn't want to know no more. As soon as we got back home I packed it in.'

He stopped for a moment and then added, 'That's how I got my scars.'

The three of them sat quietly for a while. Elliot shifted his weight around on the squeaky leather. He tried to think of a story to tell, something to compare with Zac's or Joel's. He almost began telling them how he started the Company, but decided against it. Instead he poured another glass of wine and slurped from it noisily. Eventually, he did break the silence.

'Are you two sure I can't get you anything stronger?' he asked.

Before either of them could answer, the phone rang.

'Hello, sir.' The voice on the other end was crisp and clear.

'Hello,' Elliot said.

'I believe you have some information.'

'Well, yes. Myself and two friends are stranded here in London.'

'Where?'

'West Pier Village, it's an apartment block in Wapping. We're on the top floor.'

There was a short silence.

'Were you out in the rain at all, sir?'

'Pardon?'

'The rain. Were you caught in the rain?'

Elliot was a little confused by the question.

'Yes,' he said, looking at Zac and Joel, frowning. 'I think we all got a bit wet.'

'Thank you, sir,' the voice said. 'Don't move. There'll be someone there shortly.'

55

Lyn had a funny feeling about the way things had been going at the lab. She knew that most of the senior doctors, especially Richter and Arnold, wrote her off as an Aussie hippy and for that reason she had been feeling a little alienated, but that wasn't the problem. She firmly believed that what she had told both of the senior men was true and she was certain that the chimps had sensed some impending danger that the humans at the lab were oblivious to.

That certainty had become even more solid when she had seen the big man striding through reception. She had just stepped out of the ladies toilet when she saw him burst out of Richter's office and power-walk through the lobby and out of the door. She had seen his gun clearly. He made no effort to hide it. She had walked to the door herself just in time to see the man climb into a long, black Mercedes which had immediately left the car-park and sped off in the direction of Oxted.

'Who was that man?' she asked the receptionist.

'I don't know. He came with Mr Travis from the Ministry. Doctors Richter and Walid went with them.'

'Really?' She tried to piece together the clues she had, but wasn't able to form a coherent conclusion. Nothing seemed to really add up.

Lyn had always been an impulsive person. From the incident at Brisbane zoo when she was eleven, to three years ago when she and a friend had streaked at a Rugby international in

Sydney, she had always done things because she felt like it. Something, somewhere inside her mind, nagged and gnawed at her.

Without analysing what she was doing she headed out of the front door and into the car park. She walked all the way around, until she came to the back of the observation lab. The back door to the observation area was locked with a pass code. It was only the senior doctors and the zoology team who knew it. She tapped it in and listened as the air hissed out of the door seal. She stopped short of actually opening it and, feeling better, she began to walk back round to the front of the building.

Major was sitting on a low branch of a Giant Redwood. He heard the air escaping from the door seal and turned his head. His eyes sparkled. The dark, grey speckled fur on the back of his head and neck began to move, prickling, standing on end. He leapt four feet to the ground and beat his chest.

'Aaah!' he screamed, jaws wide open to reveal his long incisors, 'Aaah, Oooh, aaah, aaah, aaaaaaaah!'

'What the hell...' Margaret, watching the monitor, saw Major's sudden behaviour change. She began to speak but was struck on the head by a piece of the collapsing ceiling and died instantly. As she started talking, Arnold swivelled quickly to see what the commotion was, but before he had time to say anything, he was flung ten feet across the room against a wall, completely smashing his back and neck and severing his spinal chord.

He lived for about four seconds after that and before his brain shut down completely, he saw the building in which he had spent most of the last two years crumble around his ears.

The explosives could probably have been placed better. The saboteur had known that at the time, but didn't feel that he really had a free choice of where to put them. Ideally, the main lab would have been the best place, as the central area of the building and the one that needed to be destroyed more than any other. But he would have felt uneasy walking into a room with ninety-three people in it and putting twelve pounds of Semtex with a digital timer in the middle of the floor. He had satisfied himself with taping it under Richter's desk, content in the knowledge that it would be very unlikely to be found and would still destroy most of the facility.

The blast was sudden and violent and most of the upper floor of the building was destroyed instantly. Richter's office, the reception area and the data entry room were blown to atoms. One moment they existed, the next, they didn't: their destruction was complete and merciless. As for the downstairs laboratories, they were not shattered into non-existence, but rather reduced to a pile of gently smoking rubble, decorated randomly with human remains. The ceiling had caved instantly and the force of the blast had caused those standing directly below it to be hurled around the lab as if by a mischievous giant. The huge screen which separated the lab itself from the environment simulation area, where the chimps were kept, shattered into a million pieces, which burst outwards into the room like sparks from a circular saw, tumbling this way and that, until they lay sparkling on top of the rest of the wreckage. Of all the people working at the lab, the only immediate survivor was Lyn Dickens, who was just about to walk through the front door to the lobby when the blast hit her full in the face, burning her eyebrows and singeing her flesh. It sent her flying backwards, onto the square lawn in front of the facility, where she lay charred and unconscious, bleeding steadily from a head wound until the ambulance crews arrived, some thirty-five minutes later.

The medics couldn't revive her, but had they managed to, she would have been happy to learn that there were some survivors.

The force of the explosion had blown the back door to the observation lab wide open. Most of the ceiling above the artificial jungle collapsed, dragging down many of the giant trees with it. The majority of the chimps were killed instantly or pinned to the ground, squealing and squirming pointlessly beneath weights they could not move until they were crushed.

Major had heard the door being unlocked and after warning the rest of the colony, he tore through the trees and undergrowth towards it and was joined there immediately by Captain, two of the sharper females and one of the juveniles, who had heard his call and responded.

As the door was flung open by the blast, the five of them hurtled out through the car park, tearing across the tarmac on all fours. With shrapnel landing about their feet and hands, they leapt the small fence that hemmed in the lab's grounds and disappeared, not once looking back, into the Surrey countryside.

56

Janet had initially not known what to do. When she had first heard about the terrible, bizarre tragedy that had befallen London, she was horrified. But somewhere inside her there had been relief.

She had rushed into marriage as a relatively naive twenty-two year old and had realised over time, that it had been a mistake. She couldn't say that she *loved* Elliot, but rather had known from the beginning that life with him would be secure. He came from a rich family and had good social connections, but she had always felt a deep sense of dissatisfaction with her life that she had never truly had the courage to confront.

Financially, leaving Elliot would be disastrous, but she had frequently toyed with the idea when left by herself, which was often. Elliot's work and social commitments had kept him away from home for most of his waking hours, so she was able to respond to the philandering in which he had indulged since the beginning of their marriage with a string of fancy-men and toy-boys. She had grown to enjoy sexual promiscuity and looked upon it as one of her few true pleasures in life.

Some small part of her was actually quite pleased when she heard that the terrorist attack had left no survivors. If Elliot was dead, the house and money would be hers to do with as she wanted and she could set about living with the reckless freedom she had missed when in her youth.

She was just settling in to this new vision of life when Elliot's phone call threw everything back out of focus.

After allowing Carlo, her £75 per hour Personal Trainer to comfort her, she dialled '999' on her mobile. The voice on the other end was male.

'My husband is in Central London and is still alive,' she said, no emotion in her voice at all.

'Excuse me, madam?'

'My husband, Elliot Rossley, is in the penthouse of an apartment block called West Pier Village. He is alive.'

'Are you sure, madam?' the voice said. 'As far as we know there are no survivors in central London at all.'

'I've just spoken to him.'

'Madam, please make sure that you are available on this number for the next five minutes. Someone will call you back.'

She went back to her nails, half-heartedly, for a few minutes.

When the phone rang again, Janet picked it up and put it to her ear hastily.

'Hello?'

'Hello, madam.' It was a different voice this time, still male, but older and graver. 'I believe you called regarding some survivors in central London.'

'That's right,' she said.

'I'm afraid you must be mistaken,' the voice said.

'I spoke to my husband about fifteen minutes ago.'

'Grief can do strange things to you, madam. There are no survivors, I'm afraid.'

'But…'

'No survivors, madam.' The repetition seemed very final.

'Thank you,' Janet said, timidly.

She collapsed back on the sofa and started to sob again. Carlo put his hand on her shoulder.

'Come on,' he said. 'It's going to be all right.'

57

Richter had been vaguely aware of some kind of disturbance as the Mercedes sped through the country roads. He had turned his head and seen what appeared to be a broad cloud of smoke rising into the sky, on the horizon, but it was difficult to be sure as the back window was so heavily tinted.

'Is there something going on there?' he asked. Neither Ripon, nor Robinson, nor the driver said anything. Sahaal looked at him and then looked away again immediately. The car had driven to the edge of an area mainly wooded with tall, powerful oak and cedar trees and pulled up.

Ripon turned his head to speak to Richter and Sahaal.

'I make no apologies for what we are about to do gentlemen,' he said. Richter felt his face crumple. He wanted to cry. He looked down and to his left and saw that Robinson's hand was on the butt of his gun.

'Firstly, I must ask both of you to close your eyes.'

They did as they were told. Richter felt tears begin to well up behind the closed lids. He heard Ripon say, 'Robinson, if you don't mind.'

Richter clenched his teeth and waited for it to happen. He didn't know if it would be painful or not. He guessed there would be a moment, a flash of agony and then oblivion.

Robinson took the heavy masking tape from his pocket and covered Richter's eyes with it.

Richter exhaled loudly. Then Ripon spoke again.

'You are being taken to a secret location, gentlemen. Do not remove the tape until you are asked to do so. Any attempt to remove the tape and you will be killed. Is that clear?' His voice was still and soothing, like a gently flowing stream.

Richter nodded. Sahaal sat motionless. Ripon signalled to the driver and the car pulled away once again.

Richter had no idea where they went. None of the other men in the car spoke.

They drove steadily for what seemed about forty-five minutes. He was vaguely aware that for the last few minutes of the journey, the noise of the engine sounded different. It echoed slightly, as if they were in a tunnel.

Eventually the engine was switched off. Richter felt himself being grabbed by the shoulder. 'Come on,' a voice said. He was pulled up and out of the car and led away. His shoes slapped noisily on the floor, which was ever-so-slightly slippery. He guessed it was tiled. A beeping noise seemed to chirp intermittently from above his head. He was lead along the tiles for five minutes or so, occasionally making sharp left and right turns. The hand on his arm gripped him so tightly that he began to get pins and needles from the elbow down. At last, he was pushed onto a chair.

'Do you want to remove the tape yourself or would you like me to do it?'

'I'll do it,' Richter said. He peeled the tape cautiously, wincing as it pulled at his eyebrows. He was able to remove it without tugging out too much hair. He blinked for a few seconds, the lights above him stinging his eyes, then his vision cleared and he was able to focus properly on the person before him. It was Robinson.

He looked down at Richter coldly, his jaw muscles bulging from beneath his cheekbones. They gave his face a rectangular appearance.

'Wait here,' he said. 'Mr Ripon will be down to speak to you shortly.'

58

Elliot finished his bottle of wine.

'This is probably the biggest single tragedy since the extermination of the Jews in World War Two,' he said.

Zac and Joel nodded.

'It's difficult to come to terms with what's happening when you're worried about your own survival. You know, I think its just starting to sink in.'

Zac sat up slightly on his chair.

'I know what you mean,' he said.

'Do you have family?' Elliot asked. He seemed cautious, as if it might be a difficult subject.

'My mum moved to Southend five years ago,' Zac said. 'She'll be all right.'

Joel looked up, his mouth turned down slightly at the corners. 'My half brother lives in Harlesden. I haven't seen him for about ten years anyway.'

Zac and Elliot nodded slowly.

'What will you do afterwards?' Elliot asked.

Zac shrugged his shoulders. Exhaustion had carved itself into his face.

'I don't know. It's difficult to say, isn't it? What will anyone be doing afterwards? It's gonna be a long time before things in London are anything like back to normal.'

'I think I'm gonna get out of here,' Joel said.

'What, London?'

'Nah, this fucking country. I've been saying it for years, you know. The weather and the atmosphere of this place depress the shit out of me. I might go and find some sunshine to sit in.'

Zac laughed. 'That don't sound bad,' he said.

Joel turned to face him. 'You come and join me if you want.'

Zac leant back on the sofa, stretched his hands out in front of him and sighed. His knuckles cracked.

'Do you know,' Elliot said, suddenly sounding more cheerful, 'I think something positive has come out of this.'

Joel slumped back in his chair.

'Oh yeah?' Zac said.

'Well the fact is that you two saved my life, really.'

There was a brief pause. Elliot waited for confirmation or agreement, but none came.

'Okay, so you two saved my life and now, we've been sitting here, talking and we've got to know each other and I can honestly say that I feel close to both of you.'

'You don't need to say it,' Zac said, suddenly avoiding eye contact.

'But I want to,' Elliot enthused. 'I mean you're a couple of bloody builders. No offence. But before any of this I wouldn't have spoken to either of you. We wouldn't have moved in the same circles, you certainly wouldn't have been potential clients of mine. But now the three of us are sitting together in my apartment and because of what we've all been through, there's a bond between us.'

Neither Zac nor Joel said anything.

'After all this is over,' Elliot said, 'we're going to keep in touch, the three of us.' He waved a chubby finger as he spoke. 'You'll be welcome in Potters Bar any time you like.'

Zac and Joel nodded awkwardly.

'Anyway, I'm glad...'

Elliot was stopped mid-sentence by loud footsteps and

raised voices on the stairs outside. They got louder as they approached. It sounded like seven, maybe eight pairs of feet. All three men swivelled their heads in the direction of the door.

'Don't make a move unless I say so,' Zac said, alert again. His eyes fixed on the door, which suddenly splintered inwards, collapsing onto the floor. One by one, six men in black riot uniforms stepped inside the apartment and stood in a rigid line. They were well armed and wearing gas-marks. The leader of the group stepped forward, aimed an automatic pistol in the direction of the furniture suite and said:

'Stand up, very slowly. Put your hands above your head. Don't make any sudden movements.'

Zac, Elliot and Joel did exactly as they were told.

59

Richter had been sitting quietly on the hard, wooden chair for about fifteen minutes when Ripon walked in. The room he had been left in was fairly large. The walls were grey and metallic-looking, the door an uncompromising rectangle of steel. On one wall there was a glass panel, which, having seen his fair share of movies, Richter immediately recognised as a one-way mirror. About four feet in front of where Richter sat, another chair, identical to his, had been placed.

He was surprised to see Sahaal walk in, just behind Ripon. Both men were smiling as they entered the room, as if they had just shared a joke.

Ripon sat down opposite Richter and briefly offered something approaching a smile, before his small, white face became instantly cold and unreadable again. Sahaal walked to the back of the room and stood some way behind Richter, leaning against the back wall. Richter turned his head and tried to catch his eye, hoping to see friendly reassurance. Sahaal avoided his gaze.

'This,' Ripon said, 'is one hell of a mess.'

Richter nodded jerkily.

'Do you smoke, Richter?' Ripon asked, producing a packet of cigarettes from his pocket.

Richter shook his head. 'I used to. I gave up a couple of years ago.'

Ripon nodded. 'Good for you. I've never touched the things

personally. Hate them. But I thought you might. Anyway, they're there if you want them.' He tossed the packet onto the tiled floor with a book of matches.

'Now then,' Ripon continued. 'Where to begin?' He opened and closed one hand repeatedly, as if exercising his grip.

'Richter,' he said at last, 'you haven't been entirely honest with us, have you?'

'I don't know what you mean.'

'What happened in Test Study One, Richter?'

Richter scratched his chin. A light stubble had grown there.

'Not a great deal…You've read the report.'

'Yes. The report.' Ripon laughed sourly. 'Don't fuck with me, Richter!' he screamed.

Richter jolted back in his chair, so hard, that he almost fell off.

'The report written by Dr Rustermeyer?' Ripon spoke softly again now. 'How accurate would you say it was?'

'Well, I wouldn't – '

'Richter, don't embarrass yourself by trying to lie at this late stage. The fact that you are here, now, clearly indicates that we are in possession of some facts. Now tell me what I want to know.'

Richter shuffled on his seat and swallowed a few times. He looked as if he was about to speak on several occasions and then stopped, mouth half open. Eventually he looked directly at Ripon and said.

'I had to make a decision, Mr Ripon. It was not an easy de-cision to make but I made it. I made that decision in the best interests of the technicians and team who staffed my laboratory. I made that decision based on my experience in my field. The results could have been a freak, or an accident! I wasn't going to have the research taken out of our hands because of a bloody accident.' Richter seemed on the verge of tears. He was very pale. Huge, dark rings underscored his eyes.

'So what did you do, Lawrence?' Ripon leaned in so his

face was closer to Richter's.

'I...'

'Yes?'

'I...'

'What?'

Richter's chin began to shake.

'Come on Lawrence, say it.'

It all came out suddenly, like a blocked pipe bursting and spilling its filth.

'I falsified the results!' he said. 'I buried the findings of the first test study. I didn't think any of this would happen.' Richter felt like a huge pressure had been released from his chest and he began to sob quietly.

Ripon leaned back on his chair. He looked at Richter with a slightly lop-sided expression.

'Did you get that?' he called, angling his head towards the one-way mirror. Somebody on the other side tapped the glass twice. Ripon made a thumbs-up sign.

'Stop recording then, please.'

He turned back to Richter, looking satisfied.

'That's all I came in here for,' he said. Richter reached for the cigarettes from the floor, with his foot. He dragged them towards the base of his chair, picked them up, opened the packet and lit one. All the time his hands shook gently. He had stopped sniffling.

'Before I go, is there anything you want to ask me?' Ripon said.

Richter took a deep pull on the cigarette.

'How did you know?' he asked.

Ripon smiled. Not a big smile, but a tiny, tight-lipped, V-shaped one.

'Richter, did you really think we'd let someone like you handle something so important, unmonitored?'

'What do you mean, unmonitored?'

'There was a government agent working in your lab for the

entire time it was operational.' Ripon paused and then added, as an afterthought, 'And we bugged your office.'

Richter seemed to shrink into his chair.

'Who was the agent?' he asked.

'Well, first of all there was McNally. But after your toxic chemicals team managed to poison him and get him hospitalised, we had to place Walid there.'

'Walid? Sahaal Walid?'

'Yes.'

Richter looked down at the floor and took another long pull on his cigarette. He turned his head to Sahaal.

'I though you were a bloody saboteur,' he said, almost laughing. 'You lot certainly know how to play games.'

'Agent Walid wasn't so much a saboteur, more of an overseer,' Ripon continued. 'He helped to make sure that the results of Test Study One weren't repeated.'

'What?'

'You heard.'

Richter sucked at the cigarette desperately.

'If the second test study had produced the same or worse results as the first, you'd have felt compelled to process the report, there would have been security issues regarding staff leaks and we just couldn't take the chance. This whole thing was just too important. The second batch of chimps were hand picked for docility, Richter, it was all organised at a level way above your head. Don't be upset, there's nothing you could have done.'

'I see.' Richter looked hurt. His eyes were red. He finished the cigarette, and squashed it on the floor beneath his foot.

Ripon almost seemed to be enjoying himself.

'We knew you'd balls this up, you know, that's why you were chosen.' He smiled a little.

Richter sat silently.

'Did you really think we'd let some ludicrous nancy-boy handle a programme of research with importance to National

Security? You must have thought it was your bloody birthday when you landed this commission.'

Richter started to get angry. He made to get up from his chair.

'I wouldn't do that if I was you!' Ripon shouted. He pulled aside his jacket to show a gun belt, strapped across his shoulder. Noting Richter's shocked expression as he sat back down, he said, 'We all carry them during emergency.' His voice was calm again.

'I don't have much more time I can give you, Richter. Is there anything else you want to ask?'

Richter's eyes shone with hatred.

'There's one thing I still don't understand,' he said, making an effort to hold himself together. 'There has been a national catastrophe today. But you say the whole thing was organised above my head. Did something go wrong?'

Ripon looked at Richter very sharply. He paused for a few seconds.

'No,' he said.

'Well...'

'Nothing went wrong, Richter.'

'I don't...'

Ripon stood up. 'There's not much I can tell you. The situation had already developed too far. The Black Cloud Response was unavoidable. The question was not whether it was going to happen, just when. There's no room for sentimentality, Richter. We're aware of how London has been deteriorating, everyone is. Too much immigration, too many people, too much pollution, crime and drugs. The problems were just piling up. And they are unsolvable by any normal means. No government can reverse two thousand years of decay with legislation. It would have taken billions. So, something drastic was required. What happened would have happened one day anyway. The response is genetically encoded. A terrorist organisation was planning a chemical attack, which would trigger it. We thought we'd get it over with, allow it to happen. In fact, the attack was eventually carried out by one of our people. The fact is that most of the dead are pointless, average people or even worse, worthless scum. They're replaceable. London will regenerate and will come back better than before. We can learn from the mistakes of the past.'

Richter's mouth fell open.

'A chemical?'

'Thimos.'

'What?'

'That's what they call it. Formulated initially by the Americans. Tested in Vietnam. They were going to use it on Moscow, or possibly Beijing, in the 60s, but the government thought better of it after the peace movement got going. We heard that some extremists had got hold of it and were going to use it. The rest, as they say, is history.'

'But what about spread?' Richter was becoming shrill, his eyes wide. 'What's to stop the chemical getting into the national supply?'

'Thimos exists in conjunction with water for roughly twenty hours. It's been designed that way. After that time it decomposes, becomes harmless. Besides, out in the countryside, with lower population densities and less pollution, it wouldn't have the same effect.'

Richter shook his head.

'How long have we had it here?'

'A long time. The yanks gave us a sample for co-operating with them over the Turkish invasion of Cyprus in '74. We had a couple of trial runs ourselves, back in the early 80s, in a few inner-city areas, on, you know, expendable communities, but weren't sure of the effect it would have on a broader scale. That was actually the purpose of your study.'

'So population density and pollution were unimportant?'

'Side issues. You were testing a chemical weapon.'

'But…what you've done…it's…'

'I'll tell you what it is,' Ripon cut in. 'It's necessary. Power brings responsibility, Richter. Some decisions are unpleasant but necessary. That's something you've never understood.'

Ripon straightened his clothing and wiped his hand across his mouth.

'I have things I need to do, Richter. I'm sorry it's turned out like this for you. Goodbye.'

Richter felt a sudden sharp pain at the base of his skull. He tried to put his hand up there, but found he couldn't. His arm was too heavy.

Walid had used the time Ripon had been speaking to edge towards the back of Richter's chair, carefully placing his feet on the floor to make no sound. As the little man had spoken his last word, he'd jabbed a hypodermic needle into Richter's neck and compressed it.

Richter felt a strange numbness spread throughout his body. The initial sensation was actually quite pleasant and he smiled slackly as he slumped off his chair and onto the floor. Muscle by muscle, organ by organ, his body shut down and as he sucked desperately through numb lips for his last, laboured breath, he saw Ripon and Walid speak quietly, heads tilted towards one another. They left the room as they had entered it – laughing.

60

The pistol remained trained on Elliot's head. He could feel the heat from the red laser sight as it pinpointed a spot just above his eyes.

'Don't shoot,' he said, as his bladder let go and soaked his trousers in warm, wet fear.

The man at the head of the group beckoned to the soldiers behind him.

'Search the place. Any other survivors, bring 'em down here.' They spread out from behind him, covering the apartment. One to the kitchen, the rest heading upstairs.

'You're gonna kill us, aren't you?' Zac said. He stared straight at the eyes of the leader, or as much as he could see of them behind the gas mask.

The soldier said nothing.

Elliot turned his head to face Zac.

'Of course they're not, they're a rescue squad.'

'A rescue squad would have brought paramedics, in case we were injured or something. This lot are too heavily armed. They're a combat platoon, sent to kill.'

'No.' Elliot shook his head, his jowls wobbled. 'That doesn't make any sense.'

'Think about it.' Zac spoke very firmly. There's been some kind of chemical attack. They're worried that survivors are contaminated. They're gonna kill us.'

'Clear!' one soldier shouted, from upstairs.

Elliot's eyes widened. 'Now look here! Will somebody please tell me what's going on?'

'Clear!' another shouted, from the other side of the flat.

'I demand some sort of explanation. You can't just come barging in here, waving your guns around.'

'Clear!'

'This is private property and unless you have a warrant I can ask you – '

'Clear!'

' – to leave immediately. I think you should think very carefully about what you're doing.'

'Clear!'

'I'll have you bloody sacked. Who are your superiors? Do you know who I am? I run one of the biggest financial companies in London!'

'Clear!'

'Shut up!' the leader of the squad called. 'Who's the owner of the flat?'

'I am.' Elliot put his hand up meekly, as if he were in class.

'What's your name?'

'Elliot J Rossley.'

The leader turned to one of the other soldiers.

'Radio base, make an ID check.'

He kept his gun trained on the three men while the soldier did as he was told.

The squad member had a brief conversation into his radio and turned to his superior.

'Positive ID,' he said, sounding slightly surprised, 'selected for special order one.'

Elliot looked from one gas-masked face to the other, desperate for clues.

'Mr Rossley, stand aside. We've been instructed to remove you to a secure location.'

Elliot moved away from Zac and Joel. He didn't look at either of them. He allowed himself to be pushed towards the door.

They led Elliot downstairs and out into the car park. It had stopped raining. He felt enormous relief.

'Move,' the soldier said. 'Come on, move.'

Just as he climbed into a waiting jeep, he heard a brief volley of gunfire, followed by three more bursts, coming from the building behind him.

Elliot stepped inside the vehicle and sat down. Relief shook through his body, his backside juddered against the wheel-arch. He raised his head, eyes straining to see through the square of bright light that was the side window of the jeep. The sun's power stung him, forcing him to squint and blink.

A rainbow had spread across London, east to west, clear and bright.

Elliot spoke then, instinctively. He didn't know to whom or why.

'Thank you,' he said.

HER MAJESTY'S OFFICE FOR INTERNAL AFFAIRS

28th November 2004

Official Memo

1. Highly Classified

2. To be saved in secure file only

3. Report on Black Cloud Investigation – Final Phase

a) Greater London Mass Disturbances. Monday 30th August 2004

Full-scale use of acceleration chemical (Thimos) confirmed what isolated tests in the 80s suggested. Commendation recommended for Agent K Dahir for successful and undetected introduction of Thimos.

First reported disturbances at 9.30 am. Police helicopter patrolling the North Central area observed mass scenes of extreme violence after a traffic hold up. Similar reports soon made from all areas of the Greater London Conurbation. The bulk of violence seemed to occur within one hour of the first report. As anticipated, fatalities and destruction of property were large. It is estimated, at the last count, that over 7,750,000 deaths occurred.

An army roadblock was placed around the M25 to contain physical contamination.

It is believed there were fewer than 20 survivors in the Greater London area. Their names and addresses are contained in the accompanying file. Most survivors were burn victims (see below).

Survivors dealt with according to Special Order 2.

Scientific team responsible for isolating the contamination confirm that it did not reach any water systems within the Home Counties.

As anticipated, the press seized upon the terrorism angle and reported it zealously, thus creating momentum for military action.

b) Destruction of Bioscience Laboratory, Cherrington Farm, Surrey. Monday 30th August 2004

Commendation recommended to Agent G H Robinson for successful and undetected placement of explosives at above location. It was the decision of the Select Committee that the above laboratory (publicly believed to be a centre for pharmaceutical testing on animals) had become a liability to National Security. If the press and public had become aware of the true nature of the research, the entire purpose of the Black Cloud Investigation could have been jeopardised. The premises were therefore destroyed and all staff eliminated. This was believed to be the only viable solution under the circumstances.

c) Final Report on Thimos Formula

Formula Thimos proved extremely effective in densely populated, polluted urban areas. It is estimated that the Black Cloud Response occurred at least forty years in advance of its natural date of commencement. Possible future sites for use of Formula Thimos include Baghdad, Pyongyang, Beijing, Havana. Some suggestions of use in Cairo or possibly Damascus.

It is confirmed that Thimos remains effective for 18 hours whilst in contact with water, before it is broken down and neutralised. All primates are highly susceptible to Thimos, including humans. Although most potent when entering the vascular system via the stomach (i.e. after having entered the body orally), it can also penetrate via the pores. In the case of the latter, a high saturation level is required, to achieve absorption. For this reason, those with more than 15% burn / scar tissue tend to be resistant to contamination. This is an area for development, before further use.

d) **Operational Analysis**

The Black Cloud investigation began with the following objectives...

-To investigate the possibility of the response occurring in human beings.
-To determine when the response would occur.
-To investigate ways of avoiding the response.

However, initial investigation suggested that the response was genetically encoded and unavoidable.

Objectives were reformed, bearing in mind policy mistakes in previous governments and the economic realities (see attached costing analysis) which have led to London becoming irrevocably over-populated, polluted and subject to high levels of immigration from undesirable foreign nationals, particularly former colonies and Eastern Europe. Also accounted for was the fact that despite allowing the press to report on the early symptoms of the response, which manifested itself in rising violence within greater London, over the last 30 years and despite deliberate attempts by various governments to make London less attractive (high taxation, property prices, general cost of living, poor transport etc) the population continued to rise.

Objectives were reformed thus:
1. To ensure the Black Cloud Response occurred in as controlled a manner as possible.
2. To remove in one stroke the problems of over population, spiralling immigration, pollution and crime.
3. To create public support for military action against rogue states.

It is the opinion of the Select Committee that, judged on these criteria, Operation Black Cloud has been an unqualified success.

COSTING ANALYSIS REPORT

REGENERATION PROJECTS REQUIRED FOR <u>PREVENTION</u> OF BLACK CLOUD RESPONSE:

1. Clearing of inner-city areas, demolition of apartment-blocks and relocation of residents to external settlements...£590,000,000

2. Re-construction of demolished areas and conversion to spacious housing and / or open spaces...£60,000,000

3. Modification of London infrastructure in particular transport networks; road, rail etc to prevent congestion...£1,210,000,000

4. Relocation of core industries, in particular financial and commercial sector companies located in central London...£43,000,000

5. Cost of variety of welfare projects required to successfully integrate foreign nationals into population, i.e. assisted housing, special education...£14,000,000 per year.

6. Other miscellaneous (improvement of environment, lowering cost of living etc)... £33,000,000

Total...£1,950,000,000 (minimum figure)

It is impossible, at present, for the government to contemplate such a figure, without completely withdrawing funds from essential programs such as defence and espionage.

The regeneration approach is therefore considered non-viable by the Treasury.

ALTERNATIVE

Costs of clean-up operation required after Black Cloud Response has occurred:

1. Removal of bodies and mass burial... £25,000,000

2. Re-population of city to pre-set limit...   Free

3. Cost to economy through lost business...   £500,000,000

4. Offset Welfare costs (positive)   £500,000,000

Total...   **£25,000,000**

In light of the above figures, it is recommended by the Treasury that the alternative proposal is economically viable.

After

61

It was a sharp day in late winter and the wind that blew through the open door was stiff and cold. Elliot was pleased to see that the interviewer was female. He hadn't had any visitors since those two government chaps had come round a few weeks ago.

This journalist was young, probably mid-twenties and looks-wise she reminded him of a slightly less attractive version of Suzy. Her hair was less red and more blonde and her body, as far as he could tell, nowhere near as enticing, but he welcomed her in, pulling his dressing gown around him. He had no need these days to rise early and dress.

He offered her a drink, which she refused, and led her into the lounge. Elliot removed a newspaper that he had left on the sofa and placed it on the coffee table. The banner headline on the front page read:

British / US Troops Surround Arab Stronghold.
General says, 'If Warlord won't fight, we'll starve him out.'

The interviewer sat on the armchair next to the sofa and opened a small black handbag, removing a Dictaphone, which she switched on and placed on the table, on top of the paper.

'Ready?' she asked.

Elliot nodded, straightening his back.

'Susan Lockwood interviewing Elliot Rossley,' she said, for the benefit of the recording.

She faced him with a smile.

'Elliot, it is now almost six months since the tragic events of "Black Cloud Day" in London. A nation is slowly repairing itself and coming to terms with its grief. How are you, as the only survivor in the central London area, coping with life after the attack?'

Elliot gathered himself, gave a tiny smile and then spoke.

'Well, my business was decimated by the tragedy. More than half of my company's clients died and the majority of its workforce were also wiped out. I sold what was left of my business to a large American corporation for a cut-down price. So my days are fairly quiet now. I get up late, I read. I no longer wake up and travel to work. I must admit I miss the cut and thrust of the financial industry.'

'Is boredom your only problem?'

'Sorry, I don't understand the question.'

'Are you not haunted by the scenes that you witnessed?'

Elliot looked at her sullenly for a moment.

'One could never really forget the things that I have seen. But life must go on. I put them to the back of my mind as much as possible.'

'Would you mind once again going through the events of the day? I feel it is a story that needs to be told.'

Elliot sighed deeply. He noticed that a small section of scarred skin was visible and adjusted the collar of his dressing gown.

'I went to work as normal and the weather was shocking. Most of my staff didn't turn up. As the morning wore on I became concerned, so I went outside with my PA to investigate. That's when things began to go badly wrong. She was affected and attacked me at Bank tube. I ended up walking to Wapping, alone, fending off attack after attack. Eventually I made it to my flat where I was able to call for help. A rescue squad drove in to get me.'

'It must have taken considerable bravery to do what you

did.'

'When one's life is on the line, instinct takes over. It is beyond the conscious realms of bravery or courage, it is merely survival, raw and urgent. For that time, I lived by my wits.'

The interviewer raised an eyebrow. Elliot sat back, beaming. He had rehearsed the answer and was extremely pleased with it.

'A question that many of our readers ask, Elliot, is why you were unaffected. Why do you think that this terrible chemical weapon, which drove Londoners to destroy each other, had no effect on you?'

'It's a question I'm not really qualified to answer. You'd be better off talking to a doctor. I've been told that I have some sort of natural immunity.'

'You must feel incredibly lucky. Of eight million people, you happen to have natural immunity.'

'Well, yes, I suppose I do. Although I don't really believe in luck. I think it's destiny of some kind, I was meant to survive.'

'And how do you feel about those who carried out the attack?'

'I think the terrorists involved deserve whatever they're now getting. I can't stand all these bleeding hearts moaning about the war. Look what the bastards did! They're lucky we don't just launch some kind of nuclear strike.'

'How do you respond to the news that London will be operating as normal again, from next week?'

'It's great news. It shows the indomitable spirit of the British.'

'Will you be going back yourself?'

'I don't know. Maybe, for a restaurant or a play or something. I've no reason to, other than that.'

Elliot quickly grew bored of her questions. After twenty-five minutes, he told her he was tired and asked her to leave.

Janet popped another Valium and went downstairs.

She slid the biscuits out of the cupboard and took them to him. He lay on the sofa, propped up on pillows like a Roman emperor, his feet dangling over the edge and onto a padded footrest.

He was still in his personalised pyjamas, dressing gown and tartan lounge slippers, sipping coffee.

'Thank you, darling,' Elliot said, smacking her left buttock appreciatively with his free hand. She winced and exhaled noisily. He sat up slightly, opened out the newspaper and examined the second page.

'Have you seen this, Janet?' he asked.

'What?'

'Bloody chimpanzees living in the woods near Leatherhead.'

'Oh.'

She leaned over his shoulder to look at the article.

Wild Chimps Pose Problem for Scientists

It has been decided by parliament that a colony of wild chimpanzees that have been living freely in a forest in the Leatherhead area of Surrey should be captured with the aim of returning them to their natural habitat in Africa.

The primates, man's closest living relative, escaped from the government laboratory that was destroyed during the terrorist attacks earlier this year. Despite the adverse weather conditions in the UK and the absence of their typical food sources, the chimps had managed to establish a thriving colony which had integrated seamlessly into the ecosystem of which they had become a part.

Keith Weston, an expert on primate behaviour, believes this to be nothing short of a miracle. 'We have long believed that the main reason for human domi-

nance of the planet is our adaptability, our facility to prevail in nearly all weather conditions and landscapes. It had previously been thought that this adaptability was unique to Homo sapiens and was an indicator of our superior intellect. The fact that these chimps have managed to build a thriving colony in an environment considered "hostile" to their species, suggests that they also have this ability and throws up new questions about how we've come to dominate the planet so utterly.'

Mr Weston suggests that there were two factors that contributed to the chimps' survival.

Firstly, they managed to switch from an omnivorous diet to a largely carnivorous one, feeding on small mammals such as squirrels and mice. With the absence of other large predators in the area, the chimps were able to assume a position at the top of the food chain.

Secondly, they apparently used ingenuity to resist the cold temperatures of the advancing English winter. In a development that startled scientists more than any other, several of the chimps were wearing 'clothing' of some kind. For example, one of the females of the group had found a discarded tablecloth, which she used to cover her young when sleeping.

A group of protestors, calling themselves 'The Mother Nature Taskforce' say they will try to stop them being taken, claiming that the chimps have earned their right to stay.

Whether the chimps stay or go, the questions raised by their survival will remain with us for a long time.

Elliot put the paper to one side and looked over at Janet in the kitchen, busying herself among the tubs of fresh herbs that she kept there. He stretched his hands above his head, yawning, causing his pyjama shirt to rise up, exposing his belly.

'Do you think we've enough contacts left to have another

271

party? I think it's about time,' he said, grinning. 'Don't you?'

Janet looked up and smiled, which required considerable effort.

She couldn't bring herself to answer.

About the Author

Mark Turley is half-German, half-Welsh. He grew up in Croydon, but now lives North of the River with two beautiful girls (his wife and daughter). Mark started writing age four, but didn't take it seriously until about three years ago, when he finally tired of leaping around stages with his shirt off and fighting with the audience, as a drummer / percussionist in a variety of rock bands. His work has been published by *Open Wide* and *This Is It* as well as the International literary magazine, *NFG*. He is also featured in Laura Hird's 'Showcase'. One of his stories, *On Road*, appears on the reading list of short British fiction at Michigan State University.

The Rainbow Maker is Mark's first novel and he plans at least three others, including a sequel to this one, titled: *Illuminate the World*.